SURVIVING THE TRUTH

SURVIVING THE TRUTH

SHARON COLEMAN MONROE

AuthorHouse™ LLC
1663 Liberty Drive
Bloomington, IN 47403
www.authorhouse.com
Phone: 1-800-839-8640

Published by AuthorHouse 12/19/2013

ISBN: 978-1-4918-3548-7 (sc)
ISBN: 978-1-4918-3547-0 (hc)
ISBN: 978-1-4918-3546-3 (e)

Library of Congress Control Number: 2013920723

This book is printed on acid-free paper.

CONTENTS

Acknowledgements

My first and greatest "Thank You" goes to my husband Jack. You supported me from my very first sentence. You put up with me hunched over my laptop, forgetting dinner, forgetting errands and forgetting more than I should have. I'll never forget about you.

Mary Marsh—my friend and my "editor-in-chief". Thanks for keeping me on the straight and narrow! I guess those lists weren't that important.

Lloyd Funk, Sergeant with the Teton County Sheriff's Department—thanks for your valuable information on helicopter and wild land rescues.

Amanda Soliday, Testing/Training Officer, Wyoming K-9 Search and Rescue—thanks for taking the time to educate me.

Michael Elliott, Attorney—thanks for keeping me legal.

Chapter One

Saturday

"DAMN. YOU. SORRY. SACK. OF. SHI . . . !" The old guy in the Lexus did it again! He tailed closely for a few miles, changed to the passing lane, sped around, turned into the slow lane again and then slowed to exactly the speed limit! "Jackass!

It's too damn hard to quit cussing. Swearing was an issue for 53 year-old Laura Gregory. What started off at college in West Texas with a few "hells" and "damns" in the late '70s evolved into an extensive repertoire of profanity that now colored most of her speech. She always got a kick out of the swearing scenes in Whoopie Goldberg movies.

The necessity to change her speaking habits was highlighted at church when she was talking to Father Pete during coffee hour after service. She mentioned "raising a butt-load of money" selling cookbooks at the annual Aspen Falls Spring Celebration and Father Pete's slightly raised right eyebrow was enough to let her know the swearing had to stop! *Damn!* Maybe "butt-load" should be replaced by "boat-load".

So, a road trip was exactly what she needed to concentrate on amending her language. She even googled "How to stop swearing!" *What a load of crap!* It reminded her of Nancy Reagan and "Just Say No"! Some words are definitely forbidden. "G.d." is not acceptable because one should never take the Lord's name in vain; which also ruled out using the name of any other members of the Holy Family. "Son of a bitch" and the related word "bastard" aren't applicable because they actually "dis" the mother of the target instead of the target himself. All the words pertaining to bodily functions can be used quite expressively and the "f-bomb" is the most versatile of all!

Twice a year, late spring and mid-October, Laura drove 900 miles from Aspen Falls, Wyoming to Sinclair, Kansas to visit her younger sister Susan. A few times her husband James went along but after a handful of disagreements because he didn't want to be there in the first place, Laura started going by herself. He seemed happy to stay home with his tools and wood carvings and the dog; and her visits were a lot more fun without having to worry about cranky James. The long drive-time each way was therapeutic. Sometimes satellite radio helped pass the time but mostly the quiet allowed her to sift through all the junk that had piled up in her head over the past months and dispose of the negativity. She always felt clear-headed and ready to "face the day" when she returned from a Kansas road trip.

Fort Collins, Colorado lies halfway between Sinclair and Aspen Falls. It is nestled against the foothills of the Front Range of the Rocky Mountains, and is about as far as Laura can drive before her knee starts to protest. Arthroscopic surgery was recommended to clean out the debris floating around in her right knee but she never took the time for the surgery. The Alpenvale Inn was her favorite place to stay and just before 6:00 in afternoon she checked into the log-cabin style, two-storey motel. Room 112 was on the backside of the building and unloading took two trips; one to unlock the door and check out the room and the other to bring in a suitcase and the loaded pistol she kept in the arm rest between the front seats.

Laura had been around guns all her life. Handguns, shotguns and rifles were a common sight at her childhood home in Kerrville, Texas. Her father, Andy Billings, enjoyed hunting the white-tailed deer hiding in the oak motts throughout the Hill Country and Laura and Susan both bagged their first eight-point bucks before they were 12! Andy's gift to each of his daughters on their eighteenth birthday was a .38 Special. They had been target shooting under his supervision for years.

Laura didn't need to change clothes to go to dinner. Fort Collins wasn't Vail or Aspen; and jeans, a pull-over sweatshirt and hair pulled back into a Kansas University ball-cap were just fine. After putting her feet up for a brief look at a news channel she locked the handgun in the room-safe and walked across the parking lot to the Alpenvale Restaurant.

The pot roast was savory; the vegetables were tender and crusty bread and salad made everything just right.

It was early evening and the restaurant faced due west, so exiting was directly into the blinding mountain sunset. Laura lowered her sunglasses from the brim of her cap and walked back toward the motel. Halfway there the urge for something sweet made her wish she had ordered dessert.

A convenience store/liquor store was across the street so she walked over and bought a sudoku puzzle book, a Hershey Bar, a pony bottle of Pinot Noir and a 12-drawing, multi-state lottery ticket. Buying lottery tickets never required pondering numbers or a Quick Pick. Years ago she won $500 playing the numbers 6, 8, 17, 29, 42 and 46. Those numbers came from a fortune cookie she got with some take-out Chinese food. She won several more times; never as much as the $500 first-time ticket, but enough to keep choosing the same numbers. Throwing everything into her slouchy shoulder bag Laura walked back across the street and through the door of 112. She got ready for bed and called James.

"Hey, Babe!"

"Hey, yourself! Are you in Fort Collins?"

"Yeah, I got here about six. I've already eaten and I'm fixin' to go to bed. How's everything?"

"Good, everything's good. We had some excitement. A bear broke into the shed early this morning and I think he was trying to get into the freezer! I'm sure glad I put that lock on it. I woke up to Jo-Jo, barking like a maniac. The motion-detector lights came on and I saw the double doors to the workshop were wide open and one was hanging from a bent hinge. I turned on the back flood lights and stood in the doorway and started honking the air horn. I guess that was enough to scare it away because he came out of the shed and waddled on off toward the tree line. If I'd gone out on the deck I would have grabbed the gun but it didn't seem like it was interested in me at all."

Spring and late fall are the most dangerous times for bear attacks. Securing your garbage and not leaving out pet food or filling bird feeders during active bear season are the best ways to avoid a bear encounter.

"How big was it? Did it mess up your work bench?" For the next 15 minutes James talked about his world! He never asked about Susan or the trip or anything else. These conversations weren't unusual and Laura was used to the disinterest concerning most everything else but the dog and his woodworking projects!

"Well, I'm going to bed. Tomorrow I only have to drive 370 miles so I should be home early afternoon."

"Okay, it'll be good to have you home. Drive careful, I'll see you tomorrow, bye".

And he hung up. No "I love you" and no "I missed you." That was a snapshot of their marriage. Better than some, worse than others.

Chocolate and red wine is the perfect combination. The flavors complement one another and Laura savored them. Propped up under the fluffy comforter as protection against the chilly spring night the wine, chocolate and sudoku made for a cozy few hours before she relaxed enough to sleep.

Sunday

The drive up from Fort Collins to Laramie and across Wyoming to Rawlins was unsightly to some and downright ugly to others. There could have been people who liked the scenery. After all, someone must have liked it or no one would have stopped along the way during the pioneer's emigration to the Pacific Northwest. Or, maybe, that's as far as they got when their animals gave out or their wagons broke down.

Whatever the reason, there were few cities and towns, not much to look at and even less to slow down for and soon Laura was turning north at Rawlins for the two-hour trip to Aspen Falls.

The scenery changed as she got closer to the Wind River Range. The stark high desert was replaced by the breathtaking geology of the Rocky Mountains. Aspens and Ponderosa pines were interspersed with meadows of native grasses. Little streams joined with bigger ones and a few lacy waterfalls added glittering points of light to the landscape. Her first glimpse of the mountains usually evoked a sense of calm and peacefulness and this time was no different.

Aspen Falls lies on the eastern slope of the "Winds" between Lander and Fort Washakie. The center of town is at the foot of Mt. Carson and the residential areas spread up the slope to the west. Laura and James live in a restored log home located on the mountainside right above town at the edge of the city limits.

The first time Laura saw the little town she was entranced. She was with James on a business trip to meet an oil field contractor and the mountains called to her like nothing before in her life. She could relate to John Denver singing, "coming home to a place I've never been before."

"James, I don't want to leave. I've never seen anyplace so beautiful!"

When the trip was over James had transferred to the local division of his company, and Laura was working on her speech to her daughter Erin about the beautiful mountains and how she hoped she would like living in Aspen Falls, Wyoming.

Erin's reaction to the news made the transition from Kerrville easier than anticipated. Most 13 year old girls would've had to be dragged, kicking and screaming, away from their friends and the comfort and security of living in the same town since birth. However Erin was quiet, self-assured and not interested in most of the social situations marking the middle school years. There were three close friends but no agonizing drama; a few tears and sad good-byes and plans to post on Face Book and talk on cell phones.

The move for Laura wasn't as easy. She was born and raised in Kerrville and taught second grade at the same elementary school since graduating from University of Texas—San Antonio. It was hard to leave forty-four years worth of friends and colleagues and the hardest person to leave was her dad.

Andy Billings was still living in the same house where he raised his daughters. Pulmonary problems made every day a challenge and he met them with the same hard-headed determination he used to meet all the other challenges of living a regular, up-and-down, happy-and-sad life. And now, that life included an oxygen concentrator for the house and portable tanks for the car. With a small tank in a shoulder-pack, Andy's routine, including air travel, was rarely interrupted.

His daughters were the pride of his life and he encouraged them with unwavering support.

"Little Girl, that sounds great!" Laura was always "Little Girl" and Susan was "Baby Girl".

"When I was still in school I went through there on my way to Yellowstone for a summer program on volcanic geology. It's beautiful country. Y'all go on and just make sure you have a guest room 'cause when you get settled in I plan on being your first visitor!"

Laura and James had only been married a year when they moved to Wyoming. Her first marriage to George Patula endured fifteen years. Charming before the marriage evolved into verbally abusive and neglectful. Erin was born within the first five years but George seemed incapable of being a family man. He wanted his wife and child at home and separate from the friendships and activities that often took him to San Antonio for basketball tournaments or hockey games. Questioning only served up sneering and snarling and replies like "Don't worry about it! I take care of you, I pay the bills and I do what I damn well please!" Actually, Laura paid the bills and managed the finances but that never occurred to the arrogant asshole.

After a while, Laura and Erin got used to George being gone. Life, then, was calm and peaceful. Since George was never affectionate to Erin, even as a baby, she didn't realize until she was older that not all fathers were as self-centered and mean-spirited as George.

He never raised a hand to Laura or Erin; but the verbal abuse and emotional neglect cut like a knife and when Laura looked back on those days she really couldn't explain why she stayed as long as she did. Erin could retreat with homework and books and never appeared to care about what went on outside the sanctuary of her bedroom. Occasionally, the old charming George would walk through the front door and for a while things were calm and he was loving and life was "normal". But it never lasted. First thing you know, he came home at the end of the day working for the County Utilities Department, changed his clothes and walked back out with "See y'all later, don't wait up."

It never occurred to dumb-ass George that Laura was making as much money teaching 2nd grade as he was with the county. Long about year ten Laura opened up an account at a local bank, different from the one where she and George had their joint checking account. She didn't want a savings account; she didn't want to earn interest. She was trying to leave as small a paper trail as possible in case thick-headed George started looking at their tax returns with more than a cursory glance when he signed his name. She never deposited more than would be missed and she chose paperless statements that were sent to a new email account she had set up specifically for this reason.

Laura was very patient and she used the time to go back to school and get a Master's Degree in Education; this added a boost to her salary and gave her the confidence that she could take care of her daughter and make it on her own. After five years she had her master's and enough money to move out, hire a "hard-nosed" attorney, divorce the shit, sell the house and keep half the proceeds.

George's reaction was surprise! Surprise that Laura wasn't satisfied being treated like a possession instead of a wife and surprise she had enough gumption to leave him. She got special satisfaction from the look on his face when she gave him the divorce papers. After several months he moved to San Antonio. He made a few feeble attempts to see Erin but those rarely happened according to the court's schedule. Eventually he stopped and he stopped making child-support payments.

Laura was patient and instead of going to court for the back child support she went to court and got full custody of Erin and George got limited visitation rights. The paperwork was sent to his last known address and was returned with the required signatures. From then on he might as well have fallen off the face of the earth. Laura never heard from him or of him. Erin accepted her mother's explanation for the divorce and a few years later, when she had the maturity to express her feelings, told her mom that she always knew George didn't love them and wondered why Laura didn't see it sooner. The wisdom of your children! Just when you think you have them fooled, you end up being the fool!

After all was said and done Andy Billings offered up his opinion. "Little Girl, I never liked the son-of-a-bitch and I'm glad he's gone. I told myself that I wouldn't interfere in your marriage as long as you looked like you could handle it, and you handled it well for 15 years!"

Laura's reply was, "Daddy, he's not a son-of-a-bitch. That's disrespecting his mother. He's a sorry sack of shit and I just took out the trash!"

The road sign read "Aspen Falls—10 miles." She was ready to be home, ready to see James and ready to get out of the car. It had been a long drive.

CHAPTER TWO

Monday, the next day

The sun was shining on her face. She didn't open her eyes. She burrowed further beneath the down comforter until nothing was exposed but the tip of her nose and lay there listening to the familiar sounds in the log house. Spring mountain mornings were still cool enough to keep the comforter on the bed and flannel pajamas and socks were her usual sleeping attire. The smell of coffee lured her from the warmth of her cocoon and she walked into the kitchen.

James was sitting at the kitchen table drinking coffee and feeding toast to Jo-Jo. The five-year old Yellow Lab was at his feet patiently waiting for the buttered bites.

"Hey, babe! You were sawing logs in there and I didn't want to wake you. You ready for some coffee? We already ate!" He was usually up before Laura and seemed to enjoy the solitude; so he ate by himself and Laura took care of her own breakfast whenever she woke up.

She turned on the TV and sat in her recliner, her breakfast on a wooden folding TV tray in front of her. Laura was a news junkie and was happy to have the TV on all day; she didn't seem to care if she heard the same news story repeated five or six times. James was just the opposite. He could barely listen to the news stories even once, never mind over and over again with the broadcasters yelling at one another. He was much happier at his workbench or walking the dog.

Jo-Jo was 60 pounds of sweet loving dog and James was the object of her affection. She loved retrieving sticks thrown into Arapahoe Lake. She was curious and often vanished while on their walks, chasing an interesting scent or something scurrying through the under growth but soon she was back; bounding toward James with her ears flapping and her jowls in a perpetual smile. Her favorite toy at home was a squeaky rubber frog and she walked around the house carrying it her mouth.

A hiking trail started across the driveway from the house and meandered through the trees until the next block marking the edge of the city limits and BLM land took over. Bureau of Land Management oversees public lands and you're fortunate if your property borders against it. You don't have to worry about neighbors.

From the house, Arapahoe was a 45-minute hike. The bear bell attached to the leash would jingle as she tugged, ready for her freedom, and after 50 yards or so James would unhook her and she would race away, trying to chase everything at the same time.

"We're off to Arapahoe. She's ready for a run."

"Well, y'all be careful. I'm going to knit group after I get things straight around here.

When James first started taking Jo-Jo to the lake Laura would go with them but soon she felt the unspoken message he would rather make the hike alone and she stopped. He never purposely excluded her; he just seemed happier alone.

They'd been married for ten years. They met at a New Year's Eve party in Kerrville and their similar circumstances gave them something in common. Laura, forty-three, was newly divorced and James, forty-four, had just ended a relationship. They started dating and eight months later they were married. He was kind to Erin and she seemed to like him. Affection was there but not passion. Kindness and respect were there but not true devotion to one another. The marriage soon became more convenient and comfortable than anything else. She felt safe and she never suffered the old suspicions and hurts she did with George. A pat on the butt, a kiss on the cheek and an occasional "roll in the hay" were pretty much the extent of their intimacies and both seemed content.

After breakfast she quickly finished her morning chores. Dust is a perpetual adversary when you live on a dirt road and Laura performed her daily routine of dusting the flat surfaces and lampshades and all the other little spots that attracted the fine particles. The news channel playing in the background kept her up on the latest political scandals and weather catastrophes.

Monday was knit group day at the Community Center. Laura started meeting with this colorful collection of women soon after she and James and Erin moved up to Aspen Falls and she always looked forward to seeing everyone and watching the progress of their latest projects. She wasn't close friends with most of them outside the confines of the meeting room but for three hours on Monday mornings they shared a special camaraderie that included confessions and questions, laughter, tears and recipes for the latest potluck dishes and homemade soups.

Once they made the decision to move to Aspen Falls, finding a home was their first priority but there weren't a lot of properties to consider. A deserted log-house, situated on 6 lots in the foothills right above town on an unpaved city street was their final choice.

Changing jobs for Laura wasn't as easy as it was for her husband. James moved first and Laura stayed in Kerrville to finish out her contract and sell the house. He packed up his truck, moved to Aspen Falls and started work with the mining equipment division of his company. Three Pines Café on Main Street was open for breakfast, lunch and dinner so he rarely cooked for himself.

He worked on the cabin. Updating 30 years of neglect took some time. The work progressed faster once the Kerrville house was sold and Laura and Erin joined in on the work. It was easy for Laura to get a teaching job. Fremont County School District #47 always needed teachers.

Repairs and renovations transformed the abandoned house into an attractive home. They did as much of the work as they were able and used plumbers and electricians from Lander and local handy-man Rick Martinez when the job progressed beyond their talents.

When finished, the home included two bedrooms, two baths, and a small guest room/computer room with a Murphy bed. Laura planned on Andy being their first visitor. Decks surrounded the home on all four sides with seating available everywhere; the views were stunning!

The unpaved city street led up from town and dead-ended into a cul-de-sac and the driveway. The most-used entrance was on the north side of the house by the driveway through the mudroom and into the kitchen. An archway opens from the kitchen into the great room. A rustic round dining table and straight-backed chairs illuminated by an antler chandelier share the large room with a long sofa, coffee table and two recliners. Side tables and lamps make the room comfortable. Area rugs are on the hardwood floors. At the southern end of the room is a floor-to-ceiling wood-burning fireplace with a granite hearth and a river rock surround, flanked by bay windows with window seats. The ten-foot ceiling makes the room seem larger than it really is. A door leading to the deck is on the west side of the room.

On the south deck, supported by pillars of native rock, James installed a hot tub; the perfect location to relax and enjoy the view. Laura sowed wildflower seed at the edges of the property every spring. A row of spruce trees with a St. Francis statue placed in the center mark the southern edge of the property.

Everything was completed within the first five years they were in Aspen Falls. James continued working for Peterson, Laura found her niche at Sacagawea Elementary and Erin finished school, graduating third in her class.

A scholarship covering books and tuition, plus housing money provided by James and Laura enabled her to attend Western Wyoming Community College in Rock Springs. She usually came home on weekends and sometime around the middle of her freshman year she started bringing David Barnes with her. David was from Cody, working at the school library and taking a full load in Pre-Engineering. Erin's goal was an M.B.A.

Life was comfortable and predictable and there was no chaos or drama, until they came home in the middle of the week in early December of their sophomore year. They were at the house when Laura came home from school. A fire was burning in the fireplace and stew was bubbling on the stove and Laura knew something was about to change.

David had two small scholarships and was working and going to school, living in an efficiency apartment. His parents were able to send him a monthly allowance but there were three other kids still at home and he was barely making it.

He wouldn't consider school loans. The U.S. Army had programs available to pay for college and he enlisted and was scheduled to leave for Fort Polk in Louisiana in three weeks. They wanted to get married before he went to boot camp. She would continue going to Western Wyoming Community College and then join him wherever he was stationed.

They sat together on the sofa, holding hands, looking at Laura and James with the firm conviction particular to young adults.

"Young adults!" Erin was 19 and David was 20 and it was immediately obvious they'd made up their minds. There would be no turning back.

Ten days later there was a small wedding at St. Michael the Archangel Episcopal Church in Aspen Falls. Father Pete officiated, his wife Caroline played the organ and Laura and James, his parents and three sisters stood at the altar and promised to support the young couple in their new life.

His first assignment was to Joint Base Lewis-McChord, near Seattle, Washington. David was moving up through the ranks and when he served enough for his college tuition he didn't plan on re-enlisting. There were no babies, yet.

Two years ago, when he was 52, James was offered an attractive early-retirement package. He was ready to retire and he adjusted easily. Although he'd worked for the same company for 35 years, he didn't have problems breaking ties with his work buddies and it didn't take long for him to get comfortable being a loner.

He'd watched a wood-carver at work at a county fair a few years ago and wanted to try his hand. He was hooked the first time he picked up a carving tool. His workbench in the shed was his retreat. He had all he wanted or needed in there.

A year after James retired Laura got her opportunity for early retirement. It was more difficult for her to make the adjustment. It took a while for her to get used to the new routine. She was already active in a knit group. There was always something to do at church. She signed up as a substitute teacher and those days kept her busy. She and James did not grow any closer; but they didn't grow any further apart either. They just stayed the same.

Monday, a week later

It was late May and James was out with the dog. Laura was sitting on the loveseat on the south deck with a mug of coffee, enjoying the view, when the phone rang.

"Hey, Laura, this is Bobbie Jo. Honey, I've got some bad news."

Laura took a deep breath and held it; "Your Daddy died this morning. I went by to check on him a little bit ago and when he didn't answer I went on in. He was still in bed. I called the EMS but they couldn't do anything, Laura. I am so, so sorry."

Laura was still holding her breath, but when the deck started spinning she exhaled. Bobbie Jo Riley was near in age to Andy and she and her family lived next door since Laura was in elementary school. She'd been checking on Andy ever since he was diagnosed with pulmonary fibrosis. She was a good neighbor and Laura didn't worry too much about Andy once they moved to Wyoming because she knew Bobbie Jo was nearby.

Laura was glad Andy was been able to visit Aspen Falls. He came up once they finished the renovations and kept his promise to be their first guest. He'd been having breathing problems before his visit and the altitude was very hard on him. He was never able to return.

Laura sat on the deck staring at the horizon, no longer aware of the beauty surrounding her. After Andy's diagnosis she and Susan learned pulmonary fibrosis was a killer, but neither of them allowed themselves to consider it applied to Andy. He was always strong and they'd leaned on him all their lives. He was bull-headed and maintained his independence to the very end. They wanted him to move to an assisted-living facility, where there were others to see to his needs, but he wouldn't even discuss it with them. He made it clear from the beginning; he was going to live in his house and take care of himself. Now, as Laura looked at his actions realistically, she could see he also planned on dying there.

At first she worried his last hours were frightening, but she knew Andy was deeply spiritual and there was no fear of death. She prayed he died peacefully in his sleep and did not consciously struggle for his last breath.

Who to call first? Erin? Susan? James? James was out with the dog and cell coverage was never good out there. Susan, she would call Susan and then she would call Erin and sometime in the middle of all of these efforts she would push down the urge to scream.

"Susan?"

There was silence; then . . .

"No! No!" The first "no" was loud; the second "no", barely a whisper. "It's Daddy, isn't it?" Susan knew before Laura said a word.

"Yeah, babe, it is." Laura was squeezing her eyes shut, biting her lip, trying not to sob and failing miserably. The conversation proceeded through sobbing and shaking and finished with sad, shuddering breaths. They would make travel arrangements and call back as soon as they could. Laura would have to call Erin. Susan had no one to call.

By the time Erin answered the phone Laura had gained some control and was able to speak without sobbing. Half-way through the conversation James walked onto the deck with Jo-Jo. He sat down beside her and occasionally touched her hair or lightly rubbed the back of her neck while she and Erin made arrangements to get to Kerrville. David was on some kind of training mission and he wouldn't be able to make the trip on such short notice.

When she finished she put the phone down on the outdoor table and laid her head on her folded arms. James was beside her, softly stroking her back.

"I'm so sorry, Laura. I guess we all thought he had more time. What do you want me to do?"

She thought, *I want you to fucking take over, help me out here! MY FATHER JUST DIED!!! I want you to be decisive and comfort me. I don't want to do this by myself.*

She said, "I think I've got it figured out. I need to get on the phone and find flights for myself and Erin." That was the opening, the opportunity for him to say 'Don't worry, babe. I'll help you take care of everything,'

"What do you want me to do" was his way of saying *I don't want to go.* And if he didn't want to go, then he could sure as hell stay home. She had enough to deal with as it was without adding him to her list of things to manage.

The rest of the day was spent talking on the phone; to Susan, Erin, three different airlines, and finally to Father Pete. James spent the time on the edge of all the action. It looked like he was trying to be available if needed but only at the periphery. He didn't want to get sucked in at the last minute and have to go to Kerrville and get involved in the messy business of family life and death!

It wasn't that James disliked Andy. He was unable to understand the relationship Laura and Susan had with their Dad and it seemed to make him vaguely uncomfortable. Laura and Andy could talk on the phone for an hour and a few days later talk again for the same length of time. James couldn't understand what there was to talk about for so long. He was an only child and from the few details he told Laura he didn't have a bad home life, there just weren't a lot of outward expressions of love.

Chapter Three

Tuesday

James drove her to Rock Springs where she caught a flight on a little turbo-prop to Salt Lake City to meet up with Erin. He tried to be sympathetic and Laura accepted his efforts. Sometimes she would joke to herself about his "arrested emotional development". People didn't always "understand" James and sometimes she didn't either. What she did understand was that he was sincere. Even though what he could give sometimes fell short of what she needed; she accepted him as he was and did not try to change him. She stopped making excuses and justifying his behavior to others. She loved him. And he loved her.

Their flight arrived in San Antonio 30 minutes before Susan's and when she arrived they stood there, hugging and crying silently; finally walking together, holding hands, to baggage claim where Bobby Jo was waiting.

The sixty-five mile drive from San Antonio to Kerrville didn't take long. Driving past roadsides blanketed with bluebonnets and Indian paintbrush, Bobbie Jo used the time to tell them about the last two days.

"I think your Daddy knew his time was near. After the EMS came they called the coroner's office and I sat in the living room and waited. I just couldn't leave Andy alone with strangers. I know it sounds stupid but . . . Anyway, everything was neat and clean; there were a few dishes in the sink, and it really looked like he was getting ready for . . ." she paused, "well, you know. There was a folder from Wilson's Funeral Home on the coffee table and I guess Andy'd made his own arrangements 'cause his signature was on the paperwork. When the coroner got there he looked at everything and called Wilson's. I locked up the house after they came for him and I called you." Laura appreciated his foresight. She knew just walking into the house was going to be gut-wrenching and thank God there was one less thing to worry about.

Soon they were driving down Mission Lane and turning into the driveway of the Craftsman Style house. No one wanted to be the first to move and they sat staring at the house until Bobbie Jo popped the trunk and opened her door. Everyone took a collective deep breath and began opening car doors and unloading. They walked up the front stairs to the porch, shaded by deep, overhanging eaves and paused once again. The next steps over the threshold and through the door would mark a new stage in their lives. Suddenly, it was not an issue. The screen door made the same screechy-creak they'd always tried to stifle when they came in late and they didn't want Andy to hear. They went through the door and put down purses and luggage and inhaled the familiar scents of their childhood home.

"We need to call Mr. Shaffer", Laura said softly.

Bert Shaffer and Andy Billings had been friends since their college days at Texas A&M. They were Aggies, tried and true. Andy was Bert's first client after he finished law school.

"Hey, Mr. Shaffer, this is Laura Gregory, Andy's daughter."

"Oh, hey Laura! I just heard about your daddy and I'm sure sorry. I would've called you earlier but I've been up at the ranch and I just got back to Kerrville a little bit ago." He paused and Laura heard his voice crack. "We've been friends for a long, long time and this hurts like hell but I'm here for whatever you need me to do."

"We just got here, Mr. Shaffer. His will is probably his office. I'll look for it and give you a call."

"That's okay, hon'. I'm the one who drew up that will and I've got a copy. I know y'all are busy so go on ahead and take care of business. I'll stop by later."

Susan called Wilson's Funeral Home and made an appointment for 4:30, hoping to schedule the funeral for Thursday. Erin called St. Aloysius and Father John Cates would be over after 7:00.

It wasn't long before the neighbors were knocking on the door and soon the kitchen was filled with the usual array of bereavement food.

Bobbie Jo knew they had appointments to keep so she came over and dealt with the condolence calls.

Andy's white pick-up was parked in the garage and the keys were hanging on a hook by the back door. Laura, Erin and Susan left Bobbie Jo in charge and drove his truck over to Wilson's Funeral Home.

Joe Wilson greeted them in the foyer of the funeral home. It was decorated in "formal funeral" décor; overstuffed floral sofas, wing-back chairs in coordinated stripes and solids, Queen Anne styled coffee tables and lamp tables and sofa tables of highly polished cherry wood. Monotonous music played softly in the background and the air was lightly scented with sandalwood.

Joe led them into his office, arranged in the same décor, with a large desk and leather office chair and three fiddle-backed chairs facing the desk. A cherry side board held a silver coffee service, china cups and saucers, spoons and small linen napkins.

For some reason, Laura had the urge to giggle! *What's wrong with me? This is supposed to be a solemn occasion and here I am, trying to stifle a laugh!*

She brought the folder from home and she saw the same paperwork on his desk. A black pen and a box of tissue were the only other objects on the desktop and it appeared as if they had been set precisely, according to some funeral director's desktop template.

The three of them sat in the fiddle-backed chairs and Joe sat in his leather office chair and a receptionist served coffee. Joe reviewed Andy's arrangements as they balanced the cups and saucers on their knees. Andy's arrangements were thorough, nothing extravagant or pompous. *That's why I have the urge to giggle! Joe Wilson and his funeral home are a little on the pretentious side.* That kind of stuff always irked Andy.

The burial service would be at St. Al's on Thursday afternoon. Flowers would be limited to the bouquets normally decorating the altar. Donations could be made in Andy's name to the Texas A&M Geology Department, the American Lung Association or St. Aloysius Episcopal Church. His ashes would be committed into the columbarium located in the churchyard and after the interment everyone would be invited to a reception at the fellowship hall.

A few signatures, sincere handshakes all around and they were out the door. Laura did not giggle. She was totally baffled by her reaction.

I thought Daddy would've wanted his ashes spread somewhere around Enchanted Rock and to hell with all this funeral stuff. Andy was a geologist professionally and a "geology nerd" personally and his favorite place to explore was the Llano Uplift, known to Texans as Enchanted Rock. But it wasn't her decision. He wanted his ashes at St. Al's so that's where they would go.

They were back at the house two hours later. Visitors had been asked to give them some private time, so condolence calls wouldn't start until Wednesday afternoon *Thank. You. God. For. Bobbie. Jo. Riley*!

Father John Cates stopped by at 7:15. He had only served St. Aloysius for the last six years so he really didn't know Andy's daughters very well. They saw him when they came to Kerrville to visit their dad and were always impressed with his kindness and the joy he expressed during the services.

When Laura answered the door he was standing there with a gift basket: four bottles of wine; two reds and two whites, a wheel of brie and boxes of crackers. Although there was an age difference of almost thirty years, he and Andy were close friends; visited often and shared more than a few bottles of wine while discussing topics both spiritual and secular.

He stayed long enough to firm up plans for the funeral and to pray with Laura, Susan and Erin, thanking God for his friend Andy Billings and asking for strength and peace.

That night Susan and Laura slept on the twin beds in Susan's old room and Erin slept on the double bed in Laura's old room. No one slept in Andy's room.

Wednesday

Wednesday afternoon was certain to be busy. Friends and neighbors would be coming by and they needed to be ready to greet them. They had a few unscheduled hours in the morning and after coffee and pastry courtesy of the previous day's offerings Susan and Laura decided to start going through Andy's office. Erin called some girlfriends from her high school days and they planned a long visit.

Andy's office was dominated by a large, old, oak desk. The high-backed wooden swivel desk chair with the cracked leather seat had been behind his desk for as long as they could remember. Susan and Laura would sit in it as little girls and spin and spin until they were dizzy. A filing cabinet and twin barrister bookcases held professional journals and Aggie memorabilia. Two wing-back chairs faced the desk and on the opposite side of the room was a tall gun safe. Geology credentials, diplomas and various framed photos of Susan and Laura were displayed on most of the wall space. Two sets of antlers were mounted among the photos, evidence of their first "eight-pointers".

It was hard to know where to start. Laura finally sat down behind the desk and Susan stood in front of the filing cabinet and opened the top drawer. It was stuffed haphazardly with manila folders and papers and presented a time-consuming task to whoever would eventually clean it out.

Laura opened the shallow middle drawer above the knee-hole. A 5x7 picture frame was pushed face-down toward the back of the drawer and she gasped as she turned it over. A young, anxious-looking Susan was sitting in front of a dark-haired young woman with a tremulous smile. *Who is this woman with Susan?* She had never seen it before. The name of the photography studio and a date were stamped in gold at the lower right hand corner.

Susan was suddenly standing next to the open drawer and when she saw the photo, the frame was snatched from Laura's shaking fingers. "NO!" she screamed.

"God dammit! Where did that come from? NO!!" She threw it into the trash can beside the desk. The glass shattered and made little clinking sounds as it dropped from the frame to the bottom of the trash can.

Laura sat frozen to the desk chair. Her sister's reaction was frightening. Susan turned and fled to the middle of the room and it was as if she hit a brick wall; she could go no further. She covered her face with her hands and racking sobs blew snot and tears from between her fingers. She stood there, a quivering bundle of misery.

Disturbed by her sister's behavior, Laura rose and walked to her side, touching her shoulders gently and guiding her to one of the chairs. Susan continued to sob and as she sat she moved her hands from her face and crossed her arms over her waist and began to rock back and forth. Her face was flushed crimson and her eyes were streaming tears.

"WHY? Daddy! Why do you have a picture of her?" she screamed toward the ceiling, on the edge of hysteria.

Laura knelt in front of her, took her hands and began to stroke her face, pushing her hair away from her eyes. She made soft shushing sounds. After several minutes the shaking subsided and her sobs lessened to shudders.

Susan was finally able to take a deep breath and she looked at her sister. There was a terrified look in her eyes. "Laura, I can not talk about this and you can NOT make me!"

"It's okay, Baby Girl! You don't have to." *Hell, yes you do have to talk about it! What just happened?* "It's okay, it's okay."

A few more quavering breaths and the flush began to slowly leave her face. Susan refused to say anything about the picture. The rest of the morning was spent on the glider on the shady back porch; Susan resting her head in Laura's lap, moving back and forth, not talking; each of them trying to comprehend what just happened, besieged by questions, not even knowing where to begin to look for answers.

Early afternoon the visits began. Susan, Laura and Erin were armed with smiles and conversation about old times and the afternoon passed until 5:00 when the visits slowed to a stop. Everyone needed to get back to their own homes and families and there was an hour where they sat in the living room with their shoes off and their feet propped up on the coffee table, telling stories of times gone by and laughing. The phone rang and Laura answered it.

"Laura?"

"Yes?"

"Hey you, this is Kaurie!"

"Kaurie? Kaurie!" Her voice filled with pure joy. "Oh, honey it is SO GOOD to hear from you! I miss you, miss you, miss you!"

"I just read about your dad. I get the Kerrville Times online and I know this sounds morbid; but over the last couple of years I've started reading the obits right after the front page!

Laura laughed and said "Don't apologize. Surely it has nothing to do with our age!"

"Babe, I'm so sorry. I won't be able to make it to the funeral. I just can't get a flight scheduled in time."

"It's really okay, Kaurie. This shindig has been thrown together fast and we're practically meeting ourselves coming and going. And besides, if you came all I'd want to do is sit in a room with you and talk, talk, talk. People would be really pissed because I'd be neglecting my duties. I'm dreading the next few days." There was a slight quiver in her voice. "I know Daddy's gone, but . . . it just hasn't sunk in yet. I keep having to remind myself I'll never see him again or talk to him again and it's hard."

"Laura, I know what you and Susan are going through." Kaurie's mom died a year ago. The major difference was Kaurie was an only child and she had to handle everything all by herself. "Listen, I know you're busy! I'm already making you neglect your duties!" They talked for a few more minutes and Laura promised to call her once she got back to Wyoming.

She and Kaurie Hidalgo taught 2nd grade together for 15 years. Even after Laura moved to Wyoming they kept up their friendship and got together every year or so. They might not talk for six months and then one or the other would call and it was like they had just spoken the day before.

Bert Shaffer came at 6:00 with a bottle of bourbon and Andy's will. "Bourbon and branch", bourbon and water to most non-aficionados, was Bert's signature drink, emphasizing his roots in Bourbon County, Kentucky and even after being in Texas for more than sixty years, his Kentucky accent was still recognizable.

"Okay, here it is." He opened a folder. "Have y'all seen this before?" The filing cabinet in Andy's office remained unexplored, so . . . no, they had not seen it.

The next two hours were spent in the living room with Bert sipping bourbon and branch, Susan and Laura drinking wine, reviewing the will and discussing the steps they would have to take to settle the property and carry-out Andy's wishes. The will was straight-forward. The house had been paid off for years. There were a few bills which would be coming in over the next month. Laura and Susan could keep the house and contents or it could be sold and the profits divided between the two of them. Although this was their childhood home, neither one planned on moving back to Kerrville and the decision to sell was easy.

"Andy wanted me to take care of everything but it's really your decision now. If you want me to I'll be happy to do it." Laura and Susan nodded in unison.

"Of course we want you to do it!" said Susan. "You know as much about Daddy as we do." *Except for the picture.*

Bert hesitated a moment longer than necessary before continuing. "Okay then, here is a key to the safety deposit box at the bank. Your names are on the signor's card so there'll be no problem getting into the box. There should be a life insurance policy in there and I can take care of the paperwork and the insurance company'll send you a check. Several death certificates can be ordered from Wilson's. I'll use what I need and send the rest to you. I'll find a realtor and get the house on the market and then y'all can handle it from there. Andy made three bequests; $2,500 each to the A&M Geology Department, St. Al's and the American Lung Association. Y'all can take care of those when you get the insurance money. I'll go through his filing cabinet for you and see if there is anything else to include."

"It's okay, Mr. Shaffer. We'll do it." Laura replied quickly, noting Susan's eyes widen slightly.

"I'll be glad to do it for you."

"No, sir, thanks, we'll do it later."

Bert did not persist and continued. "He designated $4,500 to cover legal fees and the costs of settling everything but I really don't think it'll take that much. Don't worry about paying me now. I'll just bill y'all when everything's finished. I know you're good for it, and besides, I know where you live!" He winked and finished his drink.

Thursday morning they went to the bank and opened Andy's safety deposit box. Inside was an envelope containing $1500, extra keys to the house and the truck, the combination to Andy's gun safe and Bert's business card. No insurance policy. They gathered it all and closed out the box.

Chapter Four

Thursday—Andy's Funeral

"O God of grace and glory, we remember before you this day our brother Andrew. We thank you for giving him to us, his family and friends, to know and to love as a companion on our earthly pilgrimage. In your boundless compassion, console us who mourn." Father John Cates intoned the prayer and those gathered there responded "Amen."

The Church was a significant, active part of their lives. Laura loved the beautiful liturgy of the Episcopal Church and though this occasion was heartbreaking there was consolation in the words and actions. She read and responded to The Burial of the Dead; soothed by the litany. And though the signs and symbols of her faith surrounded her and brought her comfort; neither she nor Susan were able to address the mourners. They were unable to speak without tears.

Father John prayed alone before the service. He prayed for guidance, what should he do? Should he continue to honor Andy's wishes? Would continuing to keep his secret be good for Laura and Susan; especially for Susan? He prayed he could offer them comfort and solace, and he asked the same things for himself. This wasn't an ordinary burial service. He was burying his friend and his heart was heavy.

John was able to immerse himself in the words and maintained his emotions until the Committal. It was then his tears flowed as he said "In sure and certain hope of the resurrection to eternal life through our Lord Jesus Christ, we commend to Almighty God our brother Andy, and we commit his ashes to the ground;"

"earth to earth," Laura and Susan and Erin sprinkled handfuls of dirt upon the urn,

"ashes to ashes" John took slow deep breaths, praying silently for wisdom,

"dust to dust." He received the strength to conclude the service.

"The Lord bless him and keep him, the Lord make his face to shine upon him and be gracious to him, the Lord lift up his countenance upon him and give him peace." And those gathered there responded; "Amen."

The kitchen in Franklin Fellowship Hall at St. Aloysius was overflowing with food and drink and buzzing with the background conversations that arise at any funeral. The ECW members were moving back and forth between the kitchen and the dining room and the church yard, serving the mourners. The attendance at the funeral was larger than Laura and Susan expected but the Episcopal Church Women were prepared; just as women in every other congregation or parish are prepared for occasions of bereavement or celebration. Andy had been a member of St. Al's for more than 60 years, so there were lots of friends and colleagues in attendance. Many of them were near in age to him so there were folding chairs available in the dining room and under the oak trees in the church yard to support aging knees and creaky backs. Little ones ran and played among the trees and hedges and seated guests; enjoying themselves; oblivious to the reason for the gathering.

Susan and Laura and Erin were the only family members left. Their Aunt Geneva, Andy's sister, died more than 20 years ago. They only had one another.

Andy did not want a wake the night before the funeral so this occasion served as a time for remembrance as well as mourning. There were stories and laughter among the people flowing in and out of the fellowship hall. The atmosphere was comfortable and casual and Susan and Laura and Erin learned a lot about Andy they didn't know before. Lots of Aggies were in attendance and very eager to enlighten them as to his college antics. They were able to visit with old friends and catch up with the happenings in Kerrville. Wine was available in the kitchen and quite a few took the opportunity to imbibe, even though it wasn't yet 5 p.m.! "Hey, it's 5:00 somewhere!" was the mantra of more than one mourner.

Following the reception Susan, Laura and Erin returned to Andy's house along with Bert and Father John.

"We spent many a night right here, solving the problems of the world," Bert remarked from the sofa, once again sipping a bourbon and branch, tie loosened and suit jacket draped on the back of a chair.

John Cates laughed and added, "Yes we did! I think if the three of us had been in charge things would be running a lot smoother!" He was more casual as well, his clerical collar tucked into a pocket of his suit jacket, hanging on the coat tree by the front door.

The next few hours were spent reminiscing and laughing and crying and getting a little smashed. It was obvious how much both men cared for Andy.

"How long will y'all be here, Laura?" John Cates spoke from the overstuffed chair into which he'd settled with a glass of red wine.

"Erin's going home in the morning. Susan and I are going to stay for a few more days. Mr. Shaffer's taking care of the will and selling the house for us, so we really don't need to stay a lot longer. There are a few things we want to keep. We all have homes and don't need any furniture. So . . . . it'll be easier to let him take care of everything."

"What about your dad's office? Do you need any help cleaning it out?

"No, we're good and I'm glad you brought that up! Mr. Shaffer, we know how important the Aggies are to you and Daddy. The three of us talked and we want you to have all his Aggie stuff."

Father John looked at the floor and Bert Shaffer began to tear up. "Y'all know how close your dad and I are . . . were." He was seated, leaning forward with his forearms resting on his knees and the tears started to fall. "Not everybody has a friendship like me and Andy, and I'll never have another one. It takes a lot of life to grow a friendship like ours and I have neither the time nor the inclination for it." He took a deep breath and stared into the past for a moment. "It means a whole lot that y'all want me to have it all; a whole lot. I've got a picture of us taken on the day we graduated; grinning like idiots and holding up our diplomas. All his stuff will go on my bookshelf with that picture." He took another deep breath, "Thank you."

They all sat quietly for a few minutes, staring into the spaces and not the faces. Erin rose to put her wine glass in the kitchen and everyone refocused. Laura and Susan stood up as Father John and Bert were rising.

"I know everyone's tired. I'll call y'all tomorrow; I need some signatures so I can start taking care of business." Bert's face was flushed and Laura didn't know if it was from the tears or the bourbon.

"I'm going on home, too. We'll talk in a few days" John Cates said kindly. "I think his Bible's in his office somewhere and I'd like to write a few things in it."

"I'll get it to you, Father John; that would mean a lot to us."

Hugs and pats on the back and they were gone. The porch light was turned off and Susan and Laura and Erin had the house to themselves. There wasn't a lot to do. Bobbie Jo came by before the funeral and straightened up the kitchen. A lot of the food brought by neighbors had been taken to the church to feed the multitudes but enough was left for them to eat on for the next few days.

The stress from the past several days plus the wine from tonight had taken their toll and suddenly Laura was so tired she didn't know if she had the strength to take one more step. Erin kissed them both goodnight and Susan walked into the kitchen to lock up and turn out lights. Laura did the same in the living room. As she turned off the interior light switch she glanced out of the 6-paned window in the front door and saw movement out on the sidewalk next to the street. Father John and Bert Shaffer were standing at the curb, talking. Without looking toward the house they clasped hands, patted shoulders, walked to their cars and drove away.

CHAPTER FIVE

Friday—Sunday

Laura and Susan took Erin to the airport in San Antonio in Andy's pick-up and, despite her protests to be let out at the curb; they parked and walked with her to the Security Check. Laura wanted to wait until her plane took off, but Erin shooed them back to the parking lot, "There's no sense in paying for more parking than you have to. I am fine, Mom! David and I'll see y'all at Thanksgiving," she said as she hugged her mother. "And Aunt Susan, you better be there, too!" She gave Susan a big hug. "I'll be ready for snow and long soaks in the hot tub! Y'all have had to deal with so much and I know there's still a lot more to do! So, go on!"

Erin had always been very confident and resilient and that was, in Laura's opinion, the chief reason George Petola didn't leave any lasting scars on her psyche. She wore a wise expression on her face the day she was born. Nothing really seemed to intimidate or discourage her for very long. Somehow she'd managed to go through elementary, middle-school and high-school without getting too caught up in the comedy and tragedy most kids accept; embrace even, as a rite of passage to adulthood.

After saying goodbye, they were once again driving to Kerrville, once again passing the fields of wildflowers; stunning swathes of blue and orange, a unique color combination seen nowhere else but Texas. Laura was driving and Susan was staring straight ahead, not really seeing the flowers or the road; or anything else for that matter.

"Laura?"

"Yes?" She had been hoping for this conversation, praying for this conversation, dreading this conversation.

"I emptied the trashcan."

"Yes, I know."

"I threw it all away. It's gone. It's gone, forever."

"Yes, I know."

"I never saw that picture before but I got a really bad feeling. I know the woman is our mother but I can't think about it now and I'm not going back in Daddy's office."

"You don't have to. I'll take care of it."

"And I don't want anybody else to know anything either." Susan let her breath out slowly, audibly, through her nose, as if she were releasing deep-rooted toxins from her body. Her shoulders relaxed, she no longer focused inward and she was able to appreciate the beauty of the Texas spring day.

Laura had happy, ordinary memories of home and childhood; of Susan and Daddy and her friends and her schools; of hunting and target practice and hiking and exploring; of holidays with Aunt Geneva and Uncle Bill, of boyfriends and the typical dramas associated with growing up. She had no recollection of her sister being anxious or sad and Andy was always strong and protective; always steadfast. She had only fleeting memories of her mother; vague images of a quiet woman rather than actual events or conversations. She hadn't remembered what she looked like until she saw the picture. She had no memories of being frightened or puzzled about her mother, or missing her after she was gone.

She didn't even remember exactly when she was no longer there! It occurred to her that she was never very concerned about the subject of a mother. Now she remembered that a long time ago Daddy told her something to the effect of "Mama loves us but she decided it would be better if she went to live somewhere else and she told us not to worry about her." She was never spoken of again. Apparently their home was thoroughly cleansed of any evidence of her. She no longer existed. What puzzled Laura was that she never again asked about her. Why didn't she miss her own mother? Once she was a teenager, why didn't she even ask about her mother? Her friends all had mothers. Why was hers so easy to forget? How could she have been so oblivious? Were there clues that she missed somehow? What about Susan's reaction to the picture?

Bert Shaffer knocked on the door soon after they returned. They discussed ideas for disposing of the household contents: garage sale, estate sale, consignment shop. They agreed the money to be made from those endeavors wasn't worth the time commitment.

They decided to keep the things that were meaningful and donate the remainder to a thrift shop in downtown Kerrville. This made it a lot easier for Bert and the thrift shop was in for a big donation. Andy's truck would be donated to the American Lung Association. Bert had offered to call a document shredding company to come and take care of his old business records and professional journals. Laura had other plans.

"Let me know when y'all are ready to leave," Bert said. "I called the thrift-shop and they're chomping at the bit, anxious to get over here and get busy. I'll call the medical equipment company to pick up the concentrator and the tanks. I've directed document shredding before and it's no big deal. They come in with big containers and load up whatever I tell them, cart it outside to the truck and everything is shredded right there. So, can I help you do anything else?"

"No, sir," said Susan. "Thank you for everything. We're so blessed that you were here for us. We've got all this household stuff to sort through so I guess we might as well get busy." It was time to get all this over and done with.

Saturday

On the way back from taking Erin to the airport Laura stopped at a FedEx store and purchased eight large document boxes. She wanted to go through Andy's filing cabinet and desk and decide for herself what was and wasn't important. So, she dumped all the contents into the document boxes and got them ready ship home. There she could sift through everything without feeling so rushed; without having to worry about Susan. She found Andy's Bible and his Book of Common Prayer in his bedroom in the night stand next to his bed. Although she had seen him reading them many times while she was still living at home, she never picked them up herself. In Andy's bible the Family History section was located right after the Table of Contents and there, all on one page, was her family: names written in blanks arranged in a family-tree style.

Andy, his parents Joe and Mattie Billings, his sister Geneva, her husband Bill. There were blanks for births, deaths and marriages, and dates had been written in most of them. Branching out were more blanks and beside "Andrew Carter Billings" was "Grace Everett Billings". *My mother's name was Grace!* Her parents were listed; their birth and death dates; she had no brothers or sisters. Their wedding date was listed. The year of her death was listed as 46 years ago; coinciding with the year stamped on the picture. Laura and Susan and their important dates were listed below Andy and their mother. She did not call John Cates. He did not need to see this information and right now neither did Susan.

They looked through their old bedrooms but those had been cleaned out years before and there was nothing there they wanted to keep. Susan was working in the kitchen. Most of the cabinet doors and drawers were open and she was looking through the contents. A few knickknacks were stacked on the table. Things were pretty casual around their house and Andy owned no fine china, silver or crystal. Sets of dishes and glasses and flatware were replaced over the years whenever cups or plates became chipped and fork tines no longer pointed in the same direction. The gun safe was opened; Laura and Susan chose the guns they wanted and put sticky-notes on them. They closed the safe and hid the combination under the desk pad on Andy's desk. The keepsakes and Andy's bible and Book of Common Prayer, along with a few things they found in other rooms were wrapped in paper and packed in the boxes for shipping to Wyoming. FedEx was called and they took care of everything.

Bobbie Jo came over once. When she saw Susan and Laura going through their dad's possessions she began to cry. Normally, she would have pitched right in and helped out with whatever was needed but this was too hard so Susan saved a few things she thought Bobbie Jo would like to keep. Everything went faster than they anticipated and by Saturday afternoon there was nothing else for them to do. It was time to go home.

Sunday

Flights had been scheduled for Sunday afternoon. Laura called Father John and told him a Big Fat Lie; she had not found Andy's bible. He wanted to take them to the airport but Sunday church duties prevented it. Laura said not to worry; Bert had offered to take them

For probably the last time in their lives, Laura and Susan made the trip from Kerrville to San Antonio. Andy had been the main focus in Kerrville and now . . . well, now there was no reason to go back. They walked out the front door for the last time, locked it and gave the key to Bert and went next door to see Bobbie Jo. She couldn't bear to say goodbye to them at Andy's house. They gave her the mementos they had chosen for her and promised to keep in touch. They all knew that would not happen.

They convinced Bert to let them off at curb-side check-in and he seemed relieved. He was in good health for his eighty-one years but he did get out of breath more often now and walking around the San Antonio airport wasn't exactly a leisurely stroll. He popped the trunk and Laura and Susan wrestled their suitcases out as he stood by.

"Okay, Mr. Shaffer." Susan said. "I wish I knew how to tell you just how much your help has meant to me and Laura."

"Yes, sir. It has." Laura hugged Bert. "It took a big load off our shoulders once we knew you would go through his office. We would never have been able to figure out what was important and what wasn't." *A Big Fat Lie!* "We chose what we wanted to keep from the gun safe and labeled them for you to ship to us along with whatever else you find that you think we might want. There're a few guns left so feel free to take what you want and donate the rest. The combination is written on a piece of paper we hid under his desk pad."

"I'll ship the guns and if I find anything personal in all that business stuff I'll send it as well." Bert never blinked when he told his Big Fat Lie. Big Fat Lies all around it seems! He hugged them both and got back into his car.

"I just let them off at the airport. I should be there in an hour."

"Okay," said John Cates. "I'll meet you at the house."

Once Susan's flight departed Laura called James to make sure he knew when to pick her up. She had called him every night and he listened to her talk about Andy and Bert and Father John. She told him about their decisions for the house, about talking to Kaurie, about the funeral. He told her about a bear attacking a hiker up in the Tetons, about his woodworking projects, about the dog. It was comforting to talk about routine, ordinary things. She did not tell him about Susan and the picture. The conversation ended with her saying "I love you, babe." James said" . . . love you too."

"Did everything go okay?" John said as Bert got out of his car. He had been waiting, somewhat impatiently; and was relieved they would soon put an end to everything.

"Yeah, it did. Susan should be gone in just a little while and Laura's plane leaves 45 minutes later. They asked me to let them off at the curb. Thank God, they didn't want me to go in with them. That damn airport is so big. I probably would've had to rent a scooter. I'm telling you John, I'm sure as hell glad this thing is almost over. I've laid awake nights ever since Andy died worrying about it."

"I haven't been sleeping well either. He should have told them a long time ago"

"I know, I know. Whenever I confronted him he would say that Susan was fine, she didn't remember anything, and that's the way he wanted it. I don't know why he kept the Homestead Hills file after everything was over. I was the one who handled all the payments but he insisted on keeping a list. All he would say is that he would throw it away when he didn't need it anymore". *What was 'to need'?* Bert sighed with the memories.

"Well let's get this over with." John said, anxious for Bert to unlock the door. "I didn't even think about his bible until Thursday night after the funeral. During all of our biblical conversations he had his bible and I had mine. I don't know for sure he ever wrote anything about Grace in it, I'm just afraid that he may have. Laura said she didn't find it and truthfully I don't know if she even looked for it. Once it was decided that you would take over I guess she figured if you found it you'd send it to them."

"Yeah, well if I'd heard about his death sooner I could've gone over there and searched through his office and we wouldn't have to be worrying about all this crap. He would never talk about it, even after a couple of bourbons."

They walked into the living room and, though they had been at Andy's many times, the atmosphere was different this time. Though the rooms were full and the shades were up, it felt empty, gloomy. John went into Andy's bedroom to look for the bible. Bert walked into Andy's office and heaved a sigh of relief, he was glad to see Andy's filing cabinet. He opened the top drawer.

"Oh, no!" He said quietly.

Although John was in the next room, the house was so quiet he heard Bert's remark clearly. "What?" John walked in to stand beside him. He looked into the file drawer. Except for a few paper clips and rubber bands, it was empty. All of the other drawers were empty as well.

Bert's face said it all. "Go ahead and look in his desk but I can guaran-damn-tee you it'll be empty too." It was.

"Now what?" John looked defeated.

"We wait."

Chapter Six

Two free-drink tickets made the flight home bearable for Laura. She boarded, stowed her carry-on and settled into her window seat. Flying was crowded in Economy Class and usually the window view wasn't worth the cramped conditions. However, this time she was willing to trade the roomier aisle seat for the cramped window seat; at least no one would have to walk over her to get in or out of the row. She pushed her shoulder bag under her seat, slipped off her shoes and as soon as they were airborne she reclined her seat as far back as possible and ordered two bourbon and cokes. She tried ordering three but the flight attendant said the flight was too short for her to be served three drinks. She plugged in the ear buds she purchased earlier and tuned to the elevator music. She didn't want to think; she didn't want to dream, she just wanted to check out for a few hours. She closed her eyes and when she opened them the flight attendant was instructing everyone to return their seat backs and tray tables to their upright and locked positions.

Changing planes in Salt Lake City was uneventful and soon she arrived in Rock Springs. She called James before she was off the plane and by the time she got her luggage and walked through the exit he was waiting for her. A quick hug and "I'm glad you're home" and she was resting her head against the window frame as he exited the airport and started the drive home. She slept until he turned onto their street and stopped in the driveway.

"Oh, babe! I'm so sorry. Everything finally caught up with me and I crashed and burned. I don't think I have ever been this tired." James retrieved her luggage and she walked in through the mudroom and the kitchen and into the living room where she collapsed into her recliner.

Jo-Jo came to greet her, placing her head on Laura's knee waiting to be scratched behind the ears. Laura complied and Jo-Jo was satisfied.

James picked up barbeque on the way home so they didn't have to worry about cooking. Chopped beef sandwiches, beer, kosher pickles, baked beans and peach cobbler. Laura didn't know if she was more tired than hungry or just the opposite, but she managed to eat without falling asleep in her plate. He cleared the table while she told him about the last six days, leaving out the part about the picture and Susan's meltdown. He apologized about not being there with her and she assured him (really, not a Big Fat Lie!) it was okay. She was busy from daylight till dark and she knew he would have been uncomfortable with the whole situation.

The bourbon on the plane and the beer with the barbeque at home added up to exhaustion requiring immediate sleep. She didn't even unpack and was out the second her head hit the pillow. James came in and covered her with the comforter and stood there for a few moments, stroking her hair and watching her sleep.

Monday morning

"James! I don't even remember getting into bed!" She walked out onto the back deck, wearing jeans and a tee shirt, her hair still wet from the shower. A carafe of coffee and a plate of buttered toast under a metal dome were on the deck table. A shower, coffee and toast; she was well on her way to recovery! She still felt tired but it was understandable considering the demands of the last week.

"Do you even remember coming home or having dinner?" He laughed as he fed toast to Jo-Jo. "Your eyes were open but I don't know if you were really awake and you snored!" She threw a bite of toast at him. "Like a freight train, like an avalanche, you rattled the windows!"

"Okay, okay. Enough! I don't know when I've ever been that tired. Thanks for tucking me in. Once I catch up on my sleep I'll stop snoring."

"Then you better go on back to sleep and finish catching up. I ended up in Erin's room last night because you were so loud. I miss my side of the bed!"

"And I missed you on your side of the bed. I'm ready to get back to normal!"

"Me too," he said, standing and brushing breakfast crumbs from his hands. He took Jo-Jo's leash from one of the hooks beside the door. "Go take a nap. Jo-Jo and I are on our way to Arapahoe.

"Nah, I'm good. I need to unpack and today is Knit Group. If I go to sleep now I won't be able so sleep tonight. I'll go by the store on my way home and get a pack of those anti-snore things you stick on your nose. Maybe I won't snore tonight."

James laughed and shook his head. "Yeah, we'll see! We'll be back in two hours and I bet I find you asleep." He hooked Jo-Jo to her leash and they walked across the driveway and into the forest. Laura could hear the jingle of the bear bell getting further and further away.

She loaded the dishes into the dishwasher and unpacked her suitcases. The sun was shining brightly through the windows and she felt a sense of contentment. The last week was grueling and she was happy to be home again.

She was on the road driving down to the Community Center when she passed a brown delivery truck going the opposite direction. "The boxes! They're already here? That was fast!" She made a quick U-turn and followed the truck up the road and parked beside it on the driveway.

"Are you Laura Gregory?" The delivery man said as he was getting down from the truck. He was holding a tracking scanner and when she said yes he started entering information. "You have nine boxes here. Some of them are heavy. Would you like me to bring them in for you?"

"Yes, please," and within just a few minutes the boxes were unloaded onto a hand truck and stacked in the living room. Laura signed her name on the little glass window in the scanner and the delivery man was on his way.

Knit Group was forgotten as Laura surveyed the stacks of boxes. There were four labeled "Filing Cabinet" and it was those she opened first. She didn't review the contents of each of the files. If it looked interesting she put it in a stack, if not, she threw it in a trash bag. By the time she finished the four filing cabinet boxes, she had a small stack of files and the trash bag was getting full. Then she started with the boxes labeled "Desk". Most of the contents went into the trash bag. The box from the middle drawer where she found the photograph was scrutinized closely.

The ordinary contents of a desk drawer. There was a crumpled manila mailing envelope. She did not open it.

She opened the box packed with the keepsakes. Daddy's bible was there and she took it out and put it aside. She glanced through the remaining contents and put the top back on the box.

She stood up and took the trash bag out to the large bins built onto the side of the workshop. James designed them to be "bear proof" and she had to set the bag on the ground and open several latches intended to defeat the efforts of the cleverest of bears. Whenever the bins were full James loaded the garbage bags into the pick-up and hauled them to the waste transfer station. Aspen Falls didn't provide trash pick-up as a city service. Residents could pay for private trash pick-up but James felt like they could save money by hauling it himself and paying a small fee per bag.

She came back into the living room and sat on the floor beside the stack of files. She found his will in one folder. She found her, his and Susan's birth certificates and baptismal certificates in another folder. In another one she found two life insurance policies for Andrew Everett Billings for $10,000 each. The beneficiaries were herself and her sister. A business card for the insurance agent was clipped to the folder. Within the folder was a large unlabeled envelope. Laura had no idea how to interpret what she was looking at but it listed their mother's name and an amount: $750,000! A business card from a bank in Dallas was clipped to the document. Susan was the only one who could figure this one out. She would talk to her about it later.

By this time Laura was trembling. She went into the kitchen and got the bottle of bourbon from the pantry. To hell with the time of day, she needed something to calm her nerves; something to give her the nerve to continue. She poured three fingers worth into a rocks glass, added two ice cubes and took a sip. It stung her throat as she swallowed, but it was a good sting. She walked back to the files and took another sip and sat down on the floor again.

The next folder was labeled Homestead Hills. Laura skimmed through it and then turned on her computer and googled Homestead Hills, Texas.

Homestead Hills was a private psychiatric hospital in Bristol, Texas located between San Angelo and Abilene. The website showed a sprawling, one-story building, surrounded by lawns and rock gardens, walking paths and a swimming pool. There were short-term placements available for drug and alcohol rehabilitation, offering acupuncture, exercises, yoga, Hippotherapy and psychotherapy. Long-term care was available for those patients unable to respond to the short-term treatment options.

She went back to the file and reread it. It contained two envelopes and a simple spreadsheet. At the top of the spreadsheet Grace Billings was printed in bold capital letters. There were two columns: Date and Monthly Charges. The dates started 46 years ago and the monthly charges started at $3000 and when they stopped 20 years later the charges had gradually risen to $4250. At the bottom something had been written in pencil and erased. Laura could make out "Bert" but nothing else. One envelope was addressed to Andy with Homestead Hills as the return address. It contained a letter on the Homestead Hills letterhead and dated the same date as the last entry.

Dear Mr. Billings,

Thank you for allowing us the privilege of caring for your wife, Grace. Although she was unable to respond to any of the treatments available, our staff learned to care deeply for her over the twenty years she was at our facility. Her death was a sad occasion for all of us here at Homestead Hills.

We understand why your visits were infrequent. It is difficult to relate to someone who can not speak. You were always so positive and complimentary to our staff when you did visit and our hope is that you and your daughters will be able to continue on with the assurance we did everything we could to make your wife comfortable while she was with us.

Sincerely,
Dr. Richard Nichols,
Director of Clinical Services
Homestead Hills Hospital

The other envelope contained a death certificate.

The rest of the files were reviewed and the rest of the bourbon was sipped. There was nothing else of value or interest and it was dumped into a new trash bag.

All that was left was the manila mailing envelope. It was addressed to Grace Billings at Andy's address on Mission Lane in Kerrville and was postmarked six months ago. The return address was from Carlson Photography Studio in Junction, Texas. It contained a one-page letter:

> Dear Mrs. Billings,
>
> My father was Ray Carlson, owner of Carlson Photography Studio in Junction, Texas.
>
> He recently passed away and I am preparing to sell the building. I was going through several old filing cabinets in a store room and found this photograph. Attached was an information card with your address and an invoice for a down payment of $20.
>
> It's been sitting in this filing cabinet for more than 45 years. Apparently it was moved from the front office to the store room and the folder was overlooked. It appears you may have forgotten about it. There was a Balance Due statement included with the photo but after so long I don't think that it's important anymore. I know it has been a very long time, however, I hope the photo is still meaningful.
>
> Sincerely,
> Frank Carlson

"Oh, dear God in Heaven! I have to call Susan. I have to call Bert Shaffer." Laura closed her eyes and prayed, *"What do I do now?"*

When she opened her eyes she was laying on her side on the floor beside the files and the trash bag; her head resting on the crook of her elbow. Through the bay windows she could see the sun above the horizon and shadows from the mountains were starting to creep across the valley.

Her head was pounding and her mouth tasted like crap. She'd had nothing but toast and then the bourbon. A sure-fired recipe for a nice long nap.

"A nap! James told me to take a nap, but I don't think he intended me to sleep on the floor!" She stood up and the headache shot like a hot knife from between her eyes down through to the base of her skull. *How could he let me sleep like this?* She looked at the clock and it was 7:15!

"James? Hey James, where are you?" The house was silent. He should have been back before noon! She walked through the rest of the house. He was not there. Neither was Jo-Jo.

She went back through the kitchen and mud room and out the back door. The lights were not on in the workshop but she checked the building anyway. The doors were locked and she could see where James repaired the hinges after the bear had broken in.

Now her heart was pounding. She was scared. *I'm calling 9-1-1. Something is wrong, bad wrong!* She went back into the house and looked in her purse for her cell phone. They'd never had a land line; cell phones had always served that purpose.

She found her blinking cell phone. Three missed calls from Susan! Why didn't she hear her phone? When she looked she saw she had never turned on the ringer after landing at the airport.

She had to dial 9-1-1 three times because her hands were shaking so badly.

"9-1-1, what is your emergency?"

"Opal," (Opal Robinson from Knit Group) "this is Laura Gregory. Please send someone up here right away. James is missing! He went for a hike with the dog this morning and he never came back" Normally, Opal would have gone through the scripted questions 9-1-1 operators are trained to ask, but she knew Laura and she could sense the fear in her voice.

"Hang on Laura. Frank Bell is on patrol. I'll send him right up there. Don't hang up. I'll stay on the phone with you till he gets there" Laura could hear Opal on the radio with Frank telling him to go up to Laura Gregory's place, 442 Mountainside Circle. James was missing and Laura sounded frantic.

"Okay, Laura, he's on his way. He's out by Public Works so he'll be there in less than five minutes." Opal then went into "9-1-1 operator" mode asking questions, trying to get pertinent information for the report she would later write, as well as to trying to reassure Laura. Frank drove up as she was still asking questions.

"He's here, Opal. I'll tell him everything, I'm hanging up." Frank Bell parked his cruiser behind Laura's Jeep and got out, holding a notebook and clipping his radio onto his belt. Laura was beside his car within seconds, talking too fast and crying and not making much sense.

"Whoa, Laura, whoa. Slow down, I can't understand you. Come on; let's go inside, you can sit down and I can get all the details." They walked into the kitchen and sat at the table. She started with this morning and the toast and the exhaustion from the trip and James taking the dog for a walk and her meeting the delivery man and going through all the files and having a drink to calm her nerves and falling asleep and waking up and James is gone!

"So, you had a drink this morning and passed out and didn't wake up until about 30 minutes ago?"

"Damn it, Frank!" Laura could hear the rumor mill starting up now: Laura Gregory is a drunk who was passed out on the floor while her husband went missing!

"Okay, okay. Let's start over. You are going to have to slow down and tell me again. What you have said so far is just one big jumble of words."

"Frank! It'll be dark soon, we have to go look for him; he's probably hurt and bleeding some where!" Laura heard the hysteria in her voice and took a slow, deep breath. "Frank, please! We have to go look for him!" She began the story again, speaking as calmly as she could, telling the details again as quickly as possible. Sunset this time of year was a little after 8:00 and she wanted to start looking for him as soon as she could. When the sun went down it got cold in the mountains.

"You're right about it being dark soon but we have some time to drive around. Have you called any of his friends?"

"Frank, he doesn't have any friends! I mean any close friends. He goes down to Three Pines and has coffee. He and Reggie Martin talk when he's in the café but that's about it."

"Oh, sure, I've seen him there some mornings when I stopped in. I'll check with those guys if I need to. Now, I hate to ask this next question but it's important. Did you guys have an argument or anything? Could he just be out somewhere, cooling off maybe?"

The thought never even occurred to Laura. "No! I, I . . ." she was at a loss for words. "We don't fight, we get along fine! I had to go down to Texas; my dad passed away and my sister and I had to make arrangements for his funeral so, I was down there for a week and I got home last night. He picked me up at the airport in Rock Springs and we drove back up here. He stopped and picked up barbeque and we ate when we got home. I was exhausted from the past week so I went to sleep right after we ate. I got up this morning and he was already up; he'd made coffee and toast and he left to walk the dog right after I sat down to eat. And that's it Frank, he's missing and he could be hurt. We've got to go look for him!"

"Why didn't he go to Texas with you?" Laura knew that question was coming. Any other husband would have gone with his wife to her father's funeral. Any other husband would have been right with her to support her and comfort her. She drew a deep breath and repeated the story she had used too many times to justify James' behavior. Someday she was going to have to work on a new story.

"Alright, we'll drive around and look." He walked outside and got into his cruiser and Laura grabbed her phone and purse and got in the passenger side.

"Does he have a cell phone? Have you checked to see if you missed any calls?" He didn't say " . . . while you were passed out".

"He didn't call, but you know how the coverage is out past our street! He walks the dog around Arapahoe and he usually can't get calls out there!"

"I know, I know. But check your phone anyway. Maybe there's a missed call."

Laura checked her phone again. The only calls today were the three missed calls from Susan.

They drove up and down most of the streets on the north side of town. With a population of 2,003 there weren't many streets to search. Frank radioed Jason Mitchell, the other officer on the shift and he started driving on the south side. Frank drove up and down a few of the streets and roads outside the city limits. They drove around the road one block up from Mountainside Circle. That was as close to Arapahoe as the roads went and that's where James usually took the dog off the leash. After that was BLM land. Even though the lake was just a 45 minute hike from Aspen Falls, the only roads that went there came down from further north on 287.

By 8:30 it was dark enough and the street lights came on. They stopped at the few houses on Mountainside Circle and asked if anyone had seen James or the dog. No one had seen them.

"Laura, we've done all we can do tonight. We will start at first light in the morning. I'll talk to Chief Daily. I'll stop by Three Pines; maybe those guys have seen him. I know how worried you are, but we'll find him. He probably got lost and he's hunkered down somewhere waiting for daylight. He's got Jo-Jo and when we start searching in the morning we might be able to hear her barking. Let's get you in the house and I'll be here by 8:00. What was he wearing this morning?" Frank saw the devastation on her face. "Why don't you let me bring Ivy over to spend the night?

Laura was frightened. The thought of James out there in the dark, maybe hurt, was terrifying. Ivy Bell would be good company but she needed to call Susan. Susan said she would talk about the picture someday, maybe. Well today is that someday, they had to talk about what Laura discovered in the stuff from Andy's office and she didn't need an audience for this conversation.

"No, thanks Frank. I'll be okay. I know she would be good company but I need to call my sister. I can't believe I don't even remember what he was wearing!" She fought back panic. Frank was concerned but Susan appeared resolute about staying home alone.

"Okay, I get off at midnight but I'll keep looking. I'll check by here on and off. Call the station if he shows up. Are you sure you are okay staying by yourself?"

"Yes, really I'm fine. I'm going to call my sister and then go through his closet and figure out what he was wearing. I doubt I'll be getting a lot of sleep. I'll see you in the morning."

Laura turned on the deck lights so Frank could get to his cruiser safely and stood there for a few minutes after he left, straining to hear Jo-Jo barking. She heard the wind and the sound of a truck further down towards town, but no dog. She closed and locked the door and reached to turn out the light but she changed her mind. She had never once been scared out here. Neighbors weren't more than twenty-five yards away. There was a streetlight at the end of the block. She wasn't scared, she just felt better with the outside lights on.

Chapter Seven

Sunday

There is no such thing as a direct flight from San Antonio, Texas to Sinclair, Kansas. Uncle Bob used to say "You can't get there from here" and he was right! There are no direct flights from anywhere to anywhere in Kansas!

Susan had to fly to Houston, ride a tram from one terminal to another, sit for thirty minutes, board another plane, fly to Wichita Mid-Continent Airport, find her car and drive north 125 miles to Sinclair. She was grateful for all the flying and riding and driving. It kept her focus away from the last five days. She purposely filled her thoughts with trivialities. Susan had always been very good at avoiding anxiety. She probably had less wrinkles than any other 51-year old woman in Kansas because she had the ability to ignore worry!

She turned into her gravel driveway, got her luggage from the trunk and walked up the front steps and into the living room of her lake house.

She dropped the car keys in the wooden bowl on the table by the door and her luggage was abandoned in the middle of the living room. The back wall of the living room was floor to ceiling glass overlooking a deck with a wooden pier jutting out into Milford Lake, the "Lake of Blue Water". Serene and glassy, it called her outside. She stopped long enough to grab a beer from the fridge, slip off her shoes and walk barefoot down the pier to the end where there were two Adirondack chairs and a small table. Oh, she had missed this! This was her favorite spot and she sat down, leaned back and enjoyed the view.

"Hey, Suzy-Q! Let's go for a ride!"

Susan had never seen Mama drive the green car. Daddy always drove the green car. Daddy drove the green car when he would take her and Laura to school on school days or church on church days. Susan thought it was funny 'cause school and church were at the same place. Daddy said some kids go to school in one place and church in another place but the Billings family goes to Saint Al's for everything. She and Laura even stayed there after school and in the summer and Daddy would pick them up when he finished his work. Saint Al's wasn't the real name of the church. The real name was hard to say, it sounded like Santa Wishus. Everybody just called it Saint Al's. Mama didn't go to church. Daddy said she was tired and it took too much out of her. Susan didn't know what that meant but Daddy said it a lot.

Sometimes Daddy drove the old white truck to go to his work. It made funny loud noises and smoke came out of the back. He drove the green car when they needed to go places like the grocery store or the movies or on drives to see Daddy's j'ology. Mama would go on the j'ology drives. She would sit in the front seat and look out the window. Sometimes she would talk if Daddy talked to her but mostly she would look out the window. Daddy would tell her and Laura all about j'ology. He liked j'ology.

Daddy would cook for everybody. He was always laughing and joking and teasing her and Laura and he would let them help him cook. Mama didn't cook very much. Daddy said it took too much out of her. Sometimes she would help him make French toast on Saturday mornings. She would sit in the kitchen and stir the eggs and watch Daddy but she usually went back into her and Daddy's bedroom or laid on the couch in the living room or sat on the glider on the back porch.

Sometimes she would talk to Daddy or Laura or Susan. She would eat breakfast and lunch and supper with them but she didn't eat very much and she didn't talk very much. She never stayed in the same room with the girls and Andy for very long. Daddy would always tell her "I love you, Grace" and Mama would smile a little smile. Daddy would tell Laura "I love you Little Girl. I love you bunches and bunches." And he would hug Laura. Daddy would tell Susan "I love you Baby Girl. I love you bunches and bunches." And he would hug her. Daddy always called Laura "Little Girl" and he called her "Baby Girl". Only Mama called her Suzy-Q. Everyone else called her Susan.

Sometimes when Daddy hugged her and Laura his eyes would be wet, but daddies don't cry so she guessed his eyes were just wet sometimes. She and Laura loved Daddy very, very much. He would take her into Laura's room every night and tell them some silly story they liked and then they would say prayers. They always prayed for Mama.

Today was a Big Day! It was Saturday and Laura was going to church camp for two weeks; fourteen days and nights! Camp was only for the big kids. Laura was a big kid, she was seven. The little kids didn't go to camp yet. Susan was a little kid and she couldn't go for two more years. Laura said at camp they slept on folding beds in "tent-shelters" and they went hiking and they made stuff and they went swimming and kayaking and they rode horses and they built campfires and they sang songs. Susan didn't know what kayaking meant but Laura sounded excited about it. Laura had never gone to camp before but her teacher told her all about it and that's how she knew to tell Susan all about it. Daddy was going to drive Laura to camp in the white truck because he was helping haul some of the camping gear. Daddy was always helping out when it came to his girls.

"Andy," Mama said. Daddy's real name was Andy. "I feel good today. I've been feeling good. Why don't Suzy-Q and I stay home? The truck is going to be really crowded and hot. We can stay home and make French toast!" Mama smiled and looked at Susan.

Susan thought it was a good idea. She was happy when Mama smiled. Sometimes Mama would pat her head and say "I love you, Suzy-Q" and she would pat Laura on the head and say "I love you, Laura." And they would say "I love you too, Mama."

Daddy looked at Mama and Mama smiled her little smile. He looked at Mama's eyes. Then he looked at Susan. "What do you think Baby Girl? Do you want to stay home with Mama and make French toast? I have to haul all this camping gear up to camp. I'll be gone for just a little bit. And then I'll be right back." Camp wasn't far away; it was on a river close to Kerrville.

Susan didn't want to ride in the hot, crowded truck and she liked it when she saw Mama smile so she said, "Yes, Daddy. Me and Mama can stay home. We can make French toast and we'll save some for you!"

Daddy looked at Mama, "Today does look like a good day, Grace. You think you and Baby Girl can hold down the fort while I'm gone?"

"Sure we can!" She patted Andy on the shoulder. "Y'all go on and Suzy-Q and I will have fun here and when you get back you can have French toast unless we eat it all before you get back!" Mama made a joke. Mama's little smile got bigger.

Daddy and Laura drove to camp and Susan and Mama stayed home.

"Hey, Suzy-Q! Let's go for a ride!"

"Are we gonna make French toast?'

"Well, we'll do that in just a little while. Let's go for a ride first and we'll go to the store. We need more syrup."

"Okay, Mama. Are you gonna drive the green car?"

"Sure, Suzy-Q! I'm a good driver. This'll be fun! This'll be our own little adventure, just me and you!"

Grace took the car keys hanging from the hook by the back door and got her purse from the bedroom. She was still smiling and Susan was happy to see Mama happy.

"Mama, we just passed the store, there it was!"

"Oh, dear, Suzy-Q. I missed the turn. That's okay, we'll find another one."

Grace drove west on I-10; Susan happily chattered about the j'ology they passed. Andy was a good teacher and she recognized the formations he taught her and Laura about. Soon they came to the city of Junction.

"Is the store here, Mama? Will we stop here?"

"Why look at this! Yes, we're stopping right here." Grace was going above the speed limit and she had to step hard on the brakes to make the right turn into a parking lot.

"I like this place, Suzy-Q! Let's go in here."

"But, Mama this isn't a grocery store. What place is this?"

"I wasn't planning on stopping but then I saw the sign and I knew we needed to go in here. Let's get our picture made! I want a picture of my sweet little Suzy-Q."

Grace parked in front of a small photography studio. Usually when Susan got her picture made at school Daddy made sure she had on pretty clothes and her hair was brushed. Now she was wearing shorts and a tee shirt and sandals and her hair hadn't been brushed since she got up this morning.

"Good morning!"

"Good morning!" Mama's voice sounded funny. She smiled but her smile wasn't as big as it was this morning. "I'd like my picture made with my little girl."

"Well, you've come to the right place. I don't have a sitting scheduled for another hour so I've got time to take some pictures of you and your pretty little girl!" The man at the picture place wore a big smile and his smile looked happy. Not like Mama's.

"My name's Ray Carlson and I'll be your photographer. What kind of picture did you have in mind Mrs . . . ?" He said waiting for Grace to introduce herself.

"I just want a simple picture of Suzy-Q and me together. Nothing fancy." Mama's voice was a teeny tiny bit shakier.

"Alrighty, then. Let's go to the back and see what we can do."

The picture man talked about all kinds of ways to take their picture but Mama just kept saying "No!" So finally he sat them down on a bench with Mama sitting back and Susan sitting forward and the light on his camera flashed a bunch of times.

"Well now, I'm sure I'll get a good picture from all those shots. If you'll fill out this information card I'll get in touch with you. There'll be a twenty dollar deposit. You can come back to look at the proofs and choose the one you like best."

"You mean I can't get the picture right now?" Mama's hands were shaking as she wrote her name and address on the card.

"Oh, no ma'am," the picture man said. "We send all our photos out to be developed but I can have the proofs ready for you by this coming Wednesday."

Mama's eyes got big around and she said "Why don't you just pick out the one you think is best and print that one."

"Well, uh, yes ma'am, I can do that. I'll call you when it's ready."

"No!" Mama's voice was kinda loud. "I, I don't have a phone. I'll come get it."

"But, Mama, we have a . . ."

"Shush Suzy-Q. If you don't be quiet you'll have to wait in the car." Mama had never talked like that to Susan before. She was always quiet and never used a mean voice.

"How much did you say it would be?"

"Twenty dollars, ma'am, and a balance due of twenty when you pick up your picture. Would you like me to put it in a frame for you?"

"I guess so. I assume that will be twenty more?" Mama's voice and hands were shaking.

"Oh, no ma'am, we have some nice frames for ten dollars." The picture man was not smiling anymore. Susan didn't know what his face meant.

Mama opened her purse and Susan saw money; lots and lots of money. Not the quarters and nickels you use in the coke machine; it was paper money. All in wads in Mama's purse.

Mama took two wads of the paper money from her purse and dropped them on the counter. "I'm afraid you'll have to count it out yourself." All the paper money was one-dollar bills and five-dollar bills. Daddy had taught Susan about money when they went to the grocery store.

The picture man looked at Mama and then he flattened out some of the money and said, "Alrighty, then, that's twenty dollars." He took the flat money and put it in a drawer. He didn't touch the other wads of money. Mama looked at him and scooped the money back in her purse.

"I'll be back later," Mama said very softly.

"Yes ma'am. Now you have yourself a good day." And he walked them to the glass front door and opened it for them. *What a kook,* he said to himself after the door closed. *I'm really ready for my vacation. Buddy'll have to handle her when she comes back. I've done enough.* He walked to the back to get the negatives ready to send to the developer.

Mama and Susan got back into Daddy's green car but Mama was shaking real bad and she just sat behind the wheel and squeezed the steering wheel with her hands. Her fingers looked white. In a few minutes Mama stopped squeezing the steering wheel and started the engine. She wasn't shaking so bad anymore.

"Mama, I'm hungry. We didn't eat any breakfast." Susan wasn't scared of Mama even through she was acting kinda scary.

"Oh, Suzy-Q! I'm so sorry. Of course you're hungry. What kind of a mama am I to let my little girl be hungry?" Mama tried to smile her smile. It came out kinda crooked 'cause her lips were shaking. "What would you like? How about a hamburger and a coke? Would you like that?

"Oh, yum, Mama! That sounds good, but a hamburger? For breakfast?"

"Why sure for breakfast! We're on an adventure right? And I see a place right down there where we can get you a hamburger. We'll drive over there right now. And, we'll drive up to the window and when we do will you be a little sweetie and get the money out of my purse to pay for it? You can count, right?"

"Of course, I can count. I learned to count to a hundred when I was four!" *Why didn't Mama know this? Daddy did.*

"Then will we go to the grocery store? Daddy could be back from camp now and he might be worried about us." Susan felt a little worry in her stomach.

"Why, of course we will. Let's get you that hamburger first and then we'll find the store and then we'll go home to Daddy." Mama looked straight ahead and her voice sounded high and different.

At the drive-up window Mama made Susan lean over from her side of the car and tell the lady what she wanted. "I want a junior hamburger, plain and nothing on it but ketchup and I want a coke. Please." Daddy said you should always say please. Grown-ups liked it when you said please.

"That'll be two dollars and forty-nine cents little missy." Mama looked at her purse and Susan knew to get some of the wadded up dollars out. She gave it to Mama and Mama gave it to the lady and said "Keep the change."

"Oh, no ma'am. We're not allowed to keep tips. But thank you very much."

"Just throw it out the window then, I don't want it." Mama said, not looking at the lady.

The lady didn't say anything. Then the hamburger was ready and she handed the bag and the plastic cup out of the drive-up window and Mama passed it to Susan and drove the green car away, kinda fast.

"Go ahead and eat it now, Suzy-Q. It's okay to eat in the car." Mama said while she was driving, looking straight ahead.

"What about you, Mama? You wanna bite of my hamburger?" Susan offered her hamburger to Mama.

"What a sweetie you are. No, I'm not a bit hungry. You just eat up and I'll look for the grocery store."

Mama drove and drove and Susan thought about Daddy. *He would be very worried about them.* She ate her hamburger and drank most of her coke; she spilled the rest in her lap when she tried to give some to Mama. Mama said she didn't care.

"Suzy-Q, I still can't find that grocery store, but I am getting real tired and we're going to have to stop up here." They were approaching Fort Stockton, Texas. Mama said "See that big tall sign Suzy-Q? It says $39.99 Motel. We are going to stop there so I can rest. This has taken a lot out of me. Open my purse and get out one hundred dollars. Can you count to one hundred?"

Susan just looked at Mama and reached for her purse. She already told Mama she could count to a hundred. Mama stopped at $39.99 Motel and Susan started counting out the money. Susan could count but she couldn't add the ones and fives very well and she wasn't sure if she had enough money or not so she put in some extra one-dollars just in case.

"I've got to go pay for this myself. I don't think they'll take the money from you. I'll be right back. Don't get out of this car for any reason." Mama flattened out the money like the man did at the picture place and got out of the car and went inside a little room with a blinking sign over the door that spelled O F F I C E. Susan knew her letters and some of her sounds but she couldn't read that word O F F I C E. Another sign taped on the door spelled C A S H O N L Y. Susan couldn't read that either. There was a big telephone on the wall on the outside of the glass door.

Mama walked into the little room. Susan could see her through the glass door. "How many nights will this get me?" She said softly. She was using every ounce of strength she had just trying not to shake.

The man behind the counter looked at the money and said "That'll getcha two with change."

"Then give me a key." She didn't have to fill out a card or register her car. This wasn't that kind of a motel. She hadn't been away from Andy in a long, long time. She didn't really know just how long she had been dependent on him for her every need. *Poor Andy. H's so good and I'm just worthless!*

The guy behind the counter had seen plenty of druggies like this one. He didn't care what she would be doing in the room. He did his job, minded his own business and even if he'd noticed the little girl in the car he wouldn't have given a damn.

Mama drove Daddy's green car around to the back of the building where Susan saw lots of doors with numbers on them. Mama got out of the car and put a key in the lock of a door with the numbers 1 1 6.

"C'mon, Suzy-Q. Mama needs to rest."

Now Susan was very scared. She was trying hard not to cry, but some tears were rolling down her face. "Mama, what about Daddy? Don't you think we should call Daddy?"

"No, I don't think we should call Daddy! Don't say Daddy again!" Mama's hands were shaking and her voice was shaking and her mouth was shaking. "Come into this room and shut the door. I have to get some rest and then we will find the grocery store and then go home. Don't argue with me."

Susan walked into the room. It didn't smell good. It smelled like pine trees and strange smells she had never smelled before. There were two beds and a TV on a desk. There was a bathroom with a toilet and a sink and a shower. Susan didn't like that bathroom. It smelled bad. It wasn't like their bathroom at home. Their bathroom at home smelled good and it had a window and it was light. This room didn't have a window and it was dark.

Mama turned on the TV and found a station with cartoons and funny shows Susan liked to watch. "Can you hear this?"

"Yes, ma'am."

"Okay then, you watch this channel. I'm putting the channel changer up on top of the TV, you don't need to change any channels or watch anything else. Sit on the bed and be a quiet a little Suzy-Q and Mama will rest and then we will go. Don't you dare go outside. Don't you even touch the door. Do you understand me?" Mama's voice was scary.

"Yes, ma'am."

Susan was scared and crying and Mama acted like she was scared, too. Susan sat on the bed and watched TV and Mama laid down on the other bed and put a pillow over her head and went to sleep.

Susan wanted to call Daddy. She knew her telephone number and she knew her address, but there was no telephone in this room. Susan put her head down on one of the pillows and she went to sleep, like Mama.

When she woke up the room was dark. There was light shining from under the bathroom door and Susan could hear Mama in the bathroom, talking. She couldn't understand what Mama was saying. Mama was crying and she heard banging noises.

"Mama, please come out. I'm scared Mama. Please come out." Susan was crying and her nose was running and she didn't have a kleenex and she was wiping her nose on her shirt and she was scared.

Mama got very quiet in the bathroom and then she opened the door. Susan screamed. Mama's hair was messy and her shirt was unbuttoned and she didn't have her shoes on and her face was all red. Mama yelled something but Susan was crying and she couldn't understand what she was saying. Mama shook Susan hard; so hard she started to hiccup.

"Suzy—Q you have to get into the closet. You have to get in there right now."

Susan was crying again. "Mama, please, Mama, please call Daddy."

Mama screamed at Susan again. "You get in that closet right now. Right now!" Mama took a deep breath and made her hands into fists. "Honey, please. Mama is sick and I'm afraid you'll get hurt so get in the god damn closet!" Mama was screaming again. *Daddy said you should never take God's name in vain and Mama just did.*

Mama opened the closet door and shoved Susan in and slammed it shut. It was dark and stinky and Susan was very, very scared. There was a loud bump on the other side of the door, a loud hard bumping sound.

Susan was sobbing and banging on the door when something loud, loud hit the door. "Suzy-Q you be real quiet now, you hear Mama? You be real quiet and everything will be okay, okay?"

Susan sat down on the scratchy stinky carpet and made herself stop crying. She was shaking and hiccuping but she wasn't crying. She could hear Mama outside the door, mumbling and talking and crying. Every once in a while she would hear a bump and then it got real quiet.

"Mama? Mama?" Susan said softly. "Mama, I have to go to the bathroom. Mama, I have to go real bad. Mama?

Mama didn't answer. Susan cried. She had to pee, really really bad but Mama wouldn't let her out of the closet. She stepped over to the very far corner and pulled her shorts and panties down and she peed in the corner. She was miserable and embarrassed that she had to pee in the corner. There was no tissue so she just pulled up her shorts and moved over to the other side of the closet. She pressed her ear against the closet door and listened. She could hear Mama mumbling on the other side of the door.

"Daddy, Daddy where are you?" she whispered in the dark. "Daddy, come get me." she cried in the dark.

She fell asleep again and when she woke up she could see light under the door. She heard Mama again, crying and mumbling and making banging noises. "Mama? Mama? Mama, please let me out!" Susan spoke very softly this time.

"No, Suzy-Q, Mama can't let you out. Mama loves you, Suzy-Q, you are a good little girl, but Mama can't let you out."

That was the last time she heard Mama. She stayed in the closet and peed and pooped in the corner and slept in the other corner and she pretended she was talking to Daddy. It got dark under the door and she slept again. She opened her eyes and there was light again. She didn't hear Mama. She was very, very hungry. Her stomach hurt and she threw up.

Loud banging, loud banging! "Open up in there, c'mon lady open the door." More loud banging and a scary voice yelling "Open up! I'm calling the cops if you don't open up!" Susan got really quiet. She was afraid the person with the scary voice would come into the closet and get her. Then it was quiet again.

Then the loudest banging she ever heard. Then more voices. "Awww, shit. Look at this mess, Ronnie! Hey lady, lady are you okay? Awww man, you better call an ambulance, she's whacked out big time." Susan was very quiet.

After a little while there were more voices. "Ma'am, ma'am? Can you hear me? Ma'am, can you look at me? Okay, get the gurney in here, this is bad."

"What was she doing? Why is all the furniture piled up against the closet door?"

"Well, how the hell should I know, and who the fuck is gonna clean this up 'cause I'm sure not!"

"There's her purse. Look inside for her wallet."

"Damn, look at those wads of money!"

"Ma'am, is your name Grace? Grace, can you hear me?"

"Okay, load'er up. Radio in so they'll know she's coming. I'll start an IV."

A lady's voice, not scary like that other voice; "What's the deal with all the furniture? Why is it stacked up against the closet? Let's get this stuff out of the way."

Loud banging, loud banging. Scary noises. The closet door opened suddenly and bright light streamed in.

"Oh, Mary, Mother of God! Oh Joey, look! Call another bus, now, NOW, do it now!"

"Oh, baby!" The lady knelt on the floor and reached into the closet toward Susan and Susan screamed "No, Mama! No!" She pushed her body back into the corner and flailed her arms furiously.

"Oh, sweetie, I'm not gonna hurt you. You're gonna be okay baby. I'm not your mama. My name's Annie and I'm here to help you. Honey, can you tell me your name?"

"Susan. My-my-my name is Susan."

Susan was gripping the arms of the Adirondack. Sweat was pouring down her face and her teeth were clenched together so hard her jaw was in agonizing pain. A keening, high-pitched sound was coming from her throat. The memory of those three days came with no warning and Susan could smell the smells and feel the textures. The beer bottle was on its side and had rolled to the edge of the dock leaving a trail of brown foam.

CHAPTER EIGHT

Monday night

Laura didn't turn off the light on the back deck after Frank backed his cruiser out of the driveway. She didn't know what to do first. She needed to figure out what James was wearing. She had to call Susan; there were three missed calls from her on her phone and no telling what had happened. She checked her phone; the ringer was on, alerts for the three missed calls were blinking and there were no missed calls from James. She checked her history. The last time they talked on the phone was when she called him from the plane after she landed in Rock Springs.

"Where are you, James? Where are you?" she sobbed. She sat down in a kitchen chair and laid her head on her arms on the table. Her head was splitting, she felt awful and she realized she'd had nothing today but toast and booze and that was more than 10 hours ago. She stood in front of the open refrigerator and ate cold barbeque, beans and cobbler from the containers. She threw the rest of the food into the garbage and as she put the fork in the kitchen sink she felt thirstier than she had ever been in her life. She turned on the cold water, drank straight from the faucet and splashed water on her face. Booze always made her thirsty.

She felt a little better; at least she could think more clearly. She walked into their bedroom and opened James' closet at the same time she was dialing Susan's number.

"Laura?"

"Yeah, it's me. Susan I need you, I really, really need you to come up here." Laura said at exactly the same time Susan said, "Laura, I really, really need to talk to you and I don't want to do it over the phone! What have you been doing? What took you so long to call me back?" They both stopped talking at the same time and then started and stopped again before Laura finally said "Wait, wait, stop, stop, STOP! Okay now, start all over, you go first!"

"Laura! I remember about the picture, I remember about all of it!" Susan began, sobbing and talking and blowing her nose and was totally unintelligible.

"SUSAN, please! I can't understand you. Please, take a slow, deep breath" Laura took a slow deep breath "and tell me again; the only words I understood were 'the picture'"!

"Okay, okay," She took the slow, deep breath. "I got home yesterday and went out on the dock to relax with a beer and it hit me like a freight train. Laura," Susan was crying quietly now instead of sobbing, "I remember everything about that picture, please, I need you here, I can't deal with this alone! You've got to come to Sinclair!" she paused for a moment, and then Laura heard a quick breath, "Wait, so, what, what were you trying to tell me?" Another deep breath.

Now Laura is the one sobbing, "Susan! I went through Daddy's files today and you're right, we do need to get together right now, but . . ." Laura tried to take the slow deep breath she suggested to her sister, but it turned into more sobbing and it was Susan's turn to say "Hey, hey calm down, now I can't understand you!"

"Daddy's files were delivered this morning and I found a bunch of stuff we need to talk about and I hadn't had anything but toast to eat and I was nervous and I made a drink and I fell asleep in the floor and when I woke up it was afternoon and James was missing!" The details came out in a turbo run-on sentence. "He never came home from walking the dog this morning Susan and now it's dark and he's out there all alone and he could be hurt and, and . . . ." and she couldn't talk any more. All she could do was cry. She was sitting on the floor in front of James' closet, crying and wiping her nose on the sleeve of her shirt.

"I can't come to Sinclair! You have to come here, Susan! I can't leave! The police are starting a search in the morning and I have to find James, Susan, please, please come up here. Please! I have to tell you what I found in Daddy's files!"

Susan sounded more in control than before. "What? What is it?"

Laura was more out of control than before. "It's too much to talk about right now! We can't do this over the phone! Please come Susan, I'm really scared."

"Okay, okay, look, I'm coming but I need to figure out the fastest way to get there and I need to make some phone calls. What are you doing right now?"

"I'm sitting on the floor in front of his closet. Frank wanted to know what he was wearing. I've got to figure out what he was wearing." Laura said, still crying.

"Frank? Who's Frank?"

"Frank Bell. He's the police officer that came out when I called 9-1-1. He's married to a friend of mine."

"Oh, okay. I'm going to hang up and make some plans. You stay right where you are. Go through his closet; see if you can remember what he was wearing. I'll call you back as soon as I can."

"Okay," Laura said. "I love you, Susan. Hurry and call me back, okay?"

"I love you, too. I will, I'll call you back. It's going to be okay! Okay? Don't worry!" *Don't worry! What a stupid thing to say! Why do people say "Don't worry" when they know that's exactly what you're going to do?*

Laura stared into his closet. She stood up and started moving the hanging clothes from one side of the closet to the other. She knew he was wearing jeans. It was still too cool this early in the spring for him to be wearing shorts and he usually wore long-sleeved tee shirts. But what color, which one? She walked into the bathroom and dumped all the dirty clothes out of the hamper, trying to remember which shirts were neither there nor hanging in the closet. She knew he usually wore hiking boots; high-top brown hiking boots.

She decided he was wearing jeans and a brown or green long-sleeved tee shirt and hiking boots. She put the dirty clothes back in the hamper and stacked up the boxes and folders. She had a small, two-drawer filing cabinet next to her computer desk in the guest room and she put the folders and the bible in the bottom drawer. When Susan called back it was nearly midnight.

"Okay, I got a flight out at noon. You already know it's impossible to get out of Kansas and go straight to anywhere; so I have to fly to Salt Lake City and then catch a commuter plane back to Rock Springs. When

I get there I'll rent a car and drive up. I don't want you worrying about picking me up from the airport. I should be there no later than seven. Laura, I want to know what you found. It's time for me to know."

Laura felt better. In less than 24 hours Susan would be here and by that time they will have found James. Then she and Susan would go over the files and figure out just what happened with their mother. That's the way it was going to be; Laura was firmly convinced! She slept on James' side of the bed that night, wearing one of his shirts.

Susan had a lot to do and very little time in which to do it. She had to do laundry and repack and she had to make phone calls. She was an attorney with her own law office in Junction City; The Bennett Law Firm. Susan Billings Bennett provided general legal counsel when defending her clients against legal liability from civil lawsuits, criminal or drunk driving charges, and was certified in Contract Law, Wills and Trusts.

After she graduated from high school she got a job as a "runner" at Bert Shaffer's law firm in Kerrville. A "runner" was just that. They ran to the courthouse to deliver documents, they ran to the jail to check on prisoners, they ran to city hall, they ran to the Bluebonnet Café for coffee and donuts. Susan "ran" a lot and she loved it. She met Sergeant John Bennett at the Army Recruiting Office in Kerrville where she ran to get information for one of Bert's clients. It was one of those "join the army or go to jail" plea bargains that happened for more than a few young offenders.

It wasn't exactly "love at first sight" but Johnny Bennett and Susan Billings were madly in love soon enough. They got married at St. Al's, honeymooned in Cozumel and set up housekeeping in an apartment three miles away from Andy's house. Andy liked Johnny, Laura liked Johnny, everybody liked Johnny.

Susan kept her job with Bert, Johnny continued as a recruiter for the army and they cruised Central Texas on his motorcycle on afternoons and weekends. They had been married a year when Johnny got the opportunity for career advancement and they moved to Fort Riley, Kansas; where Susan started her freshman year at Washburn University in Topeka, majoring in accounting and working part-time for a large law firm. She and Johnny had friends and an active social life. They both liked Topeka; the influences of the military and university opportunities suited them well and they were happy and looking forward to Susan's graduation when Johnny was killed in a motor cycle accident three days before the ceremony. A little old lady turned in front of him on her way to play Bingo.

Andy had never seen anyone so heartbroken. It hurt to see the misery his Baby Girl was suffering. He stayed two weeks with her in Kansas, trying to convince her to come home to Kerrville. She could get a job at Bert's law firm and have the help of her family in putting her life back together but she would have none of it. She loved Topeka, she had a home and friends and it's where she and Johnny were happy. She wouldn't leave.

She received her diploma in the mail and put it in the bottom drawer of her dresser. She had clear-cut plans about what she wanted to do and the settlement money from the little old lady's insurance company plus the part-time work at the law firm allowed her to enter Washburn School of Law, from which she graduated magna cum laude four years later. The law partners recognized her talents and were very supportive of her during those four years and she received a lucrative job offer from them six months before she graduated.

Eventually, Susan started dating. Two relationships failed; she always compared them to Johnny and they never measured up. She felt most comfortable in crowds rather than on dates. Church continued to be a significant part of her life and she belonged to St. Jerome's Episcopal in Topeka. She was an acolyte and a lay reader and had always longed to swing the censer of incense but would never do it; she was afraid she would whack the priest in the backside and have to find another place to worship.

When Susan was forty-five she bought a small law firm in Junction City, Kansas with a loan from Bert Shaffer and Andy. It came complete with a lake house 15 miles north on Milford Lake. She had a legal secretary, a clerk and a "runner" of her own. There was an established clientele and she discovered she really liked the small town setting.

Relying on her legal secretary, Lana Walters and the runner, J.T. Sanchez, she rearranged her schedule for the next few days, concentrated on getting to Wyoming and avoided concentrating on "the picture". Susan was always able to ignore a stressful situation. She just pretended it didn't exist!

Tuesday morning

Frank and Ivy Bell knocked on Laura's back door at 8:00 the next morning. Although she managed to get a few hours sleep, her eyes were puffy from fatigue and worry. Her hair was brushed and pulled back in a pony-tail and she was wearing hiking boots and jeans and was holding one of James' "gimmee" caps from the feed store where they bought Jo-Jo's dog food.

"Hey, Laura," Ivy came in first, enveloping Laura in a huge hug. "They'll find him now, don't you worry." Frank shot a warning look at his wife that Laura didn't see.

"So, okay Frank. Where do we go first, what do we do? Have you been to Three Pines yet? Did you talk to Chief Daily?" Laura was snapping off the questions, trying her best to stay calm and in control.

"Whoa, whoa, Laura. Look, here's the deal, I need you to stay home to . . . ."

"No way in hell, Frank! I'm going with you. I have to go with you; I can't sit here all day! He'll need me when you find him!"

"Laura, shhh, shhhh," he said, guiding her to one of the chairs in the kitchen. "Listen to me. I've been working out the logistics for this search since early this morning. I need you to stay here. In case he shows up, you are the one person that needs to be here! He may have gotten lost and waited till daylight to try to get home. Now, Ivy is going to stay here with you and I'm setting up at the end of your driveway. We'll let you know the minute we find anything."

Laura looked defeated. Ivy sat on the arm of the chair next to her.

"So, did you figure out what he was wearing?"

"Yeah, I think he was wearing jeans and a green or brown long-sleeved tee shirt and brown hiking boots, but I don't understand! Why do you need to know what he's wearing? He's the only one you're looking for! Why do you need to know this?

"Well, he could have wandered off in another direction; he may be hurt or confused. He could end up on a trail or a road or someplace where there are other people and the searchers need to be able to give out a description." Frank looked uncomfortable and glanced at Ivy. He didn't want to say "just in case someone finds a body we can give them a description." He also didn't tell her he had alerted the sheriff's department in Rock Springs in case they needed a helicopter. She was on the edge of panic and he needed her as calm as possible. A missing person situation like this was difficult enough without having to deal with panicked family members.

A look of fear crossed Laura's face as she continued describing James. "He usually wears a leather backpack he uses to carry pieces of wood that he picks up. He likes to carve and whittle and he collects stuff like that when he walks the dog. When he's hiking he wears a ball cap and sunglasses. I think he has his cell phone with him. I searched around last night and it's not here." She didn't say how many times she dialed his number, praying he would pick up.

"Describe what he looks like."

"He 5' 11", he weighs about 190, he has brown hair and brown eyes.

"What does he keep in his pockets?"

"Well, usually the cell phone and his wallet."

"What kinds of ID does he keep in it?"

"His driver's license and his insurance card. He has a bank card that he uses like a credit card and for the ATM machine. There are a few pictures and he keeps two one-hundred dollar bills folded up in one of the slots. He says it's just in case of emergencies. I've never seen him spend it."

"Laura, when we're done here I want you to call your bank. Find out if there have been any withdrawals on his bank card. Start from 30 days ago and go through today. Then I want you to call your cell phone carrier and ask if there have been any calls made"

"Okay, but why so far back on the bank card?"

"It will tell us if there are any unusual withdrawals and the cell phone carrier might be able to get some kind of signal from his phone."

Why would there have been unusual withdrawals that far back? Laura was afraid to think about this too carefully. Thinking caused more questions than answers.

"Where does he work?"

"He's retired. He retired two years ago from a mining equipment company."

"Tell me again about the dog."

"She's a yellow lab, about 60 pounds and her name is Jo-Jo. She's real friendly and will go right up to strangers. She wears a red collar and there is an ID number from the vet's office tattooed in her ear. I don't remember what it is." Laura was starting to tremble.

"How long have you been married?"

"Ten years."

"Was James married before? Does he have children?"

"He had two long-term relationships but he was never married and he doesn't have any children."

"Tell me about these relationships. Did you know the women? Do you know where they are?"

"No. The first one was when he was nineteen and they lived together for five years and he lived with the second one for 11 years. There was one after that but I don't think it lasted very long. All I know is that they're in Texas somewhere. We talked about that kind of stuff when we first started dating but after that we never discussed it."

"Why did they break up?"

"He said they could never really make a commitment to one another. From what he told me the breakups were amicable. We never heard from them."

By this time Laura appeared very uncomfortable and Frank decided it was time to continue with the description.

"Does he carry water with him?"

"Yeah, he always keeps a bottle of water and a granola bar. I hadn't thought about it! That's a good thing, right? Water and food? He'll be okay, right?"

"It's always a good thing to take water and a snack when you're hiking." Frank said, evasively.

Cars were pulling up and parking around the cul-de-sac. Ivy and Laura went out onto the back deck and Frank began greeting the searchers. After stopping by Three Pines Café earlier; the word spread quickly and there were plenty of people willing to help. Chief Daily was there as well as Jason Mitchell. Usually there were two or three officers on duty at any one time, depending on the time of year. The Chief okayed the overtime so Jason could help Frank coordinate the searchers while two other officers stayed on regular patrol.

A central check-in point was established at the end of the driveway under a tree, where a folding table and chairs were set up. Jason used a spiral notebook and checked in each person. An emergency first-aid kit, bottles of water and power bars were stacked on the table. By the time Chief Daily started the briefing there were more than 30 volunteers.

They brought backpacks and binoculars and some were issued walkie-talkies. Many of the experienced hikers brought sets of their own. They were divided into teams of three. Searching for a missing person in the mountains is more difficult than searching in the flatlands. In the flatlands the search begins with everyone standing side by side. They may link arms and begin walking forward. This helps to cover the area thoroughly. The mountains present a different challenge. The searchers try to stay in sight of one another but, most times, some are up on ridges while others are in ravines and the thick forest makes it easy to lose sight of someone who might only be ten feet away.

Frank, Chief Daily and Jason Mitchell stood in front of the crowd and the chief began by thanking everyone for coming together to help search for their neighbor. He made it clear that the search could take more than one day and emphasized the importance of checking in and out whenever they began and stopped searching. After discussing the preliminaries Frank Bell took over.

"It is imperative you stay in visual contact with the other members of your team. We don't want anyone else to get lost. If you find anything you think is significant, radio me and I'll give further instructions. Look for disturbances in the underbrush, pieces of cloth, anything that looks like it shouldn't be there. Scan the surrounding area with your binoculars for anything shiny or reflective. The dog is wearing a collar with tags, her leash has a bear bell and James might be wearing sunglasses. Any of these can reflect light. James is fifty-four years old, five feet eleven inches tall with brown hair and eyes. I wish he were wearing a reflective orange vest and carrying a GPS but Laura told me he was wearing a brown or green long-sleeved tee shirt, jeans and brown hiking boots. His cell phone is not here at the house so he may have it with him although he hasn't answered any calls attempting to locate him. When you get to the lake, walk the shoreline as close to the water as possible. Look for tracks and footprints. We want to be able to keep up with everyone so I want team leaders to radio in every hour."

The teams began moving north. Frank and Jason had a topographic map and were studying it closely. Most of the searchers were familiar with the area between Aspen Falls and Arapahoe and had declined when offered copies. They wanted to concentrate on walkie-talkies and binoculars and didn't want to keep up with a map when they already knew the territory. "This is going to be a long day and I don't have a good feeling about it," Frank said to Jason without looking up.

Chapter Nine

Tuesday morning

Laura and Ivy stayed on the back deck until the teams walked into the forest and Frank and Jason returned to their post. Laura was determined to be optimistic. She kept telling herself that people had gone missing in the mountains before and they were located or found their way back home by themselves. There were amazing stories of search parties finding lost hikers; television footage of them being carried back to civilization on stretchers with bandaged heads; smiling and waving weakly at the television cameras; surrounded by tired, cheering searchers clapping and slapping one another on the back. They gave interviews from their hospital beds about how they never gave up hope; how they always knew they would be rescued. Despite her efforts there was a niggling little point of doubt in the pit of her stomach which she chose to ignore. She was almost as good as Susan when it came to ignoring stressful circumstances.

They went back inside and Laura got online to her bank. There were no withdrawals after the barbeque purchase on Sunday afternoon and nothing looked unusual the whole time she was in Texas. When she called their cell phone carrier she was told there had been no calls on his phone since Monday and the cell phone was turned off. For a while Laura stared out the window until her phone started ringing and after the third or fourth call she gave the phone to Ivy. It was hard to stay positive when you had to tell the story over and over and over. Ivy was relating the details for the umpteenth time when Reggie Martin, owner of Three Pines Cafe, knocked on the back door.

"Laura!" He gave her a huge bear hug. "Frank told me about James! I couldn't get away from the café until now but I brought you something in case you get hungry." He was holding a big cardboard box and started unloading it onto the kitchen table; sandwich makings, potato salad, cole slaw, chips, cookies, and jugs of tea and lemonade.

"I'm sorry I can't help search. That would leave Billy in charge. No telling what I would find when I got back." He winked and rolled his eyes. Billy was his nephew and somewhat dependable, some of the time.

"Listen, Laura. I've seen this happen before. They'll find him. He may have fallen down into a ravine and not been able to climb out, so he's out there just waiting for someone to come looking for him. I know most of these guys and they're very experienced hikers; they're up and down those trails all the time, they know what they're doing. I bet you he'll be home tonight. Don't you worry!"

"Thanks, Reggie!" *Don't worry? Yeah, right!* "This looks great. You brought enough to feed us for a week!" She walked with Reggie to his truck and continued down to the end of the driveway to Frank and Jason. Frank was on the walkie-talkie and Jason was checking entries on the sign-in book.

"Frank? What have you heard?"

"The teams are checking in now, Laura. They haven't reported anything so far, but it's still early. One team is on the way back in because of an injury; I'm not sure what happened but we'll see when they get here and another guy needs to go on to work"

Ivy walked up behind Laura and made eye contact with Frank. A slight shake of his head was enough to tell her there was no news. Laura was fine for the moment but Frank could see it was an effort to maintain her composure so he had been updating Ivy by sending text messages to her cell phone.

"Why don't we walk to the end of the block and back, Laura? We'll still be in sight of the house in case Frank needs us and it will give us a chance for some fresh air."

They walked the hundred yards to the next street and turned around. Laura had not said a word. Her arms were crossed in front of her and Ivy didn't press her into conversation. Ivy had Laura's phone in her pocket and when it rang she answered it prepared to give the details once again.

"Oh, yes, hello! I'm answering the phone for her. Sure, she's right here. It's your sister." She said, handing the phone to Laura.

"Hey, it's me. I'm on the plane and I have to turn off my phone so I wanted to call and let you know that I'm on my way. What's happening? Have they heard anything?"

"Not so far. Frank says it's still early yet. I guess the teams are going slowly so they don't miss anything. When did you say you would get here?" Laura's voice betrayed the panic she was trying to resist.

"I'll be there at seven, I'll call you when I land and I'll call you when I'm on the road. Who's answering your phone for you?"

"Ivy, my friend Ivy Bell. We're in Knit Group together. Her husband Frank is the police officer I told you about last night. Okay, I love you too; just get here soon, okay?"

She handed the phone to Ivy. "She wants to talk to you."

Ivy took the phone and Laura could tell by the head nodding and short answers she was telling Susan that Laura was okay and yes there would be someone with her and "I'm glad you're on your way", all the usual reassuring small talk.

"Okay, yes, I look forward to meeting you too. Bye, bye"

Ivy put her arm around Laura's shoulders. "She'll be here just as soon as she can, Laura."

Laura could only nod her head. Tears were trickling down her face and all she wanted to do was get back to the house. It was hopeful there.

As they stepped onto the deck they saw two men walking across the driveway from the trail, heading toward the check-in table. One was holding a bloody elbow and limping, followed closely by his team-mate.

Laura watched as they were talking to Frank and Jason. "Oh, I hope he's okay, I didn't even think about anyone getting hurt." She was still crying as she sat down again in the recliner.

"Laura, those guys are tough. I'm sure he'll be fine. Hey, let's look at what Reggie brought. I have a feeling you haven't eaten one thing today. Why don't I fix you something? I know you may not be hungry but you need to eat a little bit, just to keep up your strength."

She remembered how awful she felt yesterday when she hadn't eaten anything and she was starting to feel that way again. Of course then, in addition to having not eaten she'd had a good-sized slug of bourbon! The bourbon sounded like a good idea but on second thought . . . .

"Okay, sure. Maybe some tea and a sandwich."

Laura was eating when Ivy got up to answer the door. Adah and Emma Davis came in, carrying knitting bags and casserole dishes. They found a place in the refrigerator for chicken spaghetti covered with foil and set two plates of brownies on the countertop next to the food Reggie brought earlier. Adah and Ivy stayed in the kitchen and Emma came into the living room as Laura stood up, wiping bread crumbs from her mouth.

"We thought you might like some company, Laura. Adah heard about James this morning at the post office." There are no mail carriers in Aspen Falls. Everyone picks up their mail at the Post Office and it's as good a place to catch up on town news as Three Pines Café or Walker Brothers Market. Adah and her twin Emma were the iconic images of rugged mountain women. They could out-knit, out-crochet, out-can and generally out-do most everyone that knew them. Adah had hair the color of brushed steel, worn in a long braid down her back. Her clear blue eyes sparkled behind rimless glasses and her usual attire consisted of jeans, western style boots and flannel shirts, topped by a leather, western-style hat with a braided leather hatband. Her sister Emma, younger by two minutes wore her silver gray hair in the same style as her sister. Their father, deceased 45 years ago, had been a hard-rock miner and later had a successful hunting guide business. The women NEVER discussed money and paid cash for everything.

Laura smiled and said, "Thanks Emma. This is so frightening. You hear about this happening on the news but you never in a million years think it could happen to you!"

She walked back into the kitchen as Ivy and Adah were talking quietly. They both looked up when she entered.

"Laura, I've got to get to work and I didn't want you to have to stay here by yourself so I called Adah and she told me she heard about James at the post office. She offered to come over with Emma to stay until your sister gets here."

"Thanks, y'all. I appreciate it. I'm going out to talk to Frank and Jason. I can't sit still." And she walked out the door and down the driveway.

Adah and Emma looked at Ivy and she updated them on the activity so far. "So far there's not been one single sign indicating James or the dog is out there. Frank sends me text messages so we don't have to talk in front of her. She's trying really hard but I can only imagine how she's feeling. I would be climbing the walls."

"He will probably come back on his own," Adah said calmly. "When we were little girls Papa went out hunting and didn't come home when he was supposed to. His horse came back to the house the first afternoon and he showed up the next day with a broken arm and scratches all over. Something spooked the horse and he fell off and the horse came back to the barn. He was sure pissed at that horse!" Adah laughed and added, "No one sent out search parties as fast as they do now! Our mother never really seemed worried. She just kept saying 'I know your Papa, kids, he'll show up'. And he did!"

"Frank, I can't stand this, have you heard anything? Anything at all?"

"I know it's hard, Laura," he said, rising and coming to stand beside her. "Teams have been checking in and out all day. The guy you saw earlier banged up his elbow pretty good and I sent him over to see Doctor Beckham at Urgent Care. We're going to keep at this, Laura. We aren't giving up. Ivy's shift starts at Walker Brothers in a little while and I need to go home and get some sleep. I'll be back on patrol tonight and Jason is here now, Chief Daily will be out in about an hour and I know your sister is coming so it looks like you'll have plenty of people here with you."

Thank God he didn't say "Don't worry"! Why in the hell do people say that? Maybe they don't know what else to say and anyway the more someone says 'Don't worry', the more you are going to do just that! She walked back up the driveway and into the house as Ivy was walking out.

"Laura, I know you're worried, I would be too, but these guys know what they're doing. A lot of them were born around here and they know every single rock and tree! I'll call you tonight." She hugged Laura, hard.

Laura was crying again and held on to her for a few seconds before saying, "Thanks Ivy. Today was awful, thanks for putting up with me."

As she walked through the kitchen she looked around at all the food on the counters and the table. *Damn, it looks like a funeral! Well, that notion can just go to hell! There's not going to be a funeral around here!* When she got back to the living room Adah was in a recliner and Emma was on the sofa and she heard the soft clacking of their wooden knitting needles. They were always working on two or three projects at the same time. Mufflers for the Special Olympic Winter Games, hats and mittens for the kids on the reservation, blankets and caps for the newborns at the hospital down in Rock Springs. These two women were multi-tasking decades before the term was ever used!

She went to the guest room which was also the sewing room and the computer room and got her yarn and a crochet hook and came back and curled up in the recliner. Potholders were a fast, easy project and it helped to pass the time. Even so, Laura was up and down, looking out the window, walking around the room and out onto the front deck, the back deck and then back to her recliner for a few more stitches.

Susan called at five-thirty. "Laura, I'm already on the road. I'll be there in an hour and a half."

Laura's voice sounded tired, "Susan, be careful. I'm so . . . just be careful, okay?" She couldn't express exactly how she felt; she was just relieved her sister was on her way.

Tuesday evening

At 6:00 Chief Daily came in from the driveway. There was so much going on, no one waited for the door to be answered. They just knocked and walked in.

"Laura, we're getting ready to stop for the day." Laura closed her eyes and just sat there. She didn't think she could even stand up. He sat on the sofa beside her and put one hand on her shoulder. "I know it's not what we wanted but we'll start again in the morning. I need a picture of James. I think it would be a good idea to post pictures of him at the café and the gas station. Tourists are starting to come through now and maybe someone will see the pictures and recognize him."

Laura closed her eyes. She felt completely drained and it was hard to comprehend what he was saying. *A picture? He wants a picture?*

Emma bent down in front of her and put her hand on her knee. "Laura? Did you hear Chief Daily?" Laura opened her eyes and stared at both of them. Yes, she heard him; she saw his lips moving, heard sounds coming from his mouth but she really couldn't understand anything. All she could hear was a loud buzzing sound. She stood up.

"Laura? Laura! Can you open your eyes?" She felt something cool and moist on her face. "Hey, there!" She was lying on the floor. Her feet were propped up on one of the sofa cushions and Chief Daily and Emma were kneeling beside her. Emma had a wet washcloth and was pressing it to her cheeks and forehead.

"What happened? Oh my God, I fainted?" She tried to get up, embarrassed to be on the floor. She had never fainted in her life!

"Hey, hey hold on now! Why don't you lie here for a minute? I think you just stood up too fast. How do you feel, do you hurt anywhere?" Chief Daily said.

"No, I'm not hurt. I'm okay. Just let me sit up." They helped her to sit up against the sofa.

Adah was standing between Emma and Chief Daily, offering her a glass of tea. "Here, Laura, drink this. I put in some extra sugar; this should help you start feeling better."

"Okay, thanks, but let me stand up. I'm okay. I think my pride is hurt more than anything else." Chief Daily helped her to stand and then guided her back into the recliner. Adah handed her the tea and she took a sip. It was cold and sweet and after a few swallows she did start to feel better.

"How about I call Joel Beckham and have him meet us at Urgent Care?"

"Oh, no, no thanks Chief. I'm feeling better. You're right. I just stood up too fast. I'll be okay." She exhaled hard and shook her head. "That just came out of nowhere! You were talking to me and next thing I know I'm looking up at y'all from flat on my back!"

"Well, you keep sipping that tea. Do you remember what we were talking about?"

She remembered. "Yes, you need a picture of James. Let me just sit here a few minutes and I'll find one for you." She felt defeated and, for the first time, hopeless. Her life had not been all sunshine and rainbows but she had always managed to confront her challenges without being overwhelmed. Now, she couldn't even decide what to do from one minute to the next.

Chapter Ten

Tuesday afternoon

Susan's drive from Rock Springs took almost as long as it was estimated, which irritated the crap out of her. In her opinion the speed limit was more of a suggestion than an actual maximum value; however, the rental car she picked up at the airport was equipped with an intricate GPS system and the agent made it very clear that reckless driving was "frowned upon"!

What a gadget! It recorded all sorts of driving data, including locations whenever she stopped and a surcharge could be added to her bill to cover any irresponsible driving habits!

The agent wasn't specific about exactly how far above the speed limit you had to go to be "frowned upon" so Susan decided five to seven miles above the limit wasn't exactly speeding, it was just hurrying and she was hurrying a little too fast when she drove into Aspen Falls.

She was concentrating on the next turn she should take when she saw the blue and red flashing lights in her rearview mirror. *No! Not now! Please God, not now!* She could just imagine the agent "frowning upon" her. At least when she pulled over it was into the parking lot of a grocery store. Maybe "they" would think she stopped for groceries instead of being pulled over for speeding.

"Good afternoon, ma'am." The officer bent forward to look into the driver's side window. "The speed limit here in Aspen Falls is forty-five and I clocked you going fifty-seven. May I see your license and registration, please?"

Susan took her license out of her wallet and reached into the glove box for the registration card. She was ready to hand over everything when she noticed his name tag. "Bell".

"Officer Bell! Are you Frank Bell?"

"Uh, yes I am. May I see your license, please?"

"Of course, yes, here you are," she said, handing everything to him through the window. "My name is Susan Bennett. I'm Laura Gregory's sister. Aren't you the officer helping search for James?"

"Oh, you're Susan? Yes, I was up at her house most of the day today. We . . . ."

"Well, I'm trying to get there right now." Susan interrupted. "I'm very sorry; I wasn't paying attention to the speed limit. I flew into Rock Springs and grabbed a rental and started driving. I was looking for the street where I'm supposed to turn when, uh . . . ." She grinned and raised her eyebrows to finish the sentence.

"I understand," he grinned back. "Why don't you follow me, I'll lead you up to her street; and, by the way, I'll be driving the speed limit!"

"I'll be right behind you; driving the speed limit!" She replied as she put her license in her wallet and started the car. She was getting anxious and wanted to get to Laura as soon as she could. She could only imagine how she was doing right now. The old adage "It never rains but it pours" defined this situation to a T. Whatever her sister discovered in Daddy's files must have been very disturbing and she didn't even know the details about the picture yet! Now, to be confronted with this situation concerning James! It was too much!

Susan walked in through the back door and around into the living room. Two older women were seated there, knitting, and Laura was tilted back in a recliner, covered by an afghan and her eyes were closed. They stood up and one put her finger to her lips; the universal signal to "shhhhhhh" and pointed toward the kitchen.

Once in the kitchen they began talking softly. "My name is Adah Davis and this is my sister, Emma. We've been visiting with Laura this afternoon. Are you Susan?" Adah immediately impressed Susan as the strong, no-nonsense type of woman and she emanated a sense of quiet, steely strength which put Susan at ease. She could see that Adah and Emma were twins, but there was something about Emma that was slightly different than Adah; she seemed softer somehow but both women seemed very concerned about Laura.

"I'm so glad you're here. Thanks for staying with Laura. I live in Kansas and after she called me last night I made the fastest arrangements I could. I almost got a ticket as I was driving into town but fortunately the cop that pulled me over was Frank Bell. I recognized his name and told him who I was and instead of a ticket I got an escort up here."

Emma said, "Frank's a good guy. He's been here nearly all day working with the searchers. He's managing quite an operation."

Susan asked about the search and Adah and Emma were giving her the details when they heard Laura calling from the living room.

"Susan?" They heard Laura walking from the living room into the kitchen. "Susan, you're here, you're here. Thank God!" She hugged Susan tightly, as if she would never let go. When she finally did, Susan could see the effects of weariness on her face. Her eyes were puffy and the skin on her left cheek, blotchy, from sleeping on the afghan in the recliner.

She started to introduce Susan to the sisters but Adah stopped her, saying, "Yes, we introduced ourselves. How are you feeling? You need another glass of sweet tea." and without waiting for an answer she put ice in a glass and poured in tea and handed it to Laura. Laura took it obediently and started sipping. It appeared Adah was accustomed to taking charge.

"We're relieved you're here, Susan," Emma said. "Laura fainted earlier this afternoon. She's fine now but I thought you needed to know. If there's anything Sister or I can do please don't hesitate to call us. Our phone number is on the Knit Group List. There's chicken spaghetti in the refrigerator, all you have to do is warm it up and there are all sorts of food on the counter including the brownies I brought. If you like I can call you tomorrow to see if there is anything you need."

"Yes, I'd like that very much," Susan replied, grateful for any help.

Adah placed both of her hands on Laura's shoulders. "Laura, you listen to me now. I know most of the men out there today and if not them at least I know their fathers. There is no one better to be looking for James. I have faith in them and you should too." She hugged Laura quickly and patted her on the back.

Emma hugged Laura and Susan and followed her sister out to the driveway.

Susan put her arms around Laura and they stood there, quietly swaying for a moment; then Susan put her hands on each side of Laura's head and kissed her gently on the forehead. "Let's sit down. Today must have been hell for you."

They sat and were silent; each one waiting for the other to begin. Laura was staring out the bay windows, lost in thought and exhaustion so Susan started first.

"Let me make sure I have the timeline straight here. You woke up yesterday morning, James was already up and after you talked he left to walk the dog. Daddy's files were delivered and you started going through them. You made a drink to calm your nerves, you fell asleep and when you woke up it was late afternoon and James was not here. He never came home from walking the dog. Am I right so far?"

Laura continued to stare out the window. "Susan how did this happen? I have to keep reminding myself this is not a dream! This is real!"

"Laura, did you hear me?" Susan was becoming concerned. "Laura, did you hear what I just said? Am I right? Is this what happened?"

Laura took a slow deep breath, "I'm sorry, I know I must sound crazy to you. Yeah, you got it right. Frank even asked me if we had a fight, if maybe James was somewhere cooling off. But you know us, we don't fight! We get along just fine!"

Susan knew this to be true. They may have had a few disagreements but she never heard of them fighting. And James wasn't the type of man to just up and leave. He always seemed so content. Happy with Wyoming and his workshop and his dog; and Laura. He was always nice and kind to her. He loved her. He didn't leave; something bad happened to James.

Laura was able to focus and she told Susan about the day; about the search party and one guy coming in injured and about friends coming out to make sure she was alright. And about the food!

"Did you see all that food in there? Damn, it reminded me of when we were at Daddy's. Except this isn't a funeral and there isn't going to be a funeral!" Her voice was a few decibels too loud.

Rather than try to soothe her Susan got loud right back! "You got it sister! Now I'm changing the subject. Emma and Adah, they're quite a pair aren't they? How old are they?" And for a few brief moments all was well with the world; James wasn't missing and Daddy didn't keep secrets.

"I am starving! Emma said there's chicken spaghetti in the fridge? Yum, reminds me of potluck Sundays at church! Why don't we get something to eat?" Susan took her sister's hand and they walked into the kitchen.

"Yep, she was right! There's a lot of food in here. Let's see if we can make a dent in it." They got busy and in no time flat they were at the table having Chicken Spaghetti, French bread with garlic butter, Chardonnay, and brownies! Luscious, moist dark chocolate brownies! Chocolate can improve almost any situation and it worked on this one for a few minutes. Then it was time to address another situation that no amount of chocolate could make better.

Laura went back to her recliner, tilted her head back and closed her eyes. Susan sat on the sofa, and through the bay windows on each side of the fire place, she could see the sun was down behind the mountains and the flat-bottomed clouds were reflecting the vivid pinks and purples of the last light of the day.

"It doesn't seem fair that this is all happening at the same time." Susan made a soft snorting sound and continued. "I remember Daddy saying 'and just who told you the world is fair, Baby Girl?' He was right but it doesn't keep me from bitching about it"

Laura opened her eyes, looked at Susan and said, "Tell me about the picture." Susan looked back and Laura said, "Really, I'm good! You're right, it's not fair, but we have to deal with it anyway so tell me what you remembered."

Susan grabbed a sofa pillow and clutched it across her middle in an unconscious defensive posture. "I got back to Sinclair from Kerrville and I went out on the dock with a beer and sat down in one of the chairs." She took a slow, deep breath. "Do you remember the first time you went to church camp, when Daddy drove you over there and hauled a bunch of camp stuff in the back of his pick-up?"

Laura nodded.

"This happened while you were gone."

Susan told her every minute detail of the memory from when they were talking about French toast until the lady rescued her from the closet. When she finished the clouds had faded to a dull gray and the room was dark. Laura switched on the lamp between the sofa and the recliner.

"I don't remember what happened after that. It's weird! I've tried to think backwards to that time but I can't. I can remember lots of things; starting first grade, birthday parties, lots and lots of other things but nothing that can connect to that memory. At first I thought I was crazy! I thought 'Oh, Susan you're just tired from everything with Daddy', but . . . . No! I'm not crazy! All of that really happened! The picture is proof that it really happened!"

Laura tried to think back; back to when she went to church camp for the first time. She remembered bits and pieces; being scared the first night, campfires and horseback riding, but that was it. Life just went on from there, nothing terrible interrupted the flow.

She walked back to her filing cabinet and retrieved the folders and the Bible from the drawer. *How did all of this happen and we not remember it! Daddy! What happened? What were you hiding from us?*

Susan poured the last of the Chardonnay into their glasses and was sitting back on the sofa. When she saw the folders Laura was holding she took a large swallow.

"The first thing I found when I went through his files was this." She opened the folder and gave Susan the life insurance policies and the unlabeled envelope. "The life insurance policies are pretty easy to interpret. We each get $10,000. The document in the envelope has our mother's name on it. Her name was Grace Everett Billings." Laura heard a sharp intake of breath from Susan when she mentioned Grace's name.

"What . . . . ? How . . . . ?" Susan stammered.

"We call the number on that insurance agent's business card and you can look in that envelope and tell me what the hell it's all about. I'm sorry Susan but I have to tell you this all at once. We can go back and review it but I can't stop. I'm afraid if I stop before I finish telling you everything I'll . . . I don't know what, but I have to tell you everything all at once!"

Susan shuffled through the policies in the folder and put it on the coffee table. She put her hands in her lap and waited. Laura picked up Andy's bible. "This is Daddy's bible. I remember seeing it in his bedroom when I was a kid but I never once picked it up. Maybe I should have." She opened to the Family History page and gave it to Susan. Susan read everything carefully, lightly touching a name here and there as she read. "She died 46 years ago? That's when I was five. Why don't we remember this?

"I don't know. The next thing is this." She handed Susan the manila envelope and the letter from the photography studio. "This explains the picture. Look at the postmark on the envelope. Daddy received it six months ago!" Susan stared at the letter. Laura found herself wishing she had been able to look at the picture closely before Susan destroyed it. She wanted to know what her mother looked like.

She sat next to Susan on the sofa and opened the next folder and gave her the spread sheet. "According to this she was in a psychiatric hospital in Bristol, Texas. I looked it up, it's still there. This looks like a record of payments made to Homestead Hills. And there's a problem. Daddy's bible shows she died 46 years ago. The last date on this spreadsheet is 20 years later, and there is a death certificate for her. It corresponds to the last date on the spreadsheet."

Susan interrupted, "Okay, wait, slow down, I need to look at all of this again. This is too much!" There were tears in her eyes.

"I'm sorry but, please let me finish and then we can go back over everything." Laura's hands were shaking. She knew she was speaking firmly but this was the only way she could stay calm. "So, the bible shows she died forty-six years ago, when you were five and I was seven; the spreadsheet and the death certificate show she died twenty-six years ago, when you were twenty-five and I was twenty-seven!

"I found this with the spreadsheet." She gave Susan the letter from Homestead Hills and waited while Susan read. Susan had to keep wiping her eyes and blowing her nose while she was reading and rereading; becoming agitated as she glanced back and forth from the spreadsheet to the letter.

"I . . . . I don't know what to say! I don't know how to put into words what I'm feeling. This is almost too much to comprehend. She lived in a loony bin for the last 20 years of her life and she never said a damn word?

"Well, I wouldn't exactly call it a loony bin, it's more like . . . ."

"Wait, she didn't do anything to you, so you can call it any damn thing you want. She fucking tried to kill me!" She stood, wild-eyed, and looked around the room. She ran out onto the south deck, with Laura right behind her, and leaned up against the railing and screamed. A piercing, heart-wrenching scream. Then she slid down to the deck into a mound of unfathomable sadness.

Laura knelt down beside her, but Susan screamed, "Don't touch me!" She took a deep breath and then spoke in a lower tone. "I'm sorry; I'll be alright, just don't touch me. I need to sit here for a minute, okay?"

Laura walked inside to the living room and got a heavy afghan from the back of the sofa and brought it out to the deck. She sat on the deck next to her sister and spread the afghan over the both of them. Some time later, reminiscent of the glider on Andy's back porch, Susan put her head in Laura's lap and Laura decided to stay there for as long as it took.

"We've got to get up; I'm freezing my ass off!" The afghan covering them was warm but their backs were against the deck railing and there was no protection from the cold air of the spring night.

They were back in the living room again; this time Susan was huddled under the afghan. Laura was in her recliner; waiting for Susan to talk.

"Uh, you know, this may sound crazy," Susan shook her head and smirked, "like we haven't already been talking about 'crazy', but that made me feel better!"

"It made me wonder if Frank Bell was going to come roaring up here with his siren wailing and his lights flashing." She smirked the same smirk.

"Laura, there's more to this than what we know. What happened? How? Why do we not remember at least a little bit?

"Bert Shaffer's name was written and erased on that spreadsheet. Did you see it?"

Susan picked up the spreadsheet and re-examined it. "That does say Bert! I think? Yes it does! That's his name! What does the rest of the smear say? Can you read it?" She held it up to the light. "He knows something! That old fossil knows something. He's known all along, and he never said one word?"

"I think he's probably waiting for us to call him." Laura said quietly. "And I think Father John 'do-you-need-any-help-cleaning-out-his-office' Cates is in on it too!"

"What makes you say that?"

"In between thinking about James, and sometimes while thinking about James, I started thinking about the whole of last week. One week ago today we went to Kerrville. That was Tuesday. That night Father John came by the house with the basket of wine and cheese. He was there to finalize the funeral service and now I have a feeling he was also trying to check out the house. Wednesday night Bert came over and we talked about Daddy's will and he kindly offered to go through Daddy's filing cabinet. I'd found the picture earlier in the day and at the time I didn't think anybody knew about it so I told him "No, thank you". Looks like I was protecting a family secret he knew more about than we did.

"Thursday was the funeral and Thursday night we were all back at the house. Father John kindly offered to help clean out Daddy's office and he asked to see Daddy's bible. He said he wanted to write something in it.

"And, I didn't think anything about it until this very minute but after they left you and I were going around the house turning off the lights. I guess I'd turned off the porch light right after they walked out, but anyway I turned off the living room lights and was standing in the dark when I looked out the window pane in the front door. Father John and Bert were standing out there on the front sidewalk, talking. They couldn't see me. I watched them for just a minute or two and then they shook hands and went to their cars. I never gave it another thought but I'll bet you my last dime they were cooking something up then. And" Laura said; the clues were falling into place! "Bert Shaffer was out of town when Daddy died! We were already there when he found out! There was no way for him to have come over beforehand and look for anything!"

Susan sat there, shaking her head back and forth and said "Well!" she sniffed. "You know when we left Daddy's house you locked the door and gave the key to him. I have a sneaking suspicion that "Bert and Ernie" went back there as soon as we were dropped off at the airport and started looking around for the very things you found."

"Okay, then!" Laura was walking back and forth in front of the fireplace. "Tomorrow they're going to find James and tomorrow night we're calling Mr. Bert Shaffer and find out what the hell is going on!"

Susan paused for a moment, not sure she should agree, "I hear you; but right now you need to give me that folder with the insurance policies. I have to look at it again." Laura handed her the folder and Susan opened it and went through it slowly, page by page. Laura continued pacing in front of the fireplace.

"Oh! My! God! This is a trust! She had a trust!"

"So, what does that mean?"

"Well, apparently this came from her parents. It was a fund set up by them to provide her with a monthly income! I need to reread it! But if Bert Shaffer's name is on that spreadsheet then I agree; he had something to do with this! That son of a bitch has a lot of questions to answer!

CHAPTER ELEVEN

Wednesday morning

Susan walked in to find Laura sitting on her bedroom floor, surrounded by photo albums and packages of pictures.

"What are you doing up? It's early yet, did I wake you?" Laura said from the floor.

"Nah. Here it may be 4:00 in the morning but my central time zone body thinks it's 5:00 and time to get up. What are you doing?

"I couldn't sleep and Chief Daily wanted a picture of James so I'm trying to find a good one. Ah Ha! Here are the ones I was looking for, from Erin's wed . . . . ! Oh, my God! I didn't call Erin! It's been two nights! I planned on calling her Monday night but I got all involved in everything and I just forgot! How could I have forgotten to call her?" Laura crossed her arms on her bended knees and put her head down.

"I told myself I wasn't going to cry today, I was going to be strong and look how I'm starting off." When she raised her face Susan was on the floor beside her.

"Susan, I'm terrified! I really thought they would find him yesterday or he would walk out on his own, with some story about getting lost like Frank said. Oh God! What if they don't find him? I prayed last night, I prayed long and hard. I know you're not supposed to make bargains with God but I bargained everything I could think of if God would only let him come home!"

Susan stood up and said "I prayed too, babe! Right now it's the best thing we can do. Finding James is in God's hands and God has entrusted it to Frank Bell and the search party. And it bugs the hell out of me that I have to rely on anyone else but myself."

Frank Bell knocked on the back door at seven-thirty and walked through the mud room and into the kitchen. Laura and Susan were sitting at the kitchen table and coffee and brownies appeared to be the menu choice for breakfast.

"Good morning!" He stood behind Laura and put one hand on her shoulder," Susan! It's good to see you again. Did you tell Laura about your escort yesterday?"

"She certainly did! Thanks, Frank, she'll drive the speed limit next time, won't you Susan!" She looked over her shoulder at Frank and then at her sister.

"Why, of course I will Officer!" she gave him a quick grin and a salute; and then said, more seriously "Thanks again from me too, Frank; no kidding, I really appreciate it."

"No problem!" He was carrying a brown paper sack and started unloading it onto the stove top. "Reggie sent breakfast tacos," he nodded toward the brownies, "just in case you need something besides brownies. There is a giant pan full outside on the check-in table. Guys are already starting to show up and this will make them very happy." Breakfast tacos were made with scrambled eggs, potatoes, refried beans, cheese and bacon or sausage and rolled up in a large flour tortilla. It was the perfect meal and you didn't need knives or forks or plates; just a big appetite.

"Frank, what about this picture? It was taken at Erin's wedding. I have another copy in case you need to keep this one." It was a picture of a smiling James standing next to Erin at the communion rail at St. Michael the Archangel Episcopal Church

"Yes, this is good and I'll get it back to you. Jason can take it to the office and work on the flyer as soon as we get everyone situated."

"Where will you post them? Can we help? It's too hard staying here; I need to do something!"

"I know. I know it's hard but here is the best place for you. You need to be here in case anyone needs information. I'll give you my number and you can just send me a text if you have a question. And I have a question now for Susan." He looked directly at her and Laura knew what question Frank was going to ask.

"Have you ever seen any indication of unhappiness in James? Has he ever said anything about being unhappy in his marriage or of another woman?"

Susan shook her head. "I saw a few disagreements between them when she wanted him to come with her to see me in Kansas, but they worked it out and Laura just started coming by herself. James didn't seem to mind her coming alone and we really had more fun without him! I never saw them fight and as far as another woman; no I never even got so much as a hint! I think something bad has happened to him. He's not the type to run off!"

"So, are we all in agreement that James didn't run off somewhere?" Laura said pointedly; ready to change the subject.

Frank nodded, saying nothing.

"Okay, then, Frank, I need you to be straight with me. Yesterday I refused to consider anything negative, but today . . . . today I need you to be up front. I'll probably get upset but tell me anyway. Tell me the truth. I understand everyone is trying to protect me and I'm grateful but I need to know what's really going on. No more texting behind my back!"

He sat at the table and pinched off a piece of brownie and put it in his mouth; an excuse while he was gathering his thoughts. "We had thirty guys out there yesterday, Laura, working in teams; looking at everything, covering every inch of horizontal ground. They walked all around Arapahoe and found nothing; no indication James had been there. This morning we'll concentrate north of the lake. Then . . ."

Laura interrupted, "You said 'This morning'. What does that mean? Does it mean you'll be stopping after this morning?" Susan reached over and took her hand.

"No, now listen to me Laura. We're not stopping! We'll just be using some different resources. I talked to the Teton County Sheriff's Department in Jackson and they can provide a helicopter and a pilot if necessary. One helicopter can cover a lot more territory than a team on foot. I called the K-9 unit in Jackson yesterday afternoon but they couldn't get anyone up here until today and I didn't want to wait to start searching. The woman who's coming is certified in Wilderness Tracking and is EMT certified in Wilderness Medicine. If James is injured she's exactly who you need out there. She knows what she's doing and has participated in rescues all over Wyoming. Her name is Mandy Howard and she and Baker will be here around eleven-thirty."

Laura was staring out the window. Frank put his hand on her shoulder. "Did you hear me, Laura? Do you understand what I'm saying?" She focused on him and he looked directly into her eyes.

"Yes, yes, I understand. I'm just so scared." She took a slow, deep breath. "So, you'll continue the search with the teams this morning and now you're looking north of Arapahoe. A K-9 person and a dog will be up here at eleven-thirty. And then this afternoon, if you have to, you'll use a helicopter."

"Right, you got it. Now, I need you to keep a grip Laura. I know you're scared, but I need you to hang on, okay?"

"Okay, I'm okay. It's just sometimes; I swear to you, I feel like I'm going to jump right out of my skin!" She took a big bite of brownie and leaned back in her chair and closed her eyes.

Another knock on the door and Jason Mitchell leaned into the kitchen door from the mud room. "We're ready for you, Frank."

Most of the teams from yesterday signed in with Jason again and were gathered in small groups, eating breakfast tacos and drinking coffee. Some of the guys were unable to come back and a few newcomers were receiving instructions from Frank and Jason, including three boys and two girls from the high school who may have been ditching class. The breakfast tacos didn't last long and soon Jason walked up the driveway with a trash bag full of cups and napkins and empty salsa packets.

"I need to call Erin. I still can't believe I didn't call her yesterday." Laura was holding her phone, sitting in the recliner. "I don't know if she's in class or at work. I guess I can send her a text."

Erin only needed four more courses to graduate with her M.B.A. She was working part time and going to school and hadn't stopped between getting her B.B.A. and starting on her master's degree. There were two miscarriages but her doctor found nothing to indicate they shouldn't keep trying to start a family. Erin was very focused on her life and her goals and wasn't easily discouraged. It would happen when it happened.

Susan walked out onto the south deck. The mountains were beautiful; nothing like Kansas, but she missed her pier and the dock with the Adirondack chairs. That's where she did her best thinking. She decided to hold off discussing the picture and Andy's files but she couldn't stop thinking about them. She'd played out so many scenarios and nothing she could think of could resolve the turmoil she was feeling. The present circumstances were dreadful and she knew she needed to be supportive but she knew she had to unlock the secrets. Soon!

She heard Laura talking to Erin on the phone and walked back inside.

"No, it's okay. Susan's here and I don't want you to miss anymore class. I'll call you as soon as they find him. You have Susan's number in case I don't pick up. I love you too, babe. Keep me in your prayers. Tell David I love him. I'll talk to you tonight, how about? Okay, yes, I'll be okay." She disconnected the call and smiled; Erin was wise enough not to say 'Don't worry'.

Jason Mitchell walked in the back door with the stack of flyers he designed. Laura saw James' picture at the top of the page underneath the bold title "MISSING". A cold chill raced across her neck and shoulders as he handed her a copy.

"This is what they look like, Laura and here's your picture. I wanted to show them to you before we started posting them." He handed her the picture and one of the flyers. A close-up of James from the original picture took up most of the space. A physical description of him and the dog, the date and where he was last seen occupied the remaining space on the page.

"We're going to use some high school kids to post the flyers. They'll go in two different cars and post in Lander, Riverton, Fort Washakie, Rawlins and Rock Springs. We're trying to cover a wide range.

"Why would he be in any of those places, Jason? Why wouldn't you just look for hikers to give the flyers to?"

"Hikers have to come from somewhere, Laura and maybe someone will have seen him walking on 287, maybe picked him up hitch hiking, something like that. We focused our search on the relatively small area between here and Arapahoe and now we need to broaden our reach. We don't want to limit our search and run the risk of missing him somehow. The teams are leaving now so I need to get back. Come down anytime you need to"

"Susan, I know you've been thinking about Daddy, on top of all this other stuff. I just want you to know I haven't forgotten about it."

"I know you haven't. We're faced with so much all at the same time; Daddy, the picture, the files and now James. I'm glad I'm here, Laura; I wouldn't be anywhere else. If you want to talk about it we can. I know you're burdened enough with James and I don't want to add anything to your load."

"The stuff with Daddy is my load, too. They'll find him today. How could they possibly not! Teams on foot, the K-9 team and the helicopter. They'll find him today and then we can concentrate on Daddy."

Susan texted Frank, "Plz come up here whn U can. We hve to talk to L re "possibilities"!

"Laura, I'm keeping up with the office." She told a Big, Fat Lie. She heard what her sister was saying and knew she was refusing to be realistic. They might find James dead or they might not find him at all.

Frank walked in from the back door and shook his head with an almost imperceptive "No" to Susan.

"I just got a call from Mandy. She got out of Jackson earlier than she'd planned and she should be here in about 45 minutes. When she called she asked me to call all the teams in and she'll explain why when she gets here; so everyone is on their way in now. Laura, I have a lot of confidence in Mandy. We were in the academy together and she's been doing this since she first got out. She was born and raised in Wyoming and I think she's the best at K9 Search and Rescue. She and Baker have been together for several years and I think you're going to like them.

"I need to talk to the teams. When Mandy and Baker get here we'll come in and talk to you. I'm sure she'll have more questions of her own."

As he was leaving he made eye contact with Susan once again and once again shook his head 'No'. Within a minute her phone buzzed a text alert. "Yes we need discuss possibilities but we need to wait for Mandy."

"Is everything okay at your office?" Laura spoke. She was staring out the bay windows and didn't shift her gaze when she asked the question.

"Yeah, I need to call in but it looks like everything is fine. I'm going to walk out on the deck and talk. Can I get you anything while I'm up?"

"What about a breakfast taco and a coke? That should round out the brownies and coffee we ate earlier." She said with a smile.

Susan went into the kitchen and picked up a taco and popped the top on a coke from the fridge and brought it back to Laura, who continued to stare out the window and only nodded her acknowledgement when her sister put the food down next to her. She walked back to the kitchen and got a taco for herself and walked on out to the back deck and sat down.

"Hey Lana, it's me. How's everything going?"

"Everything's good. Joe Blanchard's wife's attorney called and I told him you wouldn't be available until next week. He sounded a little pissed, but, oh well! How's everything there? Did they find your brother-in-law?"

Susan filled her in on the search for James and made plans to call in every day. Lana would call at other times if there was an emergency but she didn't anticipate anything happening. She was a top-notch legal secretary and Susan had complete confidence in her ability to handle everything until she returned.

She ended the call and continued to sit on the deck; searchers were beginning to come back from the trail; walking down the driveway toward Frank and Jason. She knew eventually they would have to talk to Laura about the "possibilities" and she dreaded it. Thank goodness Frank would be there. The thought of her sister completely falling apart was something she didn't think she could deal with alone.

She also needed a few minutes to think about Daddy and the picture and the files and "Bert and Ernie". She didn't know how much longer she could sit and do nothing about that situation! Laura had enough to worry about and Susan didn't want to make it worse by bringing it up but it was on her mind constantly. *Why did they not remember anything about Grace Everett Billings?*

CHAPTER TWELVE

Wednesday mid-day

Mandy Howard drove up at 11:00 and parked on the cul-de-sac. She opened the back of her SUV and Baker jumped out and followed her to where Frank and Jason were talking with some of the search teams. She'd played this scenario before. The teams developed a sense of "ownership" for the search and many were reluctant to give up their stake in the game. This was the moment where she could win the their trust or she could lose their support; in which case she would continue to follow protocol but face the additional obstacle of an uncooperative support team.

"Frank, we got here as soon as we could," she said, shaking Frank's hand. Baker came to Mandy's side and sat quietly. Baker was a beautiful female Australian Shepard, with marbled fur. She had one brown eye and one blue eye and was wearing a chain collar and a red canvas vest marked with a white plus sign and "Search Dog. Please don't pet me when I'm working." embroidered in black. Many times it was Baker that won the support of searchers and she worked her magic effectively this time, too. All she had to do was look at someone and grin that doggy grin of hers and the person was captivated.

"Gentlemen," she said, making eye contact with as many as possible. "It looks like you've got a well-organized operation here and Frank has filled me in on the excellent job you've been doing. I'm sorry you weren't able to find James but I can see it wasn't for lack of effort. I'd like to get started as soon as possible so if you will excuse us I want to meet his wife and get some information. I'd appreciate it if you'd stay here until I can speak with Mrs. Gregory. When I'm ready to begin we'll come back out here and walk around you. This will give Baker the opportunity to eliminate false scents once we're out on the trail." She hooked a woven leash to Baker's collar and waited for Frank to walk up to the house.

She and Baker won them over. They would cooperate and be dependable when she needed them. Frank directed Mandy and Baker up the driveway and left Jason to deal with the teams.

"Laura?" Frank said, coming through the kitchen and into the living room. Laura rose from the recliner and called to Susan, out on the deck.

"Laura, this is Mandy Howard and this is Baker." Laura shook hands with Mandy and she looked into the eyes of the beautiful dog.

"Oh, my gosh, you are stunning! May I pet her?" She said, looking at Mandy.

"Sure, sure. She's not working now. And thanks for asking. A lot of people want to pet her and if she's working it can be a real distraction."

Susan walked in as Laura raised the back of her hand to Baker's nose. Baker licked her hand and instantly won another fan.

"Mandy, this is my sister, Susan Bennett." With the formality of introductions out of the way Mandy Howard got busy. It was obvious she was experienced in conducting interviews and explaining procedures and she gained their confidence immediately. She didn't waste time.

"Frank's given me all the information he has. I have to tell you the ideal search would have begun yesterday before all the extra people were out on the trail; however, I was unable to get here until today and I understand why Frank wanted to start right after your husband was reported missing. We'll still be able to search, I'll have Baker walk among the searchers in order to eliminate their scents." Laura said nothing but she felt her heart pounding. They all sat down and Mandy continued.

"Before I go any further I have to ask you what may be a very uncomfortable question. Could James want to disappear? Could it be he doesn't want to be found?"

The question still stabbed her straight in the heart! "Absolutely not! He never expressed any unhappiness with our life. In fact, when I fell in love with Aspen Falls he was ready to transfer his job from Texas to here right then! We don't argue or fight and he never said anything about wanting out of this marriage. No!" *Why does everyone keep asking me this question? I think I made it perfectly clear we are happy!*

"What about you, Susan? Did you ever see James as unhappy with his present circumstances? Could he have been attracted to someone else or was having an affair?" Her question supported the "it was always the wife that was the last to know" theory.

Susan sighed, "No! I'll tell you the same thing I told Frank. I saw a few disagreements, no fights, and no drama. No indications he was unhappy and no I didn't see signs he was having an affair!" Susan was getting as tired of this question as Laura.

"I understand your frustration but sometimes this happens and now I'm satisfied that is not a concern. So! The first thing I'll need is a support person to go with me when Baker and I start searching. He or she will need to carry a topographic map and a walkie-talkie. I brought a hand-held GPS and the support will have to be able to manage it as well. Frank, I don't think it should be you; I need you to continue coordinating everything here. When I drove up there were several guys in the group with you. Would any of them be able to work as support?"

"I'll be right back," and Frank walked out.

"Now, I need two articles of James' clothing. I want one from your dirty clothes hamper and something from his closet; preferably something that has been worn once, and I need to get them myself rather than have you do it. I don't mean to invade your privacy but it works better because I know how to handle the clothing without contaminating it with other scents." Mandy was carrying a backpack and reached in and pulled out a large zip lock bag. She put on latex gloves as she followed Laura into the bathroom. She looked in the hamper and chose a light gray sweatshirt, carefully pulled it from the hamper and holding it at arm's length; put it in the zip lock bag and sealed it; a long-sleeved tee shirt was retrieved from his closet using the same careful technique.

When they walked back into the living room, Frank was there with Jason."

"Mandy, this is Jason Mitchell, another officer on our force. I think he's just who you need. We've been studying the topographic map of this area for the last two days and he's familiar with a GPS and a walkie-talkie."

"Great, then let's get busy. Is everyone back up here and out of the area?" Frank nodded 'Yes'. "Okay, I need Baker to walk around them before we hit the trail. Laura, I'll be keeping up with Frank via the walkie-talkie and I want you to know we'll do absolutely everything we can to find your husband." She walked out to the driveway, Baker following behind her.

Laura and Susan went out onto the deck and watched them walk down to the group at the end of the driveway. They weren't able to hear what Mandy was saying but all of the men stopped moving and Mandy and Baker began walking among them. Mandy handed the zip lock bag containing the clothing to Frank and continued walking; circling them, sometimes more than once. Laura felt a crushing sense of dread; she was experiencing so many emotions. She was hopeful Mandy and Baker would find James and at the same time pessimistic; how could she and the dog find someone that 30 people, searching for a day and a half, couldn't find? She literally wanted to pull her hair, she was aware of painful muscle tension in her jaws, and sometimes she felt like she couldn't take a breath that was deep enough.

"Susan, were you kidding last night when you said the screaming helped?"

Susan shook her head. "I'm sure it would take a doctor to explain why, but yeah, it did. I take it you feel like screaming?" She grinned.

"Well, that or pulling out all my hair and biting roofing nails! Honestly Susan, I feel like I could explode into a million pieces right now. Liquor would probably help, but we know where that got me last time!"

"I don't think it was just that last drink. You'd been drinking on the plane, you had beer with the barbeque, you were totally and utterly exhausted, the next morning you ate a piece of toast and then you had the bourbon. You would've probably passed out exactly the same way if you had been drinking lemonade! So, you really feel like screaming, huh?"

"Yeah, you scared me at first but then I saw what it did for you. After you went out on the deck and screamed you melted into a puddle on the floor and then later you laughed and said you felt better."

"Okay, fine, then go ahead and scream, it can't hurt anything; however I wouldn't advise going out on the deck and letting loose. You're liable to have all those guys at the end of the driveway come flying up here thinking I'm murdering you!"

"So what do I do?"

They walked back in through the kitchen and into the living room. "Here take this throw pillow, go into your bedroom, shut the door, go into your bathroom, shut the door, sit on the floor, put your face in the pillow and scream like hell! And maybe pull your hair for good measure. I really don't remember my scream but try to do the same thing. Then come back in here and lay in your recliner and see how you feel."

Laura took the pillow and walked toward her bedroom. Susan sat on the sofa and then, *Damn, I think we both must be crazy as loons. For all I know, she'll pop a blood vessel, have a stroke and then I'll have a quadriplegic sister! Maybe this wasn't such a good idea.'* As she rose to walk toward the bedroom she heard the first muffled scream.

"Hello, you must be Susan!" Susan whirled around to see two women standing at the kitchen door holding dishes covered in foil. "We knocked but I guess you didn't hear us. I'm Yvonne Beckham and this is Clara Johnson. We are in a . . ." Another muffled scream. " . . . . a knit group with Laura." She said, looking toward the bedroom. "Uh, how is she? We brought lunch."

"She's in the bathroom right now, why don't y'all put everything in the kitchen and I'll get her."

Shit, they're gonna think we're both wackadoodle! I know the minute I open this door she's going to scream again and they're sure enough gonna call Frank!

She put her hand on the doorknob and opened it quickly and went into the room, closing the door behind her. Thank goodness, no more screams. She opened the bathroom door and there was Laura; sitting on the floor, holding the pillow and taking a deep breath, about to scream again.

"Shhhht! Laura!" She whispered "We've got company!"

"What?" She looked up. "What?"

"Shhhh, be quiet," she whispered. "Two women from your knit group brought lunch. I didn't hear them knock and they just walked in. They scared the crap out of me and I think they heard you screaming!" She took the pillow from her sister and helped her to her feet. Yep, she had been pulling her hair and her face was all blotchy. "Damn, girl, when you scream you really scream!"

"What do I do?"

"Look, just splash some water on your face and brush your hair and get out there as soon as you can. They'll think you've just been crying. I'm going back out now."

Laura was standing motionless in the middle of the bathroom. "Laura! Move your ass! Hurry up!" She pushed her toward the bathroom sink.

"She'll be right out!" Susan said, a little too brightly. "She's really having a hard time, poor thing. I'm sorry, I'm awful with names. Did you say your name was Eve?"

"Yvonne, Yvonne Beckham, and this is Clara Johnson. We brought lunch." She repeated, staring closely at Susan.

Yep! They think we're wackadoodle for sure.

"This is so thoughtful of you," Susan said, guiding them back towards the kitchen. "Laura is fortunate to have friends like you. Let's see, do I need to put anything in the refrigerator."

Susan made small talk with the two ladies, purposely not looking toward the hallway leading to the bedroom. Laura was right, with all this food; it did look like a funeral. *'C'mon Laura, hurry up! I can only think up so much b.s.! Get in here and help me out.*

"Yvonne, Clara! Thanks so much for coming. Y'all are so sweet to do this."

Laura was standing in the doorway to the kitchen, looking exactly like Susan said she felt; miserable! Susan heaved a sigh of relief; Laura was talking like nothing happened; like the two women hadn't just walked in on a primal scream therapy session!

"Why don't y'all go on into the living room and I'll take care of this. It smells delicious." Mac and cheese and beef stew. It really did smell good.

Susan busied herself in the kitchen while Laura and her friends sat in the living room and talked. She could hear Laura explaining about the search teams yesterday and this morning and about Mandy Howard and Baker. Her voice sounded stronger and more controlled than it had earlier today. *Maybe there was something to this screaming after all!*

She stood for a moment at the kitchen sink staring out the window. Thoughts of Andy and the picture and the files were always on the edge of her consciousness; nagging at her and demanding to be addressed. She couldn't do anything about them now but she couldn't put it off much longer.

"Ladies, this looks so good." Susan stuck her head through the doorway into the living room. "Laura and I haven't had lunch yet and we'd really like it if you'd join us. We've been cooped up in this house for two days and some visitors would really be nice."

Yvonne and Clara were a welcome distraction and they stayed until mid-afternoon. Yvonne Beckham was born in Green River, Wyoming. Her husband Joel is the doctor at the Urgent Care Clinic. Their twin sons, aged 16, were killed in a one-car drunk driving accident, both boys were drunk. Clara Davis Johnson, widowed 30 years, was the younger cousin to the Davis sisters. She lives in town in the same small home she moved to as a bride. She lost 6-month old twin daughters to scarlet fever and had no other children. James and the search and the K-9 team were the only topic of conversation but just the addition of new voices seemed to ease some of the stress Laura was feeling. As they were leaving, Yvonne told Laura to give her husband Joel a call if she was having trouble sleeping. Joel could work her in at Urgent Care and maybe write her a prescription if he thought it would help.

At 5:45 she was dozing in her recliner and Susan was straightening up the kitchen when Frank walked in the back door with Mandy and Baker. Mandy was carrying a leather backpack.

"She's asleep in the living room." Susan couldn't take her eyes off the pack. One of the straps was broken and it was scuffed and dirty. "I guess I should wake her up."

They walked into the living room and sat on the sofa, Mandy nearer to Laura who was still sleeping. Baker curled up in front of a window seat; relaxed; eyes always on her master.

"Laura? Hey babe, you need to wake up!" Susan touched her sister's arm and then brushed her hair away from her face. "Laura? Frank and Mandy are here."

Laura sat upright immediately, her eyes focusing from Frank to Mandy and back again. Susan sat on the arm of the recliner, waiting.

"Laura," Frank said softly, "Mandy found this." He placed it on the coffee table. "Is this his backpack?"

She stared at it for a moment before she picked it up." Yes, I think so."

"Baker alerted on it," Mandy said, "I figured we needed to get back and have you look at it."

"Where'd you find it?" She said, hugging the pack close to her chest.

"We started at the point where all the searchers began circling the lake and went from there. That's where I presented the clothing. I had her on a lead and she picked up his scent north of the lake and followed it for several miles. Then she stood at the edge of a drop-off that was about twenty feet down and began barking. We looked over the edge and saw the backpack, tangled in some brush at the bottom so we brought it up, and came back to let you have a look. I looked inside but I want to get your impressions."

Laura unzipped the pack. Inside was Jo-Jo's leash. The bear bell jingled as she lifted it out. There were several small pieces of wood, a cell phone, a half-empty bottle of water and a granola wrapper."

Mandy picked up the cell phone. It had been turned off.

"Is there anything missing that should be there?"

"I'm not sure. I never really looked through it before."

"Please check his phone. Turn it on and check the call history."

Laura turned the phone on and went to Call History. The last call was from her when he was waiting to pick her up at the airport. There were no other questionable calls.

"Keep the phone charged and turned on. I know this sounds peculiar but maybe he might try to call."

It didn't sound anymore peculiar than when she kept trying to call him over and over but she'd do what ever she was told.

"So what would be in his pockets?"

"His wallet and his keys and his pocket watch. Mandy, this backpack is really messed up. What could have happened?

"Was the pack normally in this condition?" When Laura shook her head 'No', she continued. "The dirt may have come as it fell down into the ravine. I don't think the strap broke then. This is a sturdy pack and I don't think it got hung up on anything on the way down. The strap was yanked away from where it was stitched to the bottom section. Compared to the other side, it had to have been jerked hard in order to tear away. Do you see these holes in the strap?" Mandy pointed to several punctures on both sides of the strap.

Laura looked at her and said nothing; a sense of dread building up from the pit of her stomach.

"They look like bite marks. The pack may have been slung back and forth and that could have been where the scuff marks came from. It may also have been what caused the strap to tear away. I'm sorry Laura but I believe this was either a mountain lion or a bear."

"Oh, God; oh, God, oh God!" Laura's voice rose higher and higher with every word. She clutched her arms across her waist and started rocking back and forth. "A bear? Oh, please, please! A lot of damn good that bear bell did! He should have put it on her collar instead of on her leash! Do you think he's dead?" Susan was standing next to her sister throughout the conversation and she put her hand on Laura's shoulder.

"Laura, I need you to calm down and listen to me. Not from what we saw. There was no blood, anywhere; either on the pack or up above in the area close to the drop off. Where it dropped off was not on a trail. We saw disturbed underbrush but nothing else."

Laura seemed to calm somewhat at hearing this information. "So you think, maybe something attacked him and ripped his pack from his back?"

"That's what it looks like to me. It could be as it was slung back and forth the animal lost its grip and it flew off the edge to the brush down below."

"What about the dog. Did you see any signs of Jo-Jo?"

"Nothing. It looks like whatever got the backpack was unable to get to James or the dog. They could have taken that opportunity to run. Laura, now that you've seen the pack I'm ready to get back out to where we found it. We can search in the dark as well as daylight, but in this circumstance the terrain is too dangerous to navigate in the dark. I want to keep tracking him for as long as there is daylight. If we don't find him tonight, I'm prepared to call in another team tomorrow."

"Laura," Frank said, "I have some friends with ATVs and they're waiting to take everyone back to continue the search."

"Go, go now." Laura said immediately. She stood up and walked to the back door, rushing them to start searching again.

Wednesday afternoon

Jason, Mandy and Baker walked outside and Jason got on behind the driver of one of the ATVs. Mandy picked up Baker and got on behind the other driver. They started up the trail and Laura and Susan waited on the back deck until they could no longer hear the sounds of the motors.

They walked back into the house and each picked up a cell phone. Laura called Erin and Susan called Lana Walters.

"Hey girl. Sorry I didn't call you earlier while you were still at the office. How'd everything go today?"

"Everything is going according to your schedule, except Joe Blanchard's wife's attorney is now seriously pissed, but we knew that would happen."

"Oh, damn, I don't even remember his name. Get it for me and give me his phone number and I'll call him and play on his sympathy; if he has any. They still haven't found James. The K9 team found his backpack just now and it looks pretty scary. One of the straps was broken and it was all scuffed up. The K9 handler said it looked like an animal chewed on it; she speculated the strap broke when the animal took a swipe at James; but the good thing is there was no blood so I guess he got away somehow."

"Oh, man! Susan, this has got to be so stressful. Just keep calling me everyday. You're supposed to be in court for Buddy Peterson next week. What do you want to do about that?"

"I have to come back for that. I can't put it off. When is it scheduled?"

"Tuesday afternoon at 1:00."

"Then make me a reservation out of Rock Springs for early Tuesday morning. I need you to have all the files ready and I'll look at everything when I get there. Depending on when that happens I may have to meet you at the courthouse. I hope to God they will have found James by then. I can't stand to think about leaving her alone."

"Will do! I'm glad you're there Susan, I can't imagine going through all of that by myself."

"Thanks, Lana. I'm glad you're where you are. You and J.T. have made this ordeal a hell of a lot easier. I'm going to have to work something out for you two when I get back."

"Aw, thanks boss lady. But let's take care of one thing at a time, okay? I'll talk to you tomorrow."

CHAPTER THIRTEEN

Wednesday evening

Frank walked through the kitchen and into the living room as it was getting dark. "Laura, we're packing up out there and will be working from the station from now on. I've called Jackson. A helicopter is coming in the morning at seven and the best place for the pilot to land is the field behind the elementary school, so I'll come get you and Susan in time for us to be there when he lands, in case he needs to ask you any questions.

"I just talked to the kids posting the flyers. They've posted them in Fort Washakie, Lander, Riverton, Rawlins, Rock Springs, and Laramie. They went to post offices, hospitals, police stations and sheriff departments, and truck stops. These kids plastered the flyers on telephone poles and one of the kids went to homeless shelters and gave them flyers as well.

"Dex Shelton called and he's donating the gas for them so they don't have to use their own gas money. Laura, I am so impressed with how this community is pulling together to find James. We live in a great place and this only serves to underscore my feelings. Now we still have . . . ."

The sounds of the ATVs interrupted his conversation, becoming louder and louder. Everyone went out onto the deck and saw the headlights shining on the trail as they approached the house.

The ATVs pulled on to the driveway and Mandy, Baker and Jason dismounted. The ATVs were left idling and the drivers also approached. Rick Martinez came onto the deck.

"Laura, I'll help anyway I can. I'm letting everyone know I'm offering myself and my machine for whatever anyone needs, unless there's a fire of course and then I'll have to leave. Molly wants to come out and I think she and the rest of the Knit Group are coordinating food, so someone will be bringing something everyday."

Rick is a seasonal wild land firefighter. The fire season would be starting up soon and then he would be gone most of the summer, fighting fires in Wyoming and the surrounding states.

"Thanks, Rick. Please tell her how much we appreciate this and let her know she can come out whenever she wants. What you're doing means a lot." That's all Laura could say before the tears caused her to bite her lip to keep from sobbing.

"I'll be out again in the morning," Mandy said, "and another team will be coming with me. We still have a lot of ground to search and as of right now I'm not even going to say how long this will last and when we will stop."

Laura was still crying but hearing Mandy say the search would continue with no time limit allowed her to catch her breath and slow her breathing and say "Thank you, Mandy. Thank you for not giving up."

Frank said, "We're breaking down our location out here, like I told you; but we'll talk and I'll stop by everyday. So, before I leave, is there anything we can do for you and Susan?"

"No, Frank thanks for everything. I don't think there's anything you could do that you haven't done already. Please give Ivy my love and tell her thank you for everything she and the Knit Group have been doing."

"Then I'll see you in the morning."

Five minutes later, Laura and Susan were alone in the house, standing in the kitchen waiting; waiting for what? They didn't know.

"Why don't you call, Erin? I'll scrape together something to eat. I know it'll be hard since we have so little, but I'm sure I can find something!" She winked as she guided Laura to the living room and turned back to the over-flowing kitchen.

Laura picked up her phone and settled into her recliner to call Erin. "Scrape together something to drink, too. Okay? I've been a really good girl and I think I deserve vino! Look in the cabinet above the refrigerator. At this point I'm not picky, I'll drink anything!"

"Yes, ma'am! I'll get right on it."

As she moved around the kitchen, she thought about Andy and the picture and the secrets. She knew she would have to put it off for a while. She didn't want to but it was her only choice.

Thursday morning

Frank picked them up at 6:45 and they were waiting in the field behind the elementary school when the Bell Ranger landed on its skids. Laura and Susan stood away from the slowly spinning rotors but Frank ducked down and went to the helicopter to greet the pilot. The pilot got out of the aircraft and he and Frank walked over to Laura and Susan.

"Hello! My name's Lloyd Great Bear and Frank tells me you need some help."

Laura liked him immediately and Susan liked him even more; although the difference in their ages could be measured in decades. His age and the gold band on his left ring finger nipped that little interest in the bud real quick.

"Frank told me what he was wearing and that he had a dog with him. A yellow lab I believe?"

"Yes, she weighs about 60 pounds but I guess you couldn't tell that from the air"

"Oh, we can recognize all kinds of animals and her coloring will be a lot easier to spot than if she were brown or black. We can fly pretty low when we're searching and I'm taking Frank with me as an extra pair of eyes. Is there anything else you can tell me about your husband?"

"I don't think so. I've told Frank everything."

"I have one more question for you and you may find it . . ."

"Yes, we were happy, no, we didn't have a fight, no he was not having an affair, and no; he was not the kind to disappear!" Laura said as she sniffed and rolled her eyes. "Is that what you were going to ask?"

"Ohhh-kay, then, that's all I need to know. Let's get airborne and take a look around."

He and Frank walked back to the helicopter; the rotors continuing to spin slowly. Before Frank got in he exchanged his flat-brimmed hat for a helmet with a face shield and microphone attached; enabling the crew to communicate with one another above the noise of the aircraft. He pulled on a green jump suit and Lloyd gave him a "thumbs-up signal. He got in and buckled up his safety harness. The rotors began to spin more rapidly and soon they lifted off and swooped north.

Jason was waiting as Mandy and Baker arrived from Jackson about fifteen minutes later, followed by another SUV. She and Baker got out and walked toward the other SUV. A man and an unusual-looking dog joined them.

"Laura and Susan, this is Jake Richardson and his dog, Daegal." Daegal was the most imposing dog they had ever seen and he seemed not to invite friendly petting. With a long black face and black erect ears, he was large and squarer in appearance than a German Shepard. "Daegal is a Belgian Malinois and he and Jake have been together since he was a puppy. He's three years old and he and Baker have searched together before. They do very well together. Is there anything you want to ask Jake before we leave?

"Yeah," Laura said quickly. "How often do you not find the person you're searching for?"

Jake was very straight-forward. "I don't have a percentage for you. Sometimes we do and other times we don't. Unless we are told the circumstances under which the person disappeared are not survivable we search for a living person. That's why we're using trailing dogs. Otherwise, we use cadaver dogs. Sometimes we find a body months, or in some cases, years later and two of our handlers have searched on their own time for a person missing for more than fifteen years. Search and rescue members are a unique group. We don't give up easily. And now if you'll excuse us, we need to get busy."

The ATVs were idling at the trailhead beside the driveway and the handlers, dogs and Jason mounted up and headed north again.

Laura and Susan were at a loss. They wandered in and out of the house, sat in the living room, ate, wandered around again and munched again. The restlessness was beginning to wear on their nerves when Susan suggested a walk. They kept their cell phones in their pockets and started up the trail James took the day he disappeared. They could hear and sometimes see the helicopter moving back and forth in the sky above the search area. The terrain became steeper and steeper and after thirty minutes they were both breathing heavily. Laura's knee began to protest and they sat on a boulder, warm from the midday sun; giving them a welcome break.

"You mean to tell me he took this hike almost every day and we aren't even close to the lake?"

"Yeah, unless the snow was too deep. He talked about the scenery and how the dog would run back and forth. He really liked this hike and was usually gone for a couple of hours. He didn't seem to mind the difficulty. I went a couple of times but I always felt like I was intruding somehow and when I finally stopped he never asked me to go again. I guess this was his time to be alone and I tried to respect that." *I'm also not in great shape to be hiking. Maybe if I hiked more I wouldn't carry 155 pounds on my 5'3" body!*

"Laura, were you and James happy? I mean everyone else has asked so I might as well ask, too"

"Yeah," she sighed, "We were. I was never unhappy and he never acted like he was unhappy. There was just never any passion; it didn't seem like he missed me when I came back from seeing you. He was always sweet to Erin. He was never mean to me. We talked; but never about anything more than the events of the day. He never talked about his family and he didn't seem to understand ours. He didn't understand how you and Daddy and I could be so close; how we could talk on the phone and then a few days later talk to each other again. He seemed happiest working in his shop and walking the dog. He seemed happiest when he was alone."

"What about sex?" Her sister could be blunt sometimes.

"Sex was . . . . sex. It was good, not great, not very often. More of a release than anything else. He would tell me he loved me, I would tell him I loved him. He was affectionate. I never once doubted his fidelity and I hope he never doubted mine."

"So you don't think he would just disappear on purpose?"

"Dammit, Susan! I am so sick of everyone asking that question! No, he would not just up and walk away. We had it good here! We didn't have money problems. He could work in his workshop whenever he wanted! I didn't nag him and he ate my cooking! He took care of repairs around the house! No, for the last damn time! He didn't just disappear! Something bad happened to him and it terrifies me to think about it. I love him! Do you doubt that? Do you doubt that we love one another?" By this time Laura was on her feet, her hands balled into fists, raising her voice.

"Hey, hey. Calm down! I don't doubt anything. I just needed to ask, that's all!"

"Let's go back, okay. I don't like being out here. It gives me the willies!"

Thursday afternoon

They walked back in silence and when they reached the house Caroline and Pete Wilkerson were sitting on the back deck. Pete had his feet propped up on a large cooler. He was the part-time priest at St. Michael the Archangel, dividing his time between Aspen Falls and another parish up in Cody. He was an ex-Catholic priest married to Caroline, an ex-Catholic nun.

"Aw, I'm so glad you're here." Laura walked quickly toward them. "I was hoping y'all could come up but I know there are obligations in Cody. Aren't you supposed to be there this weekend?"

Pete and Caroline stood and engulfed Laura in a huge hug, pulled Susan into it and said, "Don't worry about us Laura, we're good."

With everyone still in his embrace he bowed his head and began to pray, "Father God, from whom all good things come, please protect your child James. Watch over him, give him warmth and protection and bring him back to us. Watch over your child Laura. Give her peace and hold her in your shielding embrace. All this we pray in the name of your son, Jesus Christ," and all said in unison "Amen."

Laura was crying openly, still hugging Father Pete. "Oh, Pete, I've never been more frightened in my life. The K9 team found his backpack and said it looked like it had been mauled by a bear or something. They didn't find any blood but they didn't find him or the dog either."

"Laura, I've gone on a few of those hikes with James; and sometimes we spotted bears. So, I'm not telling you that it's not a possibility. But, some of the terrain is pretty rugged. It will take some time for them to look over everything. I want to go out there myself. I think I'm the only one who has been out there with him and I'd like to talk to the K9 people. Maybe I can help."

As they were talking everyone was bringing in the cooler and bags and boxes Pete and Caroline brought with them. Pete looked around and grinned.

"I know, I know," said Laura. "It only looks like a funeral. And I have a statement for everyone. 'Thanks for the food', but here's a news flash 'There ain't gonna be no funeral!" She said in her deepest Texas accent!

"You got it! But it looks like we're going to be eating good for a few days. Plus we brought food for three days of meals and I brought your absolute favorite!"

Laura grinned, knowing what he would say next.

"Pinot Noir and Hershey Bars!"

"My hero! Let's eat. I'm actually hungry!"

The cooler was emptied and the contents put away. In addition to the food they brought paper plates and napkins, paper towels, plastic cutlery, three sizes of plastic storage bags, trash bags, boxes of kleenex and toilet paper.

"We needed this stuff or someone was going to have to make a run to Walker Brothers! Thanks so much! Did I see Lasagna? I've got Chianti and stuff for salad! Let's pretend we're Italian" Laura got busy and soon she and Caroline were producing a great Italian meal.

Pete walked into the living room with Susan. "Okay, spill. What's the real deal?" He said quietly.

"You know what we know. They've been searching since Monday night when she first called Frank Bell and said he was missing. At that time she estimated he had been missing for about seven hours. It's now Thursday. They used searchers on foot, one K9 team, a helicopter and now two K9 teams. I have to stay positive for Laura but I have a feeling deep in the pit of my stomach that he's dead; especially after finding his mauled backpack. I think something got him or else he fell over a cliff running away from something. I have a feeling in the next day or two they're going to switch from using trailing dogs to cadaver dogs."

"I want to go with them tomorrow. I might just be in the way but maybe I can see something or take them somewhere they never knew to go. Caroline and I are going to stay here until next Wednesday. I want to have a special service at church this Sunday with prayers for Laura and James and you and everyone who's been searching. I want to spread the word early so as many people as possible can attend."

"Father, if you're planning on staying until Wednesday, do you think it would be okay if I went back to Kansas for a few days? I have a trial on Tuesday afternoon and I was planning on flying back on Tuesday morning. I want to stay for church on Sunday, but then I could fly out of Rock Springs and go home and take care of some business and then make arrangements to come back on Wednesday. You said you could be here until then, right?"

"Sure, sure. That sounds like a plan and by then we may be closer to knowing something, one way or the other! That part's going to be hard on Laura."

Susan stood at the bay window with her back toward Father Pete. "I think for the first time she is at least considering the possibility he's dead and that they may never find him. When the day comes for her to be told I sure hope you and Caroline can be here. She has me and her friends here in Aspen Falls but she's going to need the kind of support and compassion I think only you can provide." She thought to herself. *I've waited this long, I can wait a little longer to find out all the stuff about Daddy.*

Pete wandered into the kitchen following the smells of lasagna and called out, "Susan, come and get it before I eat it all!" The food provided a few minutes respite from the unrelenting stress and there were smiles and little jokes that appeared to lift some of the burden from Laura's shoulders.

At 6:00 Frank, Jason and the K9 teams walked into the house. Laura never heard the helicopter. She introduced Father Pete and Caroline to everyone and after he explained his experience hiking with James they were more than happy to have him go with them the next day. Frank explained the helicopter would be coming and going from Jackson and not even stopping in Aspen Falls unless they found something or they needed more information. The helo pilot would be bringing his own spotter so Frank and Jason could get back to their duties with the police department and they all made it very clear to Laura and Susan; this was an ongoing search and no one was quitting.

The helicopter was already on its way back to Jackson and the K9 teams soon followed. They made arrangements to meet Father Pete at the house at 9:00 the next morning and then they were gone. The house was quiet.

Thursday night it started storming and a steady downpour continued until the next morning. Laura and Susan couldn't sleep and spent the night in the living room, huddled under blankets and watching the lightening out the bay windows; so sad and disheartened they could hardly speak.

Chapter Fourteen

Friday morning

On Friday morning the K9 units were on-site by 9:00. The rainy weather made Susan and Laura anxious but Mandy and Jake convinced them that they and their dogs had trailed in mud and rain before. They began to relax a little and regain some of the confidence they originally had in the teams. They stood on the back deck as the ATVs, with Pete Wilkerson riding shotgun, headed up the trail. Lloyd Great Bear was already flying a grid pattern back and forth over the search area and Susan thought this was as good a time as any to tell Laura she needed to go back to Kansas.

Susan asked, "Caroline, you and Father Pete said you were going to stay until this coming Wednesday, right?" Laura stared at her quizzically

"Yes, he's planning on a special service on Sunday and we arranged to stay on and do whatever we can. Is there something you need?"

"Well, I have a court case on Tuesday afternoon that I really can't postpone. Originally I planned on leaving Tuesday morning and coming back here on Thursday. But, if you and Father Pete are here I could stay for the service on Sunday, fly home and take care of some things and get back here late Wednesday. Would it be okay if y'all stayed here with Laura so I don't have to worry about her staying by herself? It would sure make me feel better."

"Uh, don't I have a say in all this?" Laura said sarcastically.

"Of course you do, babe. I just know how hard all this had been on you and the easier I or anyone else can make it then I want to do it."

"I need to go outside by myself for a little bit, okay?" Laura said as she was walking out onto the south deck.

"Sure, sure. We'll be right here." Caroline said. After Laura was outside Caroline said, "I think this is a good idea, Pete talked to me about it last night. I know you've already had to do a lot of schedule juggling because of your Dad's death so we would really like to stay here and fill in for you. Pete and James had a special friendship. Even though he didn't go to church with Laura he had his own spiritual beliefs and Pete looked forward to their hikes."

They looked up from their conversation. Laura was standing in the living room. "Here's my decision. Yes, I want Susan to stay through the service on Sunday and then fly back to Kansas and take care of business. Thank you Caroline for your offer and yes it would make me feel better. From what the K9 teams and Lloyd Great Bear tell me they will be searching, good weather or bad; at least the K9 teams. The helo can't search in the rain. If Susan can get back by Wednesday, that would be great. I'm not sure what will be going on after that and that's not something I'm prepared to think about right now. I know there's more business concerning Daddy that we have to attend to and we need to concentrate on that also. And now I'm going back outside with a glass of wine, by myself and I don't care if it is before noon or not. After the wine is gone I'll be ready to be friendly again. Right now I just need some time alone."

Caroline and Susan were surprised at how controlled Laura was while delivering her decision to them. They were both apprehensive about her and knowing she wouldn't be alone for the next several days eased their concerns.

Laura found the biggest wine glass in the kitchen, filled it to the brim and walked out on the deck, without chocolate and without saying another word. James was out there somewhere; either dead or alive, but out there in the mountains. This conclusion was based on more than an analysis of the situation; it was a gut-feeling. It had been at the back of her mind for the last day or two but, until today, she would not allow herself to consciously consider it.

Daddy, and the picture and the secrets in his files couldn't be deferred much longer. They would have to be addressed and she was grateful to Susan for not bringing them up more often. They had to be weighing heavily on her mind. Whatever the secrets, she and Susan would soon discover them and they would find out about their mother.

At 2:00 it started to rain again and Laura came inside. She did not share her feelings. The helicopter disappeared; Lloyd was probably flying back to Jackson. The rain was steady, not a gully washer; but nevertheless hard enough to interrupt the search. Soon the ATVs were coming back up the trail; the dogs and handlers were wet and cold.

They all came into the kitchen and Laura was ready with a large stack of towels. A big pot of coffee was brewing and there were plenty of cookies and snacks. Mandy and Baker, Jake and Daegal, their ATV drivers, Rick Martinez and Father Pete were grateful for the hot coffee and food and they discussed their progress.

"We're stopping for today. The rain is making the ground too treacherous for us. I don't know if the dogs are really trailing scents but they seemed to be eager to work so we'll be back in the morning ready to search in the mud. The helo will be flying the grid if the weather allows.

Susan went to the guestroom to call Lana and make the changes to her schedule. Laura and Caroline went into the kitchen to rearrange all the food into more manageable containers. Pete stayed in the living room, staring out the bay windows. He went into the kitchen and asked Laura if he could set up a prayer table. Her eyes filled with tears as she said, "Of course. Tell me what you need and I'll get it for you."

When Father Pete finished, he had prepared an area on the east facing wall of the living room. An end table was called into service and stood on a small green rug Pete had brought with him; covered with a green cloth. A wooden Crucifix was placed at the back center of the table. A small brass bowl containing holy water was at the left front of the table. A bible opened to Philippians 4: 4-8 was center front beside a small Book of Common Prayer. A votive candle in a red glass holder was at the back, left of the Crucifix. A small framed picture of James on an easel was placed to the right of the Crucifix; next to a tiny icon of St. Anthony, patron saint of lost things and missing persons.

Pete called to Susan and Caroline and Laura and when all were gathered in the living room he said, "Caroline and I have one of these in our home in Cody. God is everywhere and you can worship him anywhere. This gives us comfort in our home and I hope it will give you comfort here. They joined hands and Pete prayed for James and Laura and Susan and asked for God's blessings on all the search and rescue teams and the dogs.

The rain continued to fall and shortly thereafter Pete and Caroline left to stay in the little log cabin next to the church. They would stay there until Susan left and then move into the guest room until she returned.

When it was time for bed, Laura walked around the house, locking doors and turning out lights. She stopped at the prayer table, lit the candle and held the picture of James to her heart. She prayed he was safe and warm; that the searchers would find him soon and she prayed for peace for herself and Susan. She left the votive burning, a beacon in the dark; a beacon for James to follow home.

Saturday

Saturday, the rain continued to fall. Lloyd Great Bear did not fly but the two K9 teams went out again, accompanied by Pete Wilkerson. Caroline stayed for the day. She brought some knitting but neither she nor Laura could concentrate for more than a few stitches at a time before getting up and wandering from kitchen to window seats and back again.

Susan was working on some court papers on her laptop; Lana scheduled a flight for her out of Rock Springs for 4:30 Sunday afternoon. Occasionally she stopped and reviewed Andy's files. She found nothing new but it gave her something to do. The atmosphere around the house was tense and they were all just trying to stay out of each other's way.

The Knit Group divided into teams and each day brought enough food for breakfast, lunch and dinner. Today Rosie Esposito and Opal brought fixings for sandwiches and tacos, plus staples like bread, milk and eggs. Laura was past being positive; just expressed her thanks and didn't invite anyone to stay. Susan noticed she was eating less and drinking more.

She was worried and finally called Joel Beckham at the Urgent Care Clinic. He urged her to get Laura to come into the clinic for a check-up and if everything looked okay he would write her a prescription for anxiety. He wouldn't just bring out something to "make her feel better". Joel was a "by the book" doctor and he didn't write prescriptions without reason. He gave her his home and cell numbers and told Susan he would meet them at the clinic anytime they needed him. The trick now was to get Laura to see Joel.

After Laura wandered the circuit for the third time, Susan said, "Babe, I know how difficult this is on you and how hard you're trying to stay positive. I don't want you to be mad at me but I called Joel Beckham and he asked if you would be willing to come to Urgent Care and let him check you over and maybe give you something to help you with all this stress.

Laura looked at her and said, "Seems to me the wine is working pretty well!"

"C'mon, babe! You know wine isn't what you need right now. Please, let's go see Joel and see what he has to say."

"Today's Saturday." Laura said dully.

"It's okay; he said he would meet us."

"It's a good idea, Laura." Caroline added. "He might be able to give you something that would ease the anxiety."

"Sounds like y'all have already decided what's best for me. Sure, what the hell, I'll go." She rolled her eyes. "Maybe drugs are less expensive than wine." She went into her bedroom and got her purse and came back to the living room and sat on the couch. "So what's the hold-up? I'm ready whenever you are!"

Susan called Joel and he arranged to meet them at the clinic. The rain stopped and Caroline stayed at the house should anyone come by and Susan and Laura left in Susan's rental car. Joel's car was in the parking lot of the clinic and he was standing at the door. "I'm glad you came Laura. Let's see what you and I can do."

"I just don't know what you can do, Joel. I appreciate you making the effort and all but nothing can make me feel better except James coming back. And despite what my sister may have told you, I'm not drinking that much."

"Well, that's good news, I guess. Susan didn't mention your drinking but since you brought it up, how much are you drinking?"

"Oh!" *Busted!* "Well, we're going through a bottle a night; the both of us, not just me!"

"Okay, let's go into the exam room and do some general check-up tests." Blood-pressure, pulse-ox, blood glucose and temperature were all within normal range. Getting her on the scales took a little coaxing, with

Susan finally having to turn her back; Joel only noting the number and not saying it out loud. A little over-weight but considering all the food and desserts around the house and no exercise, it wasn't that bad.

"So, here is my recommendation. I believe that a prescription of alprazolam may help with the temporary anxiety and depression that you're obviously experiencing right now. I'm only writing one refill for it. If you need more I want you to come see me first. AND it's important you stop with the wine while you're taking this. It doesn't mix well with alcohol. Mixing alprazolam and alcohol can increase your risk of some serious side effects including behavioral changes. It can also slow your respiratory and heart rates and it can cause fainting. Now you told me about the one time you fainted and from what I see I don't think it's anything to worry about but if it happens again you need to call me. You also need to walk a few miles a day with someone. The exercise will do you good. You can ask somebody to stay at the house; I know there are lots of people wanting to help out and walking the few miles won't take all that long."

"If, after a few days of taking this as prescribed, you're still having problems, then call me and we'll discuss changing the dosage or the drug itself.

"I have some samples I can give you now, I'll call your script in to the pharmacy in Lander and you can go get it or send someone to get it for you. Or better yet, let me get it for you. They know me but I probably need to take your driver's license and your insurance card. What do you think?"

"I think I want all this over with. I think I want my husband back. I also think neither of these is going to happen in the next day or two so; let's go for it. I can stop having a glass of wine at night, I'm not a wino, you know! It just helps me relax and thanks for offering to pick up the script, that would be great. I want to be home when they find him."

Joel's eyes did not waver from Laura to Susan but at the same time he tensed. He knew Laura was going to have to consider the possibility of James not being found and he knew it was going to have to be soon.

He unlocked a cabinet and took out a small sample bottle. "Take one now according to my directions. I'm going to Lander and I'll bring them back out to your house".

Laura gave him her credit card, her driver's license and her insurance card. She and Susan left to go back to the house and Joel locked the clinic and drove toward Lander.

When she and Susan drove up to the house her stomach sank. She could see several people in the kitchen. When they walked in Mandy and Frank Bell and Caroline and Pete were having coffee at the kitchen table. Baker was curled up on the floor near Mandy. Laura sensed they weren't gathered to give her good news.

"Okay, let's get this over with." Laura said bluntly. "What happened? Why are you here and where are Jake and Daegal? Why did the ATVs leave?"

"Laura, this is not working anymore. Even though we and the dogs are trained to work in the rain it looks like they've lost the scent. We've been looking now since Wednesday morning with not so much as one clue since finding the backpack. I think it's time to change teams; bring in some new handlers and dogs."

"Okay." Laura said, refusing to acknowledge the inevitable. "I can see that getting new dogs up here might be a good thing. So does this start in the morning? It's stopped raining and it looks like it may not rain for the next few days."

Mandy looked down for a moment and then looked up and said "I need you to sit down, Laura."

Laura sat at the kitchen table without questioning why; her eyes shifting back and forth from person to person. Susan stood behind her and put her hands on her sister's shoulders.

"I've sent Jake and Daegal back to Jackson. I know this is going to be hard for you to hear but yes, we need to bring in new teams with new dogs. These teams are not certified for trailing like me and Baker and Jake and Daegal. These are cadaver teams. Do you understand what I'm saying?"

Laura was staring at Mandy, barely breathing. Susan tightened her hands on Laura's shoulders. No one else said anything.

"Laura?" Mandy said.

"I knew you were going to tell me this. I've felt it since yesterday. I . . . ." She couldn't say anything else. She stood and turned to her sister and hugged her, sobbing so hard the others gathered around her became concerned.

Laura stood, holding on to Susan for several minutes before sitting down again. She took several deep breaths and the sobs began to subside. No one said anything, giving her the time she needed.

"I'm okay y'all. Everyone sit down; even though I didn't want to think about it I knew this was what you were going to say. I got a bad feeling after you found his backpack but I just kept hoping and praying. I knew this was going to happen sooner or later."

Mandy looked directly at Laura. "I wouldn't give up searching for him if I thought there was any chance he could be alive; but I think it's time we brought in the cadaver dogs."

It was obvious Mandy had given this talk to many family members. She was very gentle, yet straightforward in her message and she had perfected her deliverance enough to give the sad information to the families in the most sympathetic manner possible.

"I know you and Baker and Jake and Daegal and everyone else have done everything possible to find him. Now that we're openly talking about it I want to tell you that I . . . he's probably dead! It's hard to describe, but I have a feeling, deep in my gut, that he's not alive. I don't know what happened. I don't know if he fell down into a ravine or if a bear or something got him; but I don't think he is alive anymore." Laura said this out loud. She knew that's what they wanted her to say. She didn't say what was in her heart. *There's still a chance, there's always a chance, but I'm the only one that thinks so!*

No one sitting at the table or Susan, standing behind Laura, said a word. "Thank you for everything. I think you've done everything you could possibly do. I know it's time. I know its time to look for his body." *And there's always the chance you will find him alive!*

Laura was not crying; and since she had not had time to take the anxiety pills Joel had prescribed, she wasn't talking under the influence of any medication. She sounded like she had thought it all out before telling everyone what she thought. There was a tone of resignation to her voice.

"I miss church and I need tomorrow. James needs all our prayers. Susan is here with me; y'all go home. We'll be okay.

CHAPTER FIFTEEN

Sunday

At 8:00 the next morning Susan and Laura were at the kitchen table when someone knocked on the back door and did not immediately come in; instead whoever it was waited for the door to be answered. When Laura opened it she saw two men, both tall and well-built; one black and one white, both wearing backpacks.

The black man said, "Are you Laura Gregory?" When she nodded yes, he introduced himself, "Hi, my name is Aaron Masterson and this is Randy Avery. Mandy told you we were coming this morning?"

"Yes, she did. Please come in, where are your dogs?" Each man gave a short whistle and two large Bloodhounds loped up and sat beside the men. "C'mon in, bring the dogs, I don't mind. We own a dog . . . . , she was with my husband when he disappeared and Baker and Daegal have been in and out with Mandy and Jake, so we're pretty dog friendly around here."

Aaron was more direct than Mandy. "We'd like to get started as soon as we can. My dog's name is George and Randy's dog's name is Banda. Do you have any questions?" He appeared ready to get to work and didn't seem as comfortable talking to victims families as Mandy.

"Do you need something of James' to show to the dogs?"

"No, George and Banda are specially trained, used only for searches where there is a suspected cadaver." Laura cringed. *I don't even want to know how they train these dogs!*

"It works like this; as a body decays, it produces several very distinct odors. Most people prefer to avoid them but for the dogs they're like a signature. These odors occur nowhere else in nature. *I don't think I'll tell her that placentas are used to train cadaver dogs!* Our dogs are trained to detect remains that have been buried, that are in bodies of water and even covered in cement. If they find remains they've been trained to alert by barking and bouncing in place and that's what tells us they've found something. They're trained not to alert to dead animals, only to human remains." *Shit! When will I learn not to give too much information!* "We give them verbal cues to start, "Go, George!" or "Find, Banda!" and they know to start searching. The dogs work both on and off leash and we decide which is best in specific situations. Rain is not always a factor in calling off a search, unless it makes the terrain dangerous. Then we do have to suspend searches until the ground is safer."

"Well," Laura said, crossing her arms in front of her, "I don't want to hold you up, so whenever you come back just come on in. There've been so many people in and out of here during the last week that getting up to answer the door all the time is a real pain. We're getting ready to go to church but we should be back by 12:30 or so and we'll have our cell phones with us in case . . . in case you need to get in touch with us."

"Yeah, Mandy gave us your numbers and we'd like to get started but we've got something else to do first." Aaron acted like he wanted to start right away instead of waiting for whatever. "So we'll see you later." They turned and walked toward their car.

Laura sat with her head in her hands for a few minutes. Even the word cadaver sounded horrible. She and Susan finished dressing, turned their phone ringers to vibrate and drove to church. St Michael the Archangel Episcopal was a tiny church in a small town. Ten rows with kneelers, separated by a central aisle and one stained glass window above the altar. Most parishioners dressed casually and no one was judged for the way they did or did not dress. Most times in winter Laura wore jeans and sweaters and boots. Today was a warmer, spring day so they dressed in cropped pants and shirts.

Father Pete usually based his sermon from the Lectionary in the Book of Common Prayer but today he prepared a special service, centered on James. Prayers of the People Form VI was Laura's favorite, with special emphasis on the sentence "For all who are in danger, sorrow, or any kind of trouble."

The pews were packed with the regular parishioners plus neighbors and townspeople who usually went to other churches and even those who attended no church at all. All of the local Knit Group members were there and the most touching of all was seeing the K9 teams and their dogs and Lloyd Great Bear, the helicopter pilot. The handlers stood at the back of the church and the dogs sat beside them during the entire service. Laura sat with Susan in her usual pew, third from the back on the right side; and she never felt the love of God and friends so strongly. *James, where are you? Please God, keep him safe.* Before the recessional Father Pete asked Laura and Susan to come to the communion rail where everyone stood around them and as many as possible placed their hands on them or touched others who were touching them. Once more Father Pete prayed for the safety of James and for peace and comfort for Laura and Susan.

After the service the K9 teams and Lloyd Great Bear spoke briefly with Laura before leaving. These teams were always in demand and Laura was especially grateful they took the time to come today.

The ECW arranged a potluck lunch and Laura and Susan sat with everyone for a short time. There wasn't the kind of laughter and stories that happened at Andy's funeral. That was a celebration and the time for laughter and stories. This was a more somber occasion but there was still friendly, comforting conversation.

Susan needed to get back and pack to return to Kansas. Caroline offered to help clean the parish hall and then she and Pete would come out to the house to stay while Susan was gone. Laura and Susan stayed long enough to eat ham and potato salad and deviled eggs and then made their exit.

The house was quiet and Laura was on the south deck in the sun while Susan packed for her flight back to Kansas. She sat there alone, and soon she realized what she was doing. She was practicing being alone. She knew it was next. Next was loneliness.

Susan packed the car and was sitting in the living room, gazing out the bay windows when Pete and Caroline arrived. Laura was still out on the deck; eyes closed, wrapped in an afghan.

"Thank y'all so much for staying with her. She's trying to handle everything but this has been really hard on her. The doctor gave her some anti-anxiety meds and I'm probably breaking some privacy law by telling you this but I don't care; so if you see any behavior that concerns you, try to find out if she is taking it on schedule. She does have a schedule and I reminded her about following it. Oh, and one more thing, the doctor said it wasn't a good idea to drink alcohol while she was taking these meds."

She walked out on the deck and knelt beside her sister; gently shaking her awake. Pete and Caroline couldn't hear from inside what was said but they saw Laura stand up and hug Susan. She was crying and Susan put her hands on both side of her sister's face and kissed her on the forehead and they walked back in to the living room, holding hands.

Susan couldn't stand drawing out the good-bye any longer so she hugged her once more and said good-bye to Caroline and Pete. "Y'all have my number so please call me anytime you need to."

"I'll be okay, babe." Laura said. "Go home and take care of business. It sounds like somebody named Buddy Peterson needs you right now and I'll see you on Wednesday, okay? I know you're going to need a little time to take care of things.".

"When I get back you and I will finish going through Daddy's stuff. Just concentrate on James. I love you and we'll pray for each other every night" Susan hugged her sister again.

She wasn't crying but she was close to it so she abruptly turned and walked out the door, got in her car and drove away. This time she didn't get stopped by Frank Bell and soon she was out of town and on her way to Rock Springs.

Andy and "Bert and Ernie" and all the alarming information they found in Andy's files were always at the back of her mind but she wouldn't allow herself the time to really think about it until now. She had a dreadful feeling they were never going to find James alive. Someone would have said something about him by now if they had seen the flyers the kids plastered everywhere. It was devastating when the K9 teams switched from trailing dogs to cadaver dogs but maybe now they would be able to find his body and give Laura some measure of peace. She wouldn't say "give her closure". Susan didn't think there could ever be closure in her situation.

It had been a long time since Johnny died and she never found "closure". To Susan, closure meant that something was over and you could forget about it. She never forgot about Johnny Bennett. Some days it was only a fleeting little memory; over and gone in less than a second. Other days a memory lasted longer. There were no bad memories of her husband and she knew she would never have a love like that again. She tried dating but she always ended up comparing them to Johnny and that really wasn't fair. She was happy with her life the way it was now. She considered herself fortunate to have had the opportunity to love someone so deeply. Many people lived their whole lives without that kind of love and, sadly, she included Laura with them. Laura and James never appeared to have the kind of love for one another that she and Johnny shared; but Laura never complained and always said she loved James. So, it wasn't for Susan to judge. Her happiness wasn't anyone else's happiness.

She decided once she got home and finished prepping for Buddy Peterson she would call Bert Shaffer. She planned on getting him and Father John up to Wyoming and making them explain to her and Laura the secrets they kept hidden for so long. She couldn't wait much longer.

Her trip went without incident and soon she was home and reviewing the information she would need to represent Buddy in court. It was good to be home again, to sleep in her own bed and, although she felt guilty about it; not to worry about Laura every single minute.

Late that afternoon Caroline and Laura were knitting and Pete was reading when they heard the sound of several people coming through the kitchen. By the time Laura and Caroline put down their work and Pete marked and closed his book Randy and Aaron walked into the living room with Frank Bell and the veterinarian Carl Thompson.

Before Laura could say anything Frank said, "Laura, Randy found Jo-Jo. I'm so sorry to have to tell you this but she's dead."

Laura sat back down in her chair, clutching Caroline's hand. Randy took over the conversation, "She was lying on an outcropping about 15 feet below a cliff and I noticed her when the sun reflected off the tags on her collar. We climbed down and when we saw she was dead we used the walkie-talkie and called Frank. We got her back up to the top and wrapped her in the plastic we keep in our backpacks. She was about half a mile northeast of Arapahoe."

Frank started talking then, "When they told me they found Jo-Jo and she was dead, I called Carl and arranged for everyone to meet at his office. We didn't want to call you right away. We wanted to wait until Carl could take a look at her." Frank looked at Carl and Carl took over the conversation. *This turn-taking conversation has obviously been rehearsed!*

"Randy and Aaron told me where they found her and what the surrounding area looked like and I examined her. There was a deep slash on her side matted with dried blood, there was blood on her muzzle and in her mouth and there were several broken bones," he paused.

Tears were streaming down Laura's face; she was sniffing and shaking and Caroline was on one side of her, still holding her hand and Pete was standing on her other side, his hand on her shoulder.

"Carl, don't stop. Finish telling me."

The men all found places to sit in the living room and at the dining table; except for Carl. He brought in a chair from the kitchen turned it backwards and sat directly in front of Laura.

"This is what I think happened. I agree with Mandy's theory about the backpack. The bear may have started chasing them and it looks like Jo-Jo tried to attack it; the blood on her muzzle and in her mouth may have been from the bear. The bear swiped at Jo-Jo and that's where she got the slash on her side. I think then she started running and the bear chased her and that's when she ran over the cliff and fell to the outcropping. I think she died very soon after. There was internal damage and loss of blood. I know these are hard details for you to hear, Laura. I can only say I don't think she lived very long after the fall off the cliff."

Everyone was silent, waiting for Laura to take in all that Carl was telling her.

"But the other K9 teams said there was no blood at the point where they found the backpack. How could all of this have happened and there have been no blood?"

"I think everything happened after the bear dropped the backpack and started chasing the dog. It must have happened close to where Jo-Jo fell off the cliff. The dogs found a trail of blood from the point where Jo-Jo fell, going back a few yards and since I wasn't there I'm not sure if it was the dog's blood or the bear's. Most likely it was the dog's. A bear's fur is very dense and it would have taken a pretty deep bite to make it through the thick fur and drip onto the ground."

"What about James? Did you find any evidence from him?" She couldn't bear to say the word "blood".

Carl continued, "No, they said they looked around and found nothing. You have to remember it's rained since this happened and that has corrupted the scene. In my opinion, I think James started running because the confrontation between the bear and Jo-Jo gave him the chance to get away. After the rain, the trailing dogs tried to rediscover James' scent and they couldn't. So all I can say is that I think James was able to escape during the confrontation between the dog and the bear." Carl stopped and waited for Laura to respond.

Her voice was steady when she said, "Then, I think he's still out there. You say you found no evidence that the bear got him. I think he ran and after the confrontation with the dog I think the bear chased after him. Eventually, I think either the bear got him or he fell into someplace deep." She took a deep breath.

"I'd like you to bring Jo-Jo here if you can. I think James would like her buried out next to the trail" She stopped and looked at Frank. "Frank, I don't have a good feeling about this."

Frank took over the conversation again. "Laura, all this information indicates James may not be alive. They're not going to stop searching for him, but we want you to be prepared that the chances of him being alive are slim."

"We're starting again, first thing in the morning," Aaron said. "However, this time we're driving on through Aspen Falls and starting our search further north. There's no use starting from here. That's wasting time getting to new search areas starting from areas we've already gone over."

Laura was unable to say anything. Pete walked toward the middle of the room and said, "Thank you for not giving up. Thank you for everything you're doing. Please, please . . . whatever we can do, don't hesitate to ask. We will be right here.

There was nothing more to say. Laura sat down and Pete escorted everyone outside.

"I'm going to bed. I'm exhausted. I'm so glad you and Pete are here, Caroline. Y'all just make yourselves at home. I know it's early but I don't have an ounce of energy left and I need to call my sister."

"Are you hungry? Do you want me to fix you anything before you go to bed?"

"No, I'm really not. If I wake up hungry there is so much in the kitchen, I'm sure I can find something to munch on. I'm okay. I just need to get some sleep."

"Uh, Susan said you were on some anxiety meds that you have to take on a schedule. I don't want to be pushy or invade your privacy but have you taken your meds yet?"

Laura sniffed a muffled laugh. "I have no more privacy. Everyone knows everything about me now. It's okay. I don't mind if you know. The stuff does help me relax so I'm going to take a hot shower and one of my "chill pills" and go to bed. Too bad I can't have a glass of wine. That always helped me to relax but Joel said that was a 'No-no' as long as I am taking this stuff. So . . . . I'm alright, I'm going to bed. You and Pete need to get something to eat. 'Mi casa es su casa, okay?"

CHAPTER SIXTEEN

Monday

The "chill pill" did the trick. Laura woke up the next morning a few minutes before 8:00 and emerged from her bedroom, following the smell of coffee. Caroline was sitting at the kitchen table; sipping from a steaming mug, reading her Kindle. She looked up as Laura walked in.

"Hey you! How did you sleep?"

"Nicely, thank you! I actually slept all night long. I haven't slept this late in a long time. So, what have I missed?"

"Pete's out on the trail. Frank called and said the K9 teams stopped by his office this morning; they're driving on up 287 to start searching farther north and I heard the helicopter a few minutes ago so I guess they are back on the job again, too! Have a seat, let me get you some coffee."

"No, no. Stay where you are. Thanks for the offer but I need to start doing for myself again. The coffee smells good. I think I'll start with a cup and get something to eat later."

She and Caroline sat at the table, talking and drinking coffee. Laura thought. *This is almost like normal! Will I ever have normal again?*

One of the Knit Group members called to ask if they would join the Monday meeting but Laura told her she wanted to stick around the house in case she was needed. She prayed she would be needed, needed at home when someone burst through the back door saying 'Laura, we found him, he's on his way to the hospital right now! He'll be okay!'"

This was her favorite scenario, the one she played out most often. Sometimes unwelcome conclusions intruded into her thoughts; playing themselves out despite her resistance. Those were the ones which made her think she could never bear the sadness. How could anyone endure this overwhelming sadness?

Pete came back an hour and a half later; quiet at first, standing out on the deck, looking north and finally returning to the kitchen.

"Why can't they find him? The K9 teams told me they're not always successful in their searches but it doesn't look like this should be such a difficult situation. Maybe it's because I'm a layperson and don't really know a lot about search and rescue but I just hiked the whole trail. Of course there were lots of people out there doing the same thing I was doing, plus it rained, but I'm really surprised they can't find him or at least some evidence of him, especially with the "new" teams." He didn't want to say "cadaver" in front of Laura because it sounded so discouraging, though he understood how everyone else felt about James. He didn't want to say it for another reason. Pete refused to give up his own tiny glimmer of hope that James was alive.

Sometimes Laura appeared to be doing well; other times her grip on reality was so tenuous it worried him. What would she do if, or when, the search was finally suspended? It couldn't go on much longer without finding any new evidence. These specialists were in high demand and, no matter the season, there was usually an active search in progress somewhere in Wyoming, especially in the national parks.

To Laura, the day seemed to drag. The previous days were so full of commotion. Now there wasn't as much activity and it was, in reality, more stressful. There was nothing to prevent her focusing on what she knew was the inevitable; James would not be found; James was dead.

She and Caroline took walks, leaving Pete to stay at the house in case someone came by. They kept their cell phones turned on and slowly walked a few miles roundtrip before returning. For the first time in days she began to review the many emails she'd received. A few of them she read. To most of them she responded without even reading: "Thanks so much for your concern. Keep James in your prayers. I'll update you later when I know more. Love, Laura." Her first real email was a long, detailed message to her friend Kaurie Hidalgo. All along, she had been checking her inbox several times a day hoping somehow James had tried to contact her. She knew it was stupid, unrealistic; just like the numerous times she called his cell phone until they found his backpack. She wondered how much longer she would be making improbable, unrealistic decisions.

Once she started reviewing the emails she realized she had received nothing from "Bert and Ernie", which at first she thought was rather odd. Bert would have at least followed up with a condolence message; if not a card or a letter or a phone call. Then she remembered talking with Susan; they were probably waiting for her to contact them!

She encouraged Pete and Caroline to get out; being cooped up in the house with her all the time had to be depressing. Pete hiked and used a lot of the time to work on his sermon for the coming Sunday. She talked to Erin everyday and everyday she told her daughter the same thing. "I'm fine. You don't need to miss anymore school. Yes, there's someone here with me. I love you, too. Of, course I'll call you as soon as I learn anything new. I'll talk to you tomorrow."

Food from the knit group arrived mid-day courtesy of Ivy Bell and Molly Martinez and they told her the next delivery would be in two days. That's when Laura suffered a life-size reality bite. This couldn't go on forever and no telling how long it would take to find James. She was so grateful for everyone's efforts and concern but she knew it shouldn't last much longer. She needed to restart her old routines; actually she needed to start new ones. Her old routines included her husband and try as she might to deny it; she knew deep down he wasn't coming back. James was lying dead somewhere in the mountains. Her prayers focused on God watching over him, sheltering his body in some deep protected space. Her nightmares focused on animals feeding on his remains.

She couldn't stay still for very long. She was either in the bedroom rearranging the closets, or washing clothes or munching on whatever was on the kitchen counter. She still used the computer, looking up websites on search and rescue dogs, and helicopters and survival techniques in the wilderness. She couldn't concentrate on reading books or magazines or watching television. The news shows she used to keep on non-stop were now just an irritant. No one's troubles could be half as bad as hers! It was a dumb, stupid, selfish opinion, but so what? Politics or the economy no longer mattered. The gossip journalists all sounded petty and not even world peace mattered. Nothing really mattered anymore! Caroline and Pete were kind and supportive. They made no demands. If she wanted to talk they were there for her, but if she needed quiet they didn't try to engage her. She appreciated their presence. They prayed together at the prayer table. She knew loneliness was coming but she wasn't ready for it yet. James had been missing seven days.

Susan called Monday night. Her client's case was settled out of court and she charmed Joe Blanchard's wife's attorney into waiting three more weeks. She had some things at the office needing her attention and she was flying back to Rock Springs on Wednesday morning. She should be in Aspen Falls by mid-day. *Thank you, God. Thank you for my sister Susan.*

She knew when Susan returned they would have to face Daddy's secrets. Laura did not open a file or an envelope. She could only concentrate on one thing at a time. Soon it would be time to concentrate on Daddy and their mother.

Wednesday

The days from Monday to Wednesday passed; one into the next. Time was no longer marked by hours and minutes but by phone calls and progress reports. Frank called everyday. The K9 teams and Lloyd Great Bear were reporting to him. By Wednesday, James had been missing nine days.

Two of the Knit Groupies, Opal and Rosie, brought ham and sweet potatoes and a peach cobbler. Caroline started putting everything away and Laura asked Opal and Rosie to come into the living room.

"I'll never be able to tell y'all how much you mean to me. It's more than the food, which by the way has added several pounds in all the wrong places!" She grinned and patted her hips. "Your friendship and your support are so precious to me and I don't know if I'll ever be able to thank you enough." She smiled, they smiled.

"It's time I started taking care of myself again. Those first days were hellacious and I don't know what I would've done without everyone. There were times when I would be standing in the middle of the room and someone would have to tell me what to do next. Things really aren't a lot easier now, but I am able to do more for myself. So, as much as I hate to give up on all the yummy things y'all have been bringing I think you need to concentrate on your own lives again. I pray nothing like this happens to anyone of you but I want you to know if ever you need me I'll be there." There was not a lot more to say, so Rosie and Opal walked back through the kitchen with Laura. They stopped and hugged Caroline and continued on out the back door to their car.

Susan called at 12:30. "I'm on my way. I just got my car so I should be there in two hours. Please tell Frank I'll be a good girl and drive the speed limit once I get into Aspen Falls. I don't want a big fat fine! How 'ya doin'?"

They talked for one or two minutes. Laura asked her to stop by a liquor store and pick up a few bottles of wine. When Susan protested Laura said, "I'm really not using the chill pills as often as I first did. I'll tell you about it when you get here. Drive careful. Love you." she started to hang up and then added, "and don't forget! Pinot Noir!"

As much as she appreciated Caroline and Pete staying with her, she missed her sister. When Susan got there they would move to the little cabin they stayed in when Pete was on his regular schedule. Laura was trying to get back into some kind of familiar routine but most of the time she found herself on the north deck, wrapped in an afghan, staring at the trail James took that day. She would start to make her bed and begin her usual morning routine but so far, she never finished. She always ended out on the deck. Caroline managed everything else, she cleaned, she arranged meals and everyday she and Pete and Laura held hands and prayed for James. The prayer table became a little shrine. Laura put another picture of James and Jo-Jo on the table with a few other little mementos and often during the day she found herself there, touching the pictures and wondering; *what will happen to me now, what will I do, how will I go on?*

The pills worked their magic but Laura found herself making up her own dosing schedule; one in the morning, one in the afternoon and then she toughed it out until sometime after dinner when she would have a glass of wine. She figured by then what ever was in her system was gone.

Soon, she heard the crunch of tires on the driveway and knew her sister was back. She got to the kitchen door as Susan was taking her luggage out of the trunk. She didn't wait for her to come onto the deck. She went out to the car and threw her arms around her and they held on to one another without saying a word.

"I'm so glad you're here," was all she could say. They gathered the luggage and walked into the house. Caroline was waiting in the kitchen and soon she and Pete and Laura were updating her on the latest reports.

Caroline and Pete knew Susan was coming and they packed their things in preparation to move over to the cabin. After Susan unpacked in the guest room they visited for a while and then Pete stood up.

"Okay, Susan, I'm turning her over to you. She's a handful but I bet you can do it!" He looked at Laura. "You know I'm kidding! It was an honor for us to be here with you. We're here for you whenever you need us! James and both of you are always in our prayers."

With that, they began loading up their car and in a very short time it was just Laura and Susan again. They sat out on the deck for a while until Laura said, "Uh, I didn't see the wine! You brought it, right?"

"Oh, yeah, I forgot, it's in the trunk." She walked out to the car, pointed the key remote at the trunk and popped the lid. She returned with a box containing four bottles. "This should last us for a while."

Laura looked at the box and said, "Well at least the next three or four nights!"

"Laura, look . . . ." Susan started and her sister interrupted her, "Susan, I know what you're fixin' to say. I'm okay. I know when to stop!" Her voice sounded a little edgy; a little shrill. "Look, babe, I know you're concerned about me. I'm concerned about me. I know I'm on these meds but I don't think I'm going to need them forever and I don't take near as many as prescribed." She realized how she was sounding and softened her tone.

"You're concerned about me; I would feel the same if our situations were switched. Just give me some credit, okay? I'm not overdoing the pills or the wine. I know more than three *or four* glasses a night is too much." She took her sister's hand. "I'm really okay, okay?"

Susan searched her sister's face. "Okay. But just know if I see anything I don't like I'm sure as hell telling you about it!"

"Well, then, you sure as hell should! Do you feel better now?" Laura grinned.

Susan didn't grin back. "I know this is a horrible time for you; really for both of us and I just don't want you getting into something you can't get out of."

"I understand. And I meant what I said. Say something if you're concerned! Now can we change the subject?"

"Okay, fine! I'm hungry! What did they bring today?"

Susan opened the refrigerator, investigating all the covered dishes. "This is it for the food service," Laura said. "I told them today everything has been great, we really appreciated not having to concentrate on meals, but it was time I started taking care of myself."

"Good for you! Wise decision; but I'm still hungry so let's set up some grub!" Susan grinned and patted her sister on the head and turned back to the refrigerator.

Nothing of any substance was discussed during the refrigerator raid and subsequent meal. They talked about silly stuff. Which dish was the best—peach cobbler. Which dish was not the best—beef stew, too many carrots, not enough celery. They talked about the dogs and the handlers and Father Pete and Caroline and the Davis sisters and anything else they could think of to keep their attention away from James and the search and Daddy.

They cleaned the kitchen together, just like when they were girls. They loaded the dishwasher, wiped down the table and the counters and took all the trash out to the bins James built onto the side of the workshop.

"I guess this is one of the things I'm going to have to start doing myself. He always took care of the trash on Tuesdays.

"The last time I was driving back from Kansas I called him from Fort Collins and he told me a bear got into his workshop where we keep the freezer and it broke down the door. The dog woke him up and he turned on the outside lights. He would have used the .38 if the bear had started toward the house. But he just blew the air horn and the noise was enough to make it go away."

"You never told me about that! Have you ever seen bears around the house before?" Susan sounded alarmed.

"This is bear country, babe! Everybody knows how to keep bears away from their houses. It's no big deal. They've raided trash cans and I've seen them on the side of the highway a couple of times but we've never had any real problems.

You just don't feed your pets outside and don't fill the birdfeeders during bear season. I've blown the air horn and it's pretty loud. I've never worried about it before . . . ." Laura paused. *Until now.* "C'mon, let's get back in. I'm ready for a glass of wine." Laura turned toward the house and Susan followed. She was ready to get back inside before it got dark.

They settled into recliners with glasses of wine and watched the light fade through the bay windows.

"Bert and Ernie are coming up Friday; they'll land in Rock Springs late on Thursday and drive up here Friday morning." Susan said quietly. Laura looked at her and Susan continued. "After I got back to Sinclair I called him. When he answered and I told him who I was he just took a deep breath and said 'I wondered when you were going to call me.' I told him about the picture and all the things we found in Daddy's files. He started to explain but I interrupted him and told him about James and that he and Father John needed to get their butts up here and explain it all to our faces. My tone of voice wasn't real nice and I guess he decided that was probably the best thing to do. He got off the phone and called back a few minutes later. Apparently he called Father John. I didn't give him a lot of wiggle room. I'd already made the plane reservations and arranged for the car. He might be an attorney and think he can talk me out of it, but I'm one too and I can argue better than he can. He did say they were willing to tell us everything."

Laura was quiet for a moment, and then she said "I guess we need to start calling him Father John instead of "Ernie".

"He should be glad we're calling him "Ernie" instead of "jackass"!"

CHAPTER SEVENTEEN

Thursday

Laura and Susan were drinking coffee as the sun rose. She didn't keep shades or curtains pulled in the front part of the house so the morning sun was bathing everything in a pink-orange glow. Both were silent as they poured their coffee and sat down at the table. The Aspen Falls Gazette was delivered to her post office box so there was no newspaper for distraction. The T.V. hadn't been turned on in days; there was nothing from the world outside to divert their attention from James and Daddy and the secrets.

Frank Bell sent Laura a text saying he'd be by later in the afternoon. "They're calling off the search," said Laura. "He didn't say it out loud but he's coming by this afternoon and I'll betcha a plug nickel that's what he's going to say." She put her head down across her folded arms. "I am just so tired. I want it to be over! Either find him dead or find him alive but dammit, FIND HIM ALREADY!"

Susan reached across the table and put her hand on her sister's head. "I know, I feel the same way, babe!" She knew the loneliness that was waiting for her sister. Laura was hurting and scared and she understood how she just wanted it to all be over with.

Laura sat up and rubbed her face and brushed her hair away from her eyes. "Should we go over Daddy's files again, should we get them arranged in some way? What should we do?"

"Right now? Nothing! I wrote down everything I could remember about those three days. You've got Daddy's bible and the files about Homestead and the two letters and the insurance policies and the paperwork on the trust. That's really all there is. We'll get it out tonight and have it ready for them when they get here in the morning. It's up to them to tell us what they know and from what Bert said, they're going to tell us everything."

"But how do we start, what do we say, this next question sounds totally stupid; but where do we sit? I'm at a complete loss as to how we start off this whole . . . what would you call it? Confession? Hell, I don't know!"

"You let me worry about the logistics. I've been in a courtroom enough times to know where you and I need to sit and where they need to sit and don't you worry about who is starting off this whole thing. I am! Those two are going to be the defendants and I'm the prosecutor. I don't want to get nasty but I'm not stopping until I get answers to every last question! We'll have coffee and something ready to eat in the kitchen when they get here, but I'm telling you now, Laura; I'm not wasting a whole lot of time with small talk and making nice. This crap has gone on long enough!"

"How did you get them to come up here on such short notice?"

"I'd like to say I was convincing and talked them into it but I don't think that's exactly it. I think they're just ready to come clean now that they know that we know part of the story. I told them about James and how you wouldn't leave here with everything going on. Plus, I offered to pay for the tickets."

Laura looked at her quizzically. "You what?"

"I can afford it! I did whatever it took to get them up here! They'll land in Rock Springs late this evening and drive up first thing in the morning and we'll ask questions and they'll answer them and then they can go back to Kerrville. Laura, I can't stand this much longer. I know how awful this whole thing is with James but I just can't wait anymore. I have to know!"

The rest of the day was spent killing time. They sat, they stood, they ate lunch, Laura tried to crochet, and Susan tried to watch T.V. No one activity lasted very long. Laura took one of her chill pills and it helped. She reminded herself that was the last one today. She planned on wine tonight.

They took a short walk and as they were returning they saw Frank Bell's cruiser, sitting in the driveway. He was talking on his phone and when they walked up he put the phone in his top pocket and got out of the car. Susan took her sister's hand.

"Hey Frank," Laura's voice was very quiet. "Have you been here long?

"No, I just drove up a few minutes ago." By this time they were on the deck, entering the house. Laura walked through the kitchen and sat down in the living room. She prepared herself for what he was going to say. Susan sat beside her and Frank walked to the windows and looked out for a moment, before returning to one of the recliners. He moved it so he could face them, sat down and leaned forward placing his forearms on his knees.

"Just say it, Frank!" Laura said, looking directly into his eyes. "We both know what you're going to say."

"Randy and Aaron came by the office a little while ago. We made a conference call to their office and to the sheriff's office in Jackson. Laura, everyone agrees it's time to call off the active search. James has been missing now for ten days. The last evidence found was the dog. Randy and Aaron drove up and down 287, stopping and walking a mile or so off-road, trying to get the dogs to pick up a scent. They had Baker with them and she couldn't pick up a scent either. I've called sheriff's departments and police departments in Lander, Riverton, and Fort Washakie; in all the places the kids posted the flyers. I even called the Salvation Army shelter in Rock Springs. There've been no responses. Lloyd Great Bear was in on this too, and he saw nothing from the air that looked suspicious."

"So, now what? What's going to happen now, Frank; this can't be it! This can't be the end!" Laura paused and breathed in slowly.

"We've all talked about this before and you were there when we first talked with Mandy. The active part of the search is over, but these K9 teams don't just give up. They'll come back whenever they have time and use the dogs to search some more. It's just that . . . . it's just that it's time to stop the way we're doing it now. You've said it before and I agree with you; he's out there somewhere. I don't think we'll never find him; I just know we can't find him right now. Everyone understands this is the most important thing in your life, but search and rescue resources are limited and they have given this their best effort. There are other searches needing their attention and those families need them now as much as you needed them when they first started working with you.

"Laura, never in my life have I had to do anything this hard. I sat in the car and rehearsed what I wanted to say to you. I wanted to make it as easy for you as possible but I couldn't come up with anything good enough! I couldn't find the right words to tell you all this. I'm so sorry Laura. I'm so sorry we couldn't find him."

By this time, Frank was bent forward; all you could see was the top of his head. When he faced her again Laura had never seen a man look so sad and defeated.

"We tried every thing and we couldn't find him!"

Laura reached across the coffee table and touched his hand and said, "I don't doubt for one second there was anything possible that wasn't tried, Frank. Sometimes it was overwhelming to see the effort y'all put into this. I had no idea it involved so much. You couldn't find him but it wasn't for lack of trying. You . . . . the teams; everybody did everything in their power to find him. I know it. I saw it everyday."

"I'm not really stopping, Laura. I haven't had a chance to talk to him yet but Rick Martinez said he was willing to ride his ATV all the way from here to Fort Washakie when he had the time. Maybe even take other trails when he finds them. I have a machine, too, and I'll do the same thing. The helo probably won't fly but I told you about the K9 teams."

Susan had not said a word during this whole exchange. As much as she thought she was prepared for the news; she really wasn't. Subconsciously, she thought they would find him. She couldn't say anything. Laura was the one who was being stronger and that was supposed to be her job. Here her sister was, stalwart and in control and she was just sitting like a bump on a log. She experienced the pain of losing her own husband all over again and the emotion was crushing.

"Frank, thank you. I appreciate you telling me. You're the one who started this whole thing off and I think it's only fitting you're here with me now to end it. Ten days! I can't get my head around that number. It seems like only this morning that he and the dog walked across the driveway and into the trees; and then it seems like forever ago that it happened." Laura wondered if she would ever get back to "the present". She knew not to think "normal". Her life would never be normal again.

Frank sat there; across from the two women. He didn't know what he should do next. They had been so busy the last ten days. There were always two or three things that needed his attention at the same time.

He'd been coordinating the search and working with Chief Daily to keep officers on schedule and taking care of the regular police business in Aspen Falls. All the mundane, ordinary things he did everyday had been disrupted and now it was time to set the schedule straight. It was hard to express how he felt. He didn't want to move; somehow standing up was putting a finality on everything that he wasn't ready to accept. He stood.

He and Laura and Susan walked back through the kitchen and mudroom and out onto the deck. No one said anything. Frank looked north and then turned and put his arm around her shoulder. "I need to go. I talked to Chief Daily and all the officers are going to pay more attention to your street. I know you have neighbors but the closest one is still yards away. You'll see us more often, okay?"

"Thanks, Frank. I appreciate it. I know everything has been disrupted because of this and it's time y'all got back to your regular schedules. Tell Ivy "thank you". I know this has been hard on her too."

There was nothing else to do but get into his cruiser and drive away. "Susan, you drive careful now, okay?" Susan smiled and waved. She had not spoken.

Laura turned and walked back into the house. "I can't stand to watch him drive away. Let's go inside." Susan followed, silently. Laura poured two glasses of wine and took them, along with a small tray of cheese and crackers, into the living room. She and Susan sat silently, eating and drinking and looking out the windows.

"I'm glad that part is finished and I guess Frank is too." Laura said finally. "Once I accepted the final outcome I just wanted it to be over." Susan said nothing, continuing to look out the windows.

"Occasionally, I get this niggling little thought that he's alive out there somewhere, but then reason takes over and I know it's not true. I know he's dead." She turned to look at her sister. Susan hadn't moved; was still staring out the window. Her eyes were brimming with tears.

"Laura, I . . . ." Susan swallowed hard, never taking her eyes off the windows. "I am so sorry it turned out this way. I really, really thought they would find him. With all the dogs and the helicopter and the missing posters; I kept thinking 'No way they're not going to find him. There's just no way'. I had it all played out in my head. They were going to find him, alive, while I was in Kansas and I was going to come back and everything was going to be joyous! I was going to stay with you while you cared for him; nursed him back to health; all that dramatic crap."

"You played out those little scenarios, too, huh? So did I. I thought someone would burst through the door saying they found him, he was okay, and on the way to the hospital and everything was going to be all right. Despite what I was saying out loud, I couldn't give up the tiny speck of hope deep inside me, somewhere beyond reason and logic. What do I do now? How do I just start over?"

"I don't think you "start over"; not just yet. You just "keep on keepin' on", doing the same things you were doing and the things he was doing too! Like hauling the trash and . . . . what else did he do?"

"He did a lot! He took care of all the upkeep on the house and his truck and my jeep. He repaired stuff. He built stuff. When I sit down and think about it; there's so much he did that I have no idea how to do!"

"Then you'll learn or you'll learn who to call. Didn't you tell me you used contractors to do some of the renovations on this house?"

"Yes. And we used Rick Martinez a lot, too. You remember him! He used his own ATV!"

"Okay, then. That's what you do! You go back to your Knit Group, you start subbing again at school, and you get back to your volunteer work at church. You find a reliable mechanic, in town if possible, and you take the jeep to him and have it checked over. Don't ignore any little red or yellow lights that appear on your gauges. Start up the truck once a week; drive it just enough to get the engine warm; taking the trash to the dump is a good reason. You figure out how to fix the little things and who to call to fix the big things. Make a list!"

Laura didn't say anything for a moment and then, "That's what you had to do, isn't it? That's what you had to do when Johnny . . . . died!

"Yeah, that's what I had to do. You can sit here and let everything crumble around you, but eventually you'll look around at the shambles and realize no one is coming along to do it for you; and then you'll have to do what I told you to do in the first place. I did the same damn thing! I sat there and melted into a big whining puddle. I didn't bathe, I didn't eat right; I didn't do anything! I threw myself one giant "pity party". And when it was over and I recognized I wasn't going to die from grief, I had to get off my ass and clean up and get back to doing what I should have been doing in the first place! Despite how you feel right now, you're not going to die from this Laura. It hurts like hell, but it won't kill you."

"Okay." Laura said quietly. "Before I start learning how to do things for myself can I finish my wine first?" The tiniest of smirks played at one side of her mouth.

"And that's another thing, you need to . . . ."

Then Laura smiled and arched her eyebrows. "Gotcha'!"

"Okay, fine. You just need to be careful!"

"Okay, fine! I'll just be careful, but give me a little time, okay?"

"I'm sorry, Laura. I know I sound like a bossy bitch, but I know what you'll be facing and I'm just trying to make it easier for you than it was for me."

"You're not being a bossy bitch! Bossy, maybe, but not a bitch!" Laura grinned. "Seriously, I heard everything you said and you're right. I did think that this was going to kill me. I couldn't see how anyone could possibly survive this awful feeling. Sometimes I don't know if there are even words to describe how dreadful I feel."

Susan got up and knelt in front of her sister. "You are going to get through this, Laura. The bad thing is that it isn't over. At least with Johnny there was finality to it. I don't know if this not knowing is good or bad, does it give you hope when you really shouldn't hope? I don't know. I just want you to know you don't have to go through this alone. I went through it alone and it was a stupid, selfish thing to do. I could have called Daddy; I could have called you! Instead I just let myself turn into a stinking mass of grief and it didn't have to happen that way.

"How long? How long did it take? Before you got yourself together again?"

"A few months, is all. You know me, I'm impatient with everything. Actually I saw myself in a mirror one afternoon and I looked like hammered shit. And then I looked around the house and it looked the same way. That's when I figured if I wasn't going to die then I needed to go about the business of living. I took a shower, went to a salon and had a massage, came home and cleaned up the disaster in the house. Johnny died in the car crash three days before I graduated. Daddy tried to get me to go back to Kerrville but I said no and I put myself through all that crap after he left. I got some settlement money from the little old lady that caused the crash and I kept going to school! And here I am and according to you; bossy but not a bitch!"

Chapter Eighteen

Thursday night and Friday

Thursday night they finished a bottle of wine and, to avoid a hissy fit from Susan, Laura ate a big dinner. They firmed up their strategy for Bert and Ernie and went to bed. Laura called her daughter and reported the news about James and the search. Laura assured her she was okay, Susan was there and the K9 teams would still return when they had time and the Aspen Falls people would keep an eye out for clues whenever they were hiking.

They were up at sunrise Friday morning. They ate breakfast and got coffee and banana bread ready to serve. She and Susan decided they would continue referring to them as "Bert and Ernie" in private discussion only; in their presence they would call them what they always called them: "Mr. Shaffer and Father John."

Susan arranged the living room to be somewhat uncomfortable for the "defendants". She pulled the recliners away from the sides of the sofa and arranged them facing it on the opposite side of the coffee table. There is where she and Susan would sit; their backs to the windows, the men facing the windows and the sunlight. It was almost as good as a harsh overhead light in an interrogation room. Almost; Susan didn't want to be too hard on them but at the same time she wasn't going to give them the luxury of being too comfortable either. She wanted answers and even though Bert said he was ready to tell them everything, she didn't trust him. He'd been keeping a secret for forty-six years. It's hard to go so long protecting a secret for your best friend and then suddenly tell all the details. Then, there was nothing left to do. They started the coffee and stood in the kitchen and stared at one another.

"Hurry the hell up. I can't stand this waiting." Laura said, looking out the window again. A car drove into the driveway just as she spoke. "They're here!"

"Lights, action, camera! We're ready. You answer the door, it's your house. I'll stay here." Susan stood with her hands on her hips, then crossed her arms in front of her chest, then shoved her hands into the pockets of her jeans. *They better hurry up and get in here or she'll be standing on her head* Laura thought. She didn't wait for them to knock. She went outside and met them as they walked onto the deck.

"Mr. Shaffer," she said, giving him an obligatory hug; *I should punch you in the nose, you old buzzard!* "Thanks for making the trip up here. Father John," another obligatory hug, "y'all come on in"

"Laura, we we're so sorry about James," said Father John. "Susan told us about everything. We're more than glad to come here." *He actually sounds sincere* she thought as she held the door open for them. By this time Susan was standing in the mudroom so there was another round of obligatory hugs and greetings. She escorted them through the kitchen and into the living room.

"Mr. Shaffer, why don't you sit here at this end and Father John, how about you sitting at the other end and you can use the side tables for your coffee? Are you ready for some?" Susan took one of the recliners and file folders were lying on the seat of the other one. They had no other seating choices so they sat where they were directed.

"Yes, thanks Laura I would. The coffee at the hotel this morning was little more than colored water. I'm ready for a strong cup. I take it black. How about you, John?"

"Yes, please! I'll have the same thing"

Laura returned to the kitchen, leaving her sister in the living room with "Bert and Ernie". Her hands were trembling as she poured the first mug but by the time she finished and the coffee and banana bread were arranged on a tray she was calmer. She was thankful she'd remembered to take a pill this morning. This was going to be stressful. She wanted answers as much as Susan. *Please God, stay with me, okay?*

As she walked into the living room Susan was "making nice" and talking about the view and their drive up from Rock Springs. She sat the tray on the coffee table and the next minute was taken up with everyone getting their coffee and settling in for what was anticipated to be an uncomfortable morning.

"Laura, John and I have been waiting for . . . ."

Laura interrupted, "Mr. Shaffer, we all know why we're here and again I do appreciate ya'll coming here instead of us going down to Kerrville but we have a lot of questions and we feel like both of you have the answers."

"Laura and Susan . . ." Father John started and this time Susan interrupted. "Gentlemen, why don't you let us start first? We'll tell you what we know and then we can all talk about it."

"Bert and Ernie" looked like two school boys sitting on the bench outside an office, awaiting the wrath of the principal.

Susan started, "Mr. Shaffer, you've been keeping a secret for the last 46 years and I don't know how long you've known Father John but you're in on it too!" Susan paused a moment but neither man said a word. She continued.

"We started cleaning out Daddy's office and the first thing we found was a framed photograph we'd never seen before." Bert and John looked at one another with genuine puzzlement.

"The picture was of a young woman and a little girl. The little girl was me and the young woman . . ." Susan took a slow deep breath and glanced at her sister, "was our mother! Without understanding why, I became instantly hysterical and I'm sure I scared the crap out of my sister when I walked to the middle of the room and went to pieces."

Father John and Bert were following directions. They sat quietly, listening.

Laura took over. "We instinctively knew who the woman was but it was Susan's reaction that was frightening." Laura saw Bert Shaffer sigh and look downward for a moment. "Mr. Shaffer, I have only faint memories of my mother and I can't tell you the last time I'd thought about her and I didn't know Susan had any memories of her at all."

Susan took over. "Visitors started coming and we were busy from then on. You came over that night with Daddy's will and that's when you first offered to go through his filing cabinet. I had no idea you knew anything! We thought it was something that only Daddy knew about."

"Thursday was Daddy's funeral." Laura began. "It was busy, all day long and frankly I didn't know if I could talk about it with my sister or not. I'd never seen her like that before and the hysteria frightened me. When y'all came over that night both of you asked to help clean out his files and his office and you, Father John, asked for his bible!" Laura's voice rose and got a little shaky.

"After we took Erin to the airport I stopped and bought shipping boxes. Susan had emptied the trashcan containing the picture. She was too unnerved to say anything other than she wasn't going back into Daddy's office and she never wanted to think about it again, so when we got back to the house I packed up all his files and had them shipped here. I found Daddy's bible and our mother's name was listed in the family section. Her death was noted, too. Forty-six years ago! I lied to you Father John. I told you I couldn't find it. I thought I was protecting a family secret and it turns out you two were the ones protecting the secret! A forty-six year old secret!

"On Sunday you took us to the airport, Mr. Shaffer. I guess both of you were real surprised when you finally got to go through Daddy's house, weren't you. The evidence you were trying to protect was gone!

It was Susan's turn again. They were tag-teaming "Bert and Ernie". "I flew home that day and went out on my dock to relax and that's when the memory came back!" She held a copy of her notes but once she started talking she didn't need them. The memory of those three days was as fresh as if they'd only happened yesterday. She told them every single detail. By this time both men were looking at the floor and Susan could tell they were crying. Bert looked up, took a handkerchief from his pocket, wiped his face, leaned back and rubbed his eyes. Father John took a tissue from a box on the coffee table and blew his nose.

"We're almost finished. Monday morning I got up and James and the dog went for the walk from which they never returned. The boxes were delivered and I found the final pieces of evidence to your cover-up. I found a letter from a photography studio in Junction, Texas. The envelope was postmarked six months ago. Daddy just received it." Laura paused and swallowed some cold coffee. "Another thing I found was a file containing a spreadsheet listing payments to a psychiatric hospital in Bristol, Texas, The Homestead. The payments lasted over a period of twenty years! The name "Bert" had been written in pencil in the margin and partially erased. The file also contained a condolence letter from the Medical Director and a copy of a death certificate. Apparently our mother lived there for twenty years and never spoke one word. Daddy's bible listed her death as forty-six years ago; the date on the picture of Susan and our mother was forty-six years ago! However, these records show she lived another twenty years at this hospital!"

"Twenty years, y'all!" Susan stood and interrupted loudly. "The woman who kept me locked in a closet for three days lived in a loony bin for twenty more years! And I never even knew about her? I don't remember one thing about her other than those three days!"

Laura stood and put her hands on her sister's shoulders and gently pushed her back into her seat. "Shhhh, it's almost over.

Still standing, she continued. "The last thing I found was a file containing documents. I didn't understand what one of the documents was but the amount $750,000 was printed plainly and listed the name Grace Everett Billings, our mother! I didn't even know her name until I read it in Daddy's bible! Susan said it was a trust for our mother from her parents. The other two were insurance policies and Susan and I are the beneficiaries.

"I didn't know the details about her memory and she didn't know about what I found in the files until she came up here to be with me because of James. I can't think of words descriptive enough to express how horrible we felt when we told each other what we discovered. I have only faint, fleeting memories of our mother and those memories only came back after we discovered all of this! I don't know when I last thought about her. WHY?" Laura stood, crying at the men. "What happened? Why don't we remember anything?"

It was as if Laura used her last ounce of strength! She sat down and leaned her head back and covered her face with her hands. The room was silent.

"Okay, that's it! That's what we know! Now it's your turn! Tell us why!"

"I . . . . will tell you everything you want to know, answer every question," Bert said softly, "but first, may I please have some more coffee and I need to use your bathroom."

"I'll get the coffee," Father John rose from his end of the sofa and walked toward the kitchen. Bert got up too, a little slower; he pushed on the arm of the sofa to get to a standing position and walked slowly in the direction of what he hoped was a bathroom.

Susan and Laura didn't move or speak. Susan reached out to her sister and Laura took her hand. Apparently an 81 year-old bladder takes some time to drain because they sat like that for several minutes. Father John returned from the kitchen with the coffee expecting Bert to be back on the sofa.

"I have so much I want to say to you, but I think Bert needs to go first," he said, "Is that okay?"

"Fine," Laura said, closing her eyes and breathing deeply.

Bert returned; a small wet spot on the front of his trousers. "Thanks, Laura. I have a lot to tell you and Susan and Father John has some things to say too. But, at my age, being close to a bathroom is high up on my list of priorities so I apologize for the interruption.

He sat down and stirred his coffee. It must have been to buy some time because Bert Shaffer drank his coffee black! There was nothing to stir!

"I want to start off by saying . . . . by saying that I loved your Daddy like a brother; even more than a brother. He was my best friend and I would do anything thing I could for him! And I did, even though I thought it was wrong!"

Laura and Susan said nothing.

"Andy met your mother his last semester of graduate school at A&M. He was crazy about her from the first day he met her and they were married within a year. The best way I can describe Grace is that she was fragile. Your daddy treated her like a china doll. He did everything for her. She was never sick, exactly. When they got married her father gave Andy the paperwork for the trust he set up for Grace as a wedding gift and I think he may have known more about her health than anyone else. Her parents died soon after the wedding but I can't remember the circumstances. For the reason I can only explain as pride, Andy wouldn't use the money. He had me set up a bank account and the monthly payments from the trust went into it.

"Grace got pregnant and had you, Laura, and she seemed to be doing okay. Andy still did everything for her. He hired a maid, he cooked when he got home from work; all the home duties were covered. All Grace needed to do was take care of you! All Grace did was carry you around and smile and dress you in one pretty little outfit after another. She was affectionate but she was never passionate about you. It was almost like you were a doll to her; something to play with and carry around and dress up. Andy was the one who took you to doctor's appointments and took care of your everyday needs. Grace made me uneasy but Andy was my best friend and he never voiced any concerns and the few times I said anything about it he acted like I was interfering in his private life, so I chose to overlook a lot of stuff that maybe I shouldn't have.

"Two years later you were born Susan and she was never . . . ."right" again. Now it's called post-partum depression and although it can be serious in some women, it's a recognized condition and very treatable. Back then, Andy didn't know what to do about it and for the first couple of years he took over everything. He worked full-time; still never touching her trust money. He took care of you girls, he took you to church; he was mother and father and husband and caregiver. I don't know why but he had it in his head that everything was his responsibility. He did whatever was necessary for you girls.

"Soon after you were born, Susan, he realized Grace couldn't take care of you. St. Al's had an elementary school program and one for infants and toddlers and Andy was already a member there so it was the prime opportunity for him. You and your sister were in full-time day-care by the time you were six months old.

"By this time Andy could no longer deny there was something wrong but he didn't know what it was. He talked to your family doctor, which was a big mistake; he should have talked to a specialist, but . . . . anyway, her doctor decided she was depressed and started her on medication." Laura winced at this declaration, thinking about her "chill pills". *Could this happen to me?*

"The medication may have helped a little bit. I'm not sure, really. Grace would get up in the morning and watch Andy get you ready for school but she would be back in bed before you even left the house. You stayed at school until he got off work and picked you up on his way home. He would take y'all on Sunday drives and she always went but she never said much, rarely interacted with anyone. She was real complacent, never belligerent and she spent a lot of the time in the bedroom. Sometimes she would come into the room where everyone else was but most of the time she isolated herself.

"Usually when he got home Grace would still be in bed, watching television. She was always so meek. I think she knew something was wrong but didn't know how to ask for help. A few months before . . . . before everything happened the doctor changed her meds and she started making some progress. She stayed out of bed longer and started doing a few things around the house. What she needed, we found out later, was intensive therapy and close scrutiny of her medication but nobody in Kerrville knew anything about it then."

Laura and Susan said nothing while Bert was talking. They were sitting in the recliners; Susan with her arms crossed over her stomach. Laura with her feet tucked under her, resting her head first on one hand and then the other. Their coffee was untouched and the bravado they exhibited at the beginning turned to something akin to fear.

"Grace really tried to get better and later when Andy and I talked about it, what we saw as progress was only a desperate act. She thought she knew what "normal" was supposed to look like. She smiled and tried to interact more with y'all. The last few days before everything happened were one long performance that convinced your dad that she was really better.

"That morning Andy was getting ready to take you to camp, Laura. He planned on everyone going with him but Grace talked him out of it and . . . ." Bert began to sob. "I never knew the truth about what your mother did to you until you told me, Susan. I'm so, so sorry and I'm sure Andy never knew."

Father John stood up but Bert motioned him to sit back down. "I have to finish this, John. I've carried this burden for too many years and I can't carry it one more minute."

John sat back down and waited for Bert to begin again.

"Your dad wasn't gone two hours! He drove to camp and unloaded all the camping supplies and drove straight back. He had no idea Grace even knew where the keys to the car were, much less that she would take you and drive away. When he discovered you were gone he called me and we drove all over Kerrville. We looked everywhere and finally late in the afternoon he called the police.

"How did you find me?" Susan said. She was curled up in the recliner, unaware her position mimicked the way she'd sat in the closet those three days.

"Three days later the police department in Fort Stockton called. The motel clerk and his manager broke into the room because Grace didn't check out when she was supposed to. When they got the door open they found her sitting on the floor staring off into space. She'd pushed all the furniture up against the closet door. They called the police and an ambulance. The motel clerk had no idea a child was with her." Bert paused.

Susan was curled up even tighter and Laura moved to sit on the floor in front of her and leaned against her sister's knee

"Go on, Mr. Shaffer," she said. "Don't stop now!"

"The ambulance crew got Grace onto a gurney and one of them was curious as to why all the furniture was pushed up against the closet door, so she started moving it all back and when she opened the door . . ." Bert was crying and trying to talk at the same time. He kept wiping his face with his handkerchief.

"When she opened the door, there you were, curled up into a ball in the corner of the closet. When she first tried to get you out you . . . ."

"Enough!" Susan screamed, covering her ears with her hands. "I . . . I . . . ."

"Laura, please get your sister some water." Father John stood up and walked around the coffee table to Susan. He spoke quietly, firmly. "Susan, listen to me. I want you to ease up just a little. There's more to this but the worst is over."

Laura obediently went to the kitchen and returned with a glass of water and a damp tea towel. She gave her sister the water and then gave her the towel. Susan pressed the coolness against her face.

Bert was still sitting in his spot on the sofa, his head resting forward in his hands. When John was sure Susan would be able to continue listening he returned to the sofa and sat down. Susan patted her sister's hand and said, "I'm okay. Sit down. Let's finish this."

Laura sat down and all eyes were on Bert Shaffer.

"They found Grace's purse and got her name and address from her driver's license, called Andy and he called me. The ambulance took you and Grace to Odessa and we drove straight there. Do you remember any of this part, Susan?"

"No, nothing. My memory stopped when the woman opened the closet door. Keep talking" Susan answered flatly. She pulled the afghan from the back of the recliner and wrapped herself in it.

"When we got to the hospital Andy asked to see you but the doctor wanted us to see Grace first. She was catatonic. Andy spoke her name, put his hand on her shoulder, bent down and tried to make eye contact, but it was like she was in a trance. She focused on no one, on nothing. She didn't realize Andy or anyone else was even in the room. She was sitting in a chair with her hands in her lap, unaware of anything happening around her. The doctor told him she had been that way since she arrived at the hospital.

"Then we were taken to see you. You were in bed wearing a hospital gown and an IV was taped to your arm. When Andy walked into the room you started crying and said "Daddy, I called and called for you. Where were you? Why didn't you come get me?"

"This was more than he could take and he broke down right there. "I'm sorry Baby Girl! I looked everywhere for you! But I'm here now and you don't have to worry about anything anymore."

"You started to say something about Grace but all you had time to say was "Mama . . . ." Andy pulled you close into his arms and said, "Shhhh, everything's fine. I'm here and you're going to be alright."

"I think it was the last time the word "Mama" was ever spoken between the three of you. He lay on the hospital bed with you and held you until you went to sleep. I sat there and watched the misery he was going through and I could almost physically feel the emotional pain he was experiencing.

"Once he was sure you were asleep he got off the bed and went out into the hall. He never went further than where he could still see you. The doctors talked to him about their findings. You had been combative when they first found you in the closet but calmed down after a short time. He said you would probably be frightened and anxious for a while and you might need to see a psychiatrist if you continued to have problems.

"Then Andy had to make plans for Grace. A psychiatrist came and talked to us and recommended she be transferred to the psychiatric hospital in Bristol. Your dad and I made the arrangements. We spent the night in Odessa and I got a hotel room but Andy wouldn't leave your side. He slept in a chair next to you and I went out the next morning and got some clothes for you to wear home. He called the Salvation Army and donated the car and they came and picked it up. He never wanted you to see that green car again.

"When the hospital released you we drove back to Kerrville. Andy didn't go back to see Grace for a while. He knew she was forever changed and it hurt to see her that way but what hurt him more than anything else was that he trusted you with her. He never forgave himself for it."

"What happened after that?" Laura asked.

"You were at camp for two weeks. That's when Andy made the decision to keep everything from you. He was so devastated about Susan. He didn't want either of you to ever experience that kind of anguish again, so when you got back he told you that your mother loved you but she needed to go live somewhere else. Combined with Andy's efforts and your mother's poor interaction with you to begin with; it appeared you accepted that explanation. Your Aunt Geneva and Uncle Bill were sworn to secrecy and promised to never say a word.

"Within a short time it was like your family had always contained just the three of you. And he kept it that way. By the time you got back he had stripped the house of any reminder of her. He actually went through photo albums and destroyed every picture of her and rearranged them so there were no empty slots. He gave away all her clothes. He removed all evidence that she ever existed! He was always ready with the explanation about her needing to go live somewhere else and he may have used it a time or two but that was all.

"He asked me to handle her trust. I started paying the bills for Homestead out of the trust account and when Grace died there was less than a thousand dollars left. I have all that paperwork with me. I knew Andy was keeping a record of the payments but I never understood why. That's what I wanted to look for in his office. John and I had no idea about the photograph. He never said anything about it.

"Andy made me swear to God that I would never tell y'all about this. I didn't think it was right to keep it up once you both were grown but he was adamant about it. You were to never know anything. And Father John will tell you the same thing. Andy thought he was protecting you. After he died John and I were just trying to carry out his wishes. That's why we wanted to clean out his office. We wanted to make sure there was nothing there that would have led you to the truth.

"Over the years he tried visiting her. She never spoke again. She never recognized him.

"And Susan, this is very important. The doctors at Homestead had little to go on because of Grace's catatonic state; only her previous medical records and family information. When she took you, the trip may have started with a purpose but she lost the last bit of control to which she had been desperately clinging. She probably lost the ability to make rational decisions and she was just looking for somewhere to keep you safe. Susan, we don't feel she ever wanted to hurt you. Because she was not in her right mind, she saw the closet as a way to protect you. As for the death certificate, her official cause of death was listed as failure to thrive. There were no other contributing factors."

Susan didn't say a word. She pulled the afghan closer and nodded at Bert to continue.

"Andy called the police in Kerrville and told them that everything was okay. He'd found his daughter and his wife left him. That's how things were back then. The authorities never got that involved at the beginning of a disappearance. They figured it was a domestic squabble and his explanation was enough for them; they never asked him any more questions.

He told the same story at church. He said that Grace had decided she couldn't take care of you anymore and had gone to live with family somewhere out of state. He asked that Grace not be mentioned to you; that he was trying to give you a happy childhood and he did not want you to be upset by hearing her name.

"No one except for Andy and me, and later Father John, knew any of the details.

"Susan, for a while you were having nightmares. He bought twin beds for your bedroom and slept in there with you every night for nearly a year. He never took you to a child psychologist or anything like that. He made his own decisions about you.

"Your dad was amazing! He researched everything he could about raising daughters, he talked to women at church; he was intent on doing everything for you that a mother would do. He told you about your periods, he took you to J C Penny to buy your first bras. He never acted embarrassed about telling you about your bodies. He was determined to be both mother and father and I think he did an outstanding job because you two grew up to be as well-adjusted as anyone from a two-parent family.

"Oh, don't get me wrong, you had your moments! Neither of you were perfect, but he handled everything with love. He always loved you and supported you, even after you were grown women.

"I have all the paperwork here that will help explain what you found. I do want to say again that neither John nor I knew anything about a photograph. He never said a word to either of us." He looked at Laura. "I would've liked to have seen it too."

Susan was crying openly and looked upward, "Oh, poor Daddy! You carried this awful secret all these years!" She put her head into her hands and sobbed.

"Thank you, Mr. Shaffer." Laura said. "I appreciate now why you did what you did and I can see that it was a burden. This was a horrible shock to us and we were very angry with you, with both of you." She looked at Father John.

"I've got something to say too, Laura," Father John started. "I've only been at St. Al's for six years but your Dad and I struck up a friendship immediately. I enjoyed visiting with him and we had some great conversations at his house. He was deeply spiritual and loved to argue philosophy and traditions. He rarely missed services and he was an active volunteer. We'd been friends for a couple of years and one night he invited me over, saying he needed to tell me something in confidence.

"He told me everything. Bert was his best friend and of course he knew the whole thing; but I guess Andy wanted spiritual guidance, too. After listening to him I agreed with Bert. I felt it was time you knew the history concerning your mother, but he refused my guidance as well. He loved you both so much and he was afraid that the information would hurt you somehow and I was bound by my role as a priest when he confided in me. Before he started he made me swear I would not reveal this information to anyone. He, Bert and I were the only ones that knew. He always carried the memory of what you said to him about "why didn't you come get me." Like Bert said, he never really let go of the guilt.

"When your dad died Bert and I agreed to follow Andy's wishes. We would never tell you about your mother. We met at the house after he dropped you off at the airport and when we found Andy's file cabinets empty we were very upset! I searched for his bible but I never found it and I was prepared to conceal it to keep you from seeing any information. There was nothing for us to do but wait for you to call and the wait was the hardest thing I've ever done. We knew what was going to happen and when you called we were relieved because it was time you knew the truth and sad because we were unable to keep our word to our friend. There's an explanation for the discrepancy between the date of death written in his bible and her true date of death. To Andy, she died that day in Fort Stockton. Although he visited her at The Homestead, she was no longer anyone he knew or who knew him. She was no longer Grace Billings.

I don't think the intended on leaving everything where you could find it. I'm not sure why he kept it. Maybe he went back to it from time to time; envisioning what his life might have been like and I can only guess how he felt when he got the picture in the mail. He may have been doing the same thing; imagining what might have been.

"I believe the hand of God is in this. I believe God knew better than Andy Billings! I believe God decided it was time for you to know the truth!"

And that was it. There were no more secrets. Laura felt emotions she couldn't even name. She didn't feel just one thing. It was as if every emotion in the world had come crashing down upon her, all at one time, like a giant crushing avalanche.

Susan continued to sit, curled up in the recliner.

Bert opened his briefcase and began removing files. He had several large folders containing information from The Homestead. There were invoices and doctor's reports. A special account had been set up at the facility that was accessed whenever Grace needed clothing or personal items. He had 46 years worth of bank statements regarding the trust. He reviewed the insurance policies and he brought several copies of Andy's death certificate to attach when they were cashed in.

"Keep these in your lock box at the bank. You don't want death certificates floating around. That's how identity thieves are able to open bank accounts. The money left in the trust when your mother died collected interest. Now there is $4,610.27. I divided that in half and I have a check for each of you.

"Andy's house sold before I could even get a realtor and the buyer took most of the contents. He paid $210,000 and after probate fees and closing costs you and your sister are each getting a check for $101,500.

"With the money from the trust, the sale of the house and his bank accounts I have checks for each of you in the amount of $119,884 and change."

Laura and Susan just stared at one another. Considering the present situation, they had given no thought to an inheritance. Susan had been concerned about Laura's finances; this money came at just the right time.

Chapter Nineteen

Friday, Saturday and Sunday

While the documents were being signed Father John was in the kitchen making lunch. When everything was ready he walked into the living room. "How about taking a break and having something to eat?"

As Bert rose and walked toward the bathroom once again, Father John sat across from them and said, "I've prayed about this ever since Andy confided in me. I never felt it was the best thing to do, but I made a promise and I had no intentions of ever telling you anything. I don't know what you're feeling right now but when I think about all that has happened to the two of you in the last few weeks I wonder how you were able to handle it all without falling apart."

"We did," Susan said bluntly. "Several times!"

"I am asking for your forgiveness. I know what I did hurt both of you and I am truly sorry." He reached out and offered his hands to them. "Will you please forgive me?"

Susan was silent for a moment. "Yes, Father, we forgive you." Her voice was regaining some strength. "We understand more now. The memories of those three days creep around in the back of my mind and I've relived them more than once. I don't dwell on them purposely but they pop into my consciousness uninvited" She took his hands. "Your explanation lifted a heavy weight from us and it allowed the release of intense anger; anger at you and Mr. Shaffer and even Daddy. I wish now I could remember more about our mother and in time I may, but right now I can only remember those days. I want to forget them again."

"Will you forgive me, too?" Bert returned from the bathroom, this time with no wet spot on his trousers, and witnessed John's request. "I disagreed with his decisions but I promised your Daddy and I couldn't break my promise. Do you forgive me too?"

"Like Susan said, now we understand why and I think, in time, we'll be able to accept everything that happened as Daddy's attempt to protect us. Yes, sir, we forgive you."

"There's one more person I'd like you to consider forgiving," Father John paused and looked at the prayer table in the living room, "and that is your mother."

"Why does she need our forgiveness? She's dead!" Susan was clearly disturbed at the prospect of forgiving Grace.

"It's not for her. It's for you. Forgiveness means you've made peace with the grief and you are ready to let it go. Please think about it."

Without waiting for an answer, Father John took each woman's face in his hands and kissed their foreheads.

There were a few more documents requiring their signatures and then it was finished. Daddy's estate was settled, the secrets were unveiled, questions were answered and Laura and Susan felt they were able to breath in the fresh, clean mountain air for the first time in forever! "Forever" had actually been only twelve days! *How could so much have happened in such a short time?* Laura felt a momentary pang of guilt. For a few brief moments she felt relieved, free from worry. But then reality came crashing in again. James was still missing!

With lunch over, it was time for the next step. Bert had all the information on The Homestead divided into several different folders and those were on the table. There was nothing left to do and everyone was at that awkward stage that occurs just before someone leaves.

"Susan, God's blessings on you and Laura. I am forever grateful for the friendship I had with Andy and I'm finally at peace. I don't know if you will ever have a reason to come to Kerrville again but if you do please call me. I will always pray for your peace and happiness."

"And I thank you, too." Bert began. "I have a feeling I'll never see you again and I . . . . I want you to know how grateful I am I could help you understand why everything happened the way it did."

There was nothing more to say. They got in their car and drove away.

"He was right," Susan said, looking over her shoulder as they walked back into the house. "I don't think we will ever see them again and I don't think we need to."

Laura went to the cabinet and got out two glasses and the wine. "Can we go out on the deck and sit in the sun? I know there's more to do but I just want a few minutes of peace. And before you say anything, I had one pill at 5:00 this morning. Please Susan, just a few minutes, okay? Then I'll be ready to face whatever is next."

"Okay, there's more I want to talk about but yeah, we need some time to just sit." They walked out on the south deck and sat in deck chairs, side by side. Susan touched her glass to Laura's and said, "To us" and Laura toasted back "To finding James."

Forty-five minutes later they were facing the stacks in the living room. "What should we do with these files?"

"If it's okay with you I'd like to take them home with me. I don't want to know any more details now."

"It's more than okay because I would probably burn them. Take them, but if you can, put them somewhere out of the way; some place you don't ordinarily see everyday. I worry that you'll go over them too often, looking for answers you'll never find. We're at a good place right now and I don't want to screw it up. Father John brought up something I'd never considered. How do we forgive her?"

"I don't know; that's something we'll have to work on." Susan dismissed the topic and continued, "I understand what you're saying about the files. I just want to see for myself. And here's something else; I was always called Susan but occasionally someone at school would call me Suzy-Q and it always pissed me off. Now I know why. That's what she called me." She gathered the files and took them to the guest room and crammed them into her suitcase.

When she returned Laura was standing beside the table looking at the checks. "I think I need to go to the bank and deposit these and then, can we go for a drive? I need to get out!"

"Absolutely! That's a great idea. I'd like to make a suggestion about the money. Why don't you open a new account? That way you'll be able to keep up with how you're spending it. That's what I'm going to do."

"Sounds good to me, let's go to the bank! And by the way, what's your retainer's fee? I want to hire you as my attorney!"

Susan grinned. "Uh, honey, you can't afford me! I'll just have to represent you pro bono!"

"Pro bono? What's that? It sounds like something to do with "Sonny and Cher!"

"Pro bono means "for the public good" you doofus! It means I'll do it at no charge!"

"Okay, okay! Don't get huffy with me. I didn't want to come across all presumptuous; even though I knew you probably wouldn't charge me anything!

At the bank, Laura was greeted by everyone. It's both a blessing and a curse to live in a little town. You can't even sneeze without everyone knowing and at the same time there is a kind of comfort lost in bigger towns and cities. Everyone expressed their sympathy and concern and Laura was especially appreciative no one offered her false hope. They all knew the mountains. The mountains are a beautiful place to live but they can be cruel. They can take you when you least expect it and hide you where no one will ever look.

Aspen Falls Community Bank was a branch of a bigger banking system that served all of Wyoming. Sam Richmond was the site manager and, when needed, the teller, clerk and on occasion the custodian. When he saw Laura and Susan walk in he came around the counter to greet them.

"Laura, I was so sorry to hear about James. We've all been concerned about you. What can I do for you?"

"I need to open another account. I'm not sure if you knew that my father died down in Texas."

"Yeah, I heard about that, too. You've really had it hard haven't you?" He looked at Susan. "Hi, my name is Sam Richmond; you must be Laura's sister Susan."

"Oh, I'm sorry, yes Sam this is my sister Susan Bennett."

Susan shook his hand. *My, Oh My! I bet there are no financial secrets in this town. The only way to keep your finances private is to bury it all in a coffee can or keep it under your mattress!*

"Daddy's attorney in Kerrville took care of settling the estate for us. He and a family friend came up today to explain everything."

"Sure, thing. Let's go into my office and we'll take care of everything." *I wonder why their attorney came all the way from Texas to deliver the profits? That could have been taken care of over the phone.*

It only took a few minutes to open the account. Laura didn't realize until later she filled out the paperwork in her name only. Was it her first step toward living life without James?

They drove north on U S 287, then around to Riverton, where they stopped for coffee. Riverton was the only city in Wyoming to have casinos; all supported by two Native American tribes. The Knit Group sometimes took day trips there. Laura didn't talk a lot during the trip. As Susan drove she continually scanned the roadsides; maybe James got as far as a road somewhere.

Friday night; another casserole was pulled from the freezer. Laura saw that soon she would have to go grocery shopping. More and more she was realizing she was going to be alone, doing everything for herself. The idea was daunting.

After dinner Susan began asking questions about James' finances. "I know you told me he gets a pension. Is that his only source of income?"

"Yeah, he was bringing in a comfortable income from his early retirement package and his monthly pension. He wasn't getting social security yet. I have my teacher retirement plus I sub at the elementary school so we're doing okay."

"I need to get the information on his pension. They can be pretty nasty about sending pension payments to someone who's missing. Let me take it all back home and look it over. Don't be surprised if they stop it or reduce it because of everything that's happened."

Laura walked to the computer room to retrieve the pension files. She'd never considered that his disappearance would impact his income! The house was paid for; they'd used the proceeds from selling the house in Kerrville to restore the cabin and the title was free and clear. They didn't have car payments and they were living comfortably.

"When are you going back home?" Laura knew Susan would have to leave eventually, but she didn't want to think about it.

"Sunday morning, it's the only flight I could get out. I don't want to leave you so soon!"

"You have to. I need to start learning to do things for myself. I'm good; have faith in me, okay?"

"I do. I'm only as far away as your phone."

Sunday

Susan left at 6:00 Sunday morning to make the drive to Rock Springs in time to catch her flight. Laura was able to maintain while Susan was putting her luggage in the car. "I'll be fine. Call me when you get to Rock Springs, okay?"

The departure was especially difficult for Susan because she knew the heartbreaking sadness Laura would be facing.

Laura got back into the house and collapsed into her recliner, her body wracked with sobs she feared would never stop. She sat there, staring out the windows. It was Sunday; she wanted to go to service and that was her impetus to get up and get into the shower.

At 10:15 she drove down to St. Michael the Archangel Episcopal Church. James had never gone to church with her so going alone was not a new experience. When she walked into the sanctuary she was relieved to see no one sitting in "her pew". She genuflected, put down the kneeler and put her head on the back of the pew in front of her. She couldn't put a prayer into words so she asked God to look into her heart and figure it out for himself. A few of the parishioners came to her and welcomed her back but the church bells began ringing, signaling the time for quiet meditation, and everyone took their seats. The music started, the acolytes and Father Pete proceeded to the altar and the service began.

It was harder than Laura had expected and as soon as the Eucharist was over she slipped out the door. She still wasn't prepared for all the condolences. Caroline followed her out and touched her shoulder as she was going down the stairs to her car.

"It will get easier Laura. I'm glad you came. Stay as long as you can and leave when you need to. Pete and I are here for you, as well as everyone else at St. Michael's."

"Thanks, Caroline, I thought I could stay but this is as much as I can take right now. Susan left this morning."

"You do what you need to do. Would you like Pete and me to come by before we leave to go back to Cody?"

"No, thanks, I need to be by myself. I'll see y'all in two weeks, okay?"

Caroline hugged her and went back into the church. Laura drove home and sat in her jeep for several minutes before she finally got out and walked into the house. Was she going into the house as a . . . . what? Widow? No, James might still be alive! So she wasn't a widow. What was she? She was alone.

Susan called. She'd made it to Rock Springs and was getting ready to board her plane. Laura heard the boarding call and Susan had to hang up. She called and checked in with Erin. The rest of the day was spent in her recliner, staring out the windows. She started taking the anti-anxiety meds as written on the bottle. They did seem to make her less anxious but she felt as if she was swaddled in cotton. She didn't have a glass of wine that night.

Susan called when she got home to Sinclair. They spoke for a few minutes and then hung up. Laura was exhausted; she didn't want to talk. She didn't want to do anything.

Monday

She must have fallen asleep in the recliner because when she woke up the mountains were reflecting the sunrise. It was Monday morning. She made it through her first night alone. James had been missing since June 18th; 15 days.

The phone rang at 8:45. It was Adah Davis calling to ask if she was coming to Knit Group. "Even if you only come by for a few minutes, we would love to see you." Then Adah put on her bossy hat! "Getting out will be good for you so we'll see you at 10:30!" She hung up. There was no arguing with Adah Davis.

Laura needed to go to the grocery store so she decided a drop-in visit to the Knit Club would be okay. She got up intending on making coffee and toast. *How do you make coffee for one!* That task was too much to face. She ate toast and drank a glass of milk standing at the kitchen sink and got ready to face the first of many hurdles.

The visit to the Knit Club was brief. Hugs all around were about as much as she could take. Some of the summer people had returned and everyone offered help. She promised to ask when she needed anything. The next hurdle was the grocery store. She sat in the parking lot, realizing she had not made a list. *I'll just get whatever I need for the next couple of days.*

She shopped as quickly as she could, hoping she wouldn't meet anyone she knew. This was hard enough and she didn't want to melt into a sobbing mess in the middle of Walker Brothers! She picked up a few items, including a giant chocolate bar.

The cashier was new and only smiled and asked her if she found everything she needed. Laura nodded politely and was in and out of the store in 15 minutes. A quick stop at Lone Pine Wine and Spirits for Pinot Noir and she was back home. She sat in her jeep; her heart was pounding and she held the steering wheel in a death grip. When she noticed her knuckles turning white she eased off and took a few slow deep breaths. She made it! *I can do this! But this is enough for today!*

She was putting away the last of her purchases when her cell phone rang. It was Susan.

"Hey you, how are you?" Laura told her about her accomplishments for the day.

"I've done a lot of research on James' pension. There's quite a bit of paperwork you're going to have to do. I looked at my calendar and I can't come this Friday but I can come the following Friday, the 12th."

"Babe, thank you so much. I couldn't have made it this far if you hadn't been with me but you're doing a lot of flying and it's expensive. Can't we take care of this over the phone?"

Susan could have taken care of everything over the phone but she wanted to see for herself how Laura was doing and two weeks would be a good indicator as to her progress.

"Not really, there are several options we need to talk about, I really need a face-to-face to make sure we get everything right" *A big, fat lie.* "So, is it okay if I come in on the 12th?"

"Sure, I'd like that. I bet by then I'll have changed the sheets on the guest bed! I think one chore a day will be good for me and my chores for today are finished. I'm not starting anything else!"

"Sounds good, I'll see you then. I love you. Make it through today and worry about tomorrow in the morning!" Susan planned on calling every other day, in the evening. She didn't bring up the anti-anxiety meds and the wine but calling her in the evening might give her an idea of how her sister was coping.

Chapter Twenty

Tuesday

On Tuesday Laura called Kaurie. It was a marathon conversation; lots of tears in California and Wyoming.

"Laura, please come visit me! Whenever you're ready, please, please come. I'm not your doctor; I'm not your priest, but I am your friend and I think it would be a good thing. Think about it, okay? I've got a great deck overlooking the ocean and we could settle in with wine and chocolate and not move if it's what you want to do."

Laura promised she would think about it. After she ended the conversation she became conscious that she was delaying leaving the house for any significant amount of time. *What if James found his way home!* She wanted to be here. His truck was parked in the same place he left it. Her jeep was parked beside it. She wanted everything to remain the same. *What if he came back and things looked different? He might think I was no longer here!* No! She wasn't ready to go away anywhere.

She decided the call to Kaurie was her chore for the day. She did nothing else. The phone rang several times. Thank goodness for Caller ID. She only answered when Erin called. Everyone else left messages. She didn't bother to review them. They would call back; or, they wouldn't. Either way she didn't really care. Pills and wine took turns; one night one, the next night the other.

Friday

The days passed slowly, Tuesday through Friday. Laura's goal of one chore a day did not take place and by Friday morning dishes were piled in the sink, trash needed to be taken out and her perpetual adversary, dust, obviously prevailed. Her bed was made because she spent every night in the recliner. After 5 nights her back was telling her to *Get a grip! Go sleep in your own bed!*

She surveyed the mess and prioritized the tasks. What could she not stand one more minute and what could she put off one more day? The trash won out. A big black trash bag was soon deposited in the bin outside. One more bag and it would be time to put them in the back of James' truck and haul them to the dump. She wasn't ready for that, yet. She'd have to learn to create less garbage.

After taking care of the trash she thought she might as well tackle the kitchen. When she finished, there were stacks of bowls and platters and plastic containers on the kitchen table, labeled with the various names of those who'd brought food. All were from Knit Group and church. Returning everything could wait until tomorrow or Monday.

Sunday service was Morning Prayer. Laura came in late, and before taking her seat, put the containers from the church people in the kitchen. She slipped out early and was grateful for the consideration from her church family.

Sunday night she slept in her bed. That night she took two pills and made sure she was thoroughly exhausted before attempting to pull back the sheets and get into bed.

Everyday she paused for a few moments at the prayer table. Her prayer was always the same. *Please God, keep James safe. Watch over him. Please help him find his way back home.* She had a hard time giving up hope.

Before leaving on Monday she taped a note on the back door. "James, I had to run an errand, I'll be right back." She stopped by Knit Group with all the containers; she didn't stay and no one objected. It would happen soon enough.

She kept the note and the few times she left the house she taped it to the door. She ignored the futility of the action and didn't leave unless she absolutely had to.

Finally it was Friday and Susan returned. She brought groceries and snacks and spa footies. No wine and no mention of it or pills. Laura looked tired but it was to be expected. Susan was prepared to do whatever she could to make this time easier for her sister, but she knew there really wasn't much she could do; Laura would have to get through the days one at a time. No one could do it for her. She was still in the first stages of grief; Susan didn't say anything when she found the note to James on a shelf in the mudroom beside the back door.

Saturday

By this time Laura figured out how to make coffee for one, but she was glad to make a full pot. She and Susan savored their coffee until Susan suggested going out for breakfast.

"No, I don't think I want to do that, let's just stay here. I can make breakfast for us. I don't want to leave unless I have to. James might . . . Oh, I can't stand this!" Laura screamed, "I really can't!"

"Yes, you can." She said quietly. "You will get through this. Laura you have two choices! You can deny your feelings or you can face them head on. Denying them won't help. It only postpones them. You'll end up dealing with them anyway. You can drink and take pills to deaden the pain but when you are clear again the pain will still be there. You have to go through this, babe; you have to go through this to get to the other side!"

"The other side? The other side of what? I should have been awake that day. Maybe if I hadn't passed out I would have realized he was missing a lot sooner! Maybe we could have found him if I hadn't passed out. This is entirely my fault!"

"It's not your fault. Whether you were awake or asleep the outcome would still be the same! Something happened to James out there and you could not have prevented it, no matter where you were."

Susan did not say "I went through the same thing you are going through. I made it and you will too!" Laura didn't need to hear how someone else handled their pain right now. She needed to concentrate on her own.

"The other side of this agony is what I was talking about. You'll get through it. I know you don't believe me, but you will."

"I hear you but I don't see it. I don't see anything but loneliness. I don't want to feel all this shit! Why can't it just go away?"

"It'll go away, I promise! Now here's what we're going to do. I'm making breakfast, then we're going to talk about James' pension, then we're going to take a walk and you can put the note on the door if you want to." Laura winced. "Yeah, I saw it! Do it for a while if it makes you feel better. Then we're going to have lunch and make some more plans and then we are going OUT to dinner!"

"Good lord! You're as bossy as Adah Davis!"

"I knew there was something about that woman I liked!" Susan got up and took their cups into the kitchen. She poured her sister another cup and brought it back. "You stay here. I'm cooking and then we need to talk about this pension business."

"How about you cook and I sit there and talk to you? And then we eat and then you clean up the kitchen?"

Susan could tell Laura had made it over one more of the many hurdles she still had to clear. Laura talked, ate and watched her sister clean the kitchen. Then Susan spread several file folders on the kitchen table and they sat down.

"So, here's what I found. It looks like James took a lower payment than what he qualified for so you could continue to receive payments after his death; a very smart move on his part. Yes, I know what you're going to say but whatever else, this is what you're going to have to do. You need to call the company on Monday. I've highlighted the phone number. Tell them the facts. They will probably start the lower payments immediately. It looks like he received his payments on the first Monday of the month. He disappeared on the 17th of June. He was missing when they deposited his July check and now it's two weeks into July. Those guys aren't going to give you a penny more than what they think you deserve so I'm sure they are going to want some of their money back. I'm not sure how they will demand it.

"Now listen carefully and don't freak out on me. The law says you can't declare someone dead . . ."

Laura interrupted "I have no intention of declaring him dead, Susan!"

"Let me finish! The law says a person must be missing for seven years before he can be declared legally dead, unless he disappeared under dangerous circumstances. Like a tornado or a natural disaster; something like that. James didn't disappear under those circumstances, but if you wait that long to tell the pension people it could come back and bite you in the butt. You need to tell them now. Then if he shows up, you call them and they'll tell adjust the payments.

"He isn't receiving social security yet, so I don't think that's going to be a problem because the government doesn't take social security out of pensions. Just to be on the safe side though, you need to call them too. I've got the number for that highlighted for you, too."

"And . . . . have you been paying your bills?

"Oh! Uh, yeah! Oh, my gosh, I haven't even thought about them! Even when we went to the bank! I think I've lost my mind!"

"No, you haven't lost your mind, you've just been thinking about other things. Now focus! Have you paid your bills?"

"Yes! Everything is set up at the bank through electronic bill-pay. Every bill is covered. I use the debit card for anything else and I write a check to the church once a month.

"Oh, no! I haven't gone to the post office since . . . I don't know when my box was last checked! I think I remember someone bringing me mail but for the life of me I don't remember when! There's a pile of stuff in the living room and I haven't even paid attention to it!"

"Okay, good. Don't worry about the post office. Go there on Monday and check your box. We'll find the pile you talked about. Don't make any changes on your health insurance or your life insurance. Call those companies, tell them what happened and ask what you should be doing about the payments. God is watching over you, Laura! The money from Daddy came just in time!"

Laura crossed her arms. "You said we were going for a walk. Don't you think it's time? I'm on overload and I need a break."

As they walked out Laura taped the note to the back door. She didn't look at Susan and Susan said nothing. She started toward the hiking trail. Susan said, "Wait, let's go another direction. Let's go this way."

The rest of the day was spent taking care of business. Susan made several lists, different things Laura needed to do starting on Monday.

They went to Three Pines for dinner and Laura was able to enjoy her meal for nearly an hour before she said she needed to go home. One more step in the right direction.

No wine before bed and only one pill. Susan saw nothing alarming. She could see light at the end of the tunnel.

Susan left early Sunday morning. Laura went to church and she managed to stay through the recessional but walked out behind the last acolyte. She stayed longer this time. She was ready to face one more day.

Chapter Twenty-One

James has been missing 29 days. Susan left a list and Laura followed it without protest. Sure enough, she was right about James' pension. *We're so sorry for your loss,* we *will mail you the forms, you sign, we'll retrieve our money out of the next deposit, have a nice day.*

She called social security. *Thanks for calling, so sorry for your loss. Please call us when he is declared dead, have a nice day!* Laura bet no one could be less compassionate than the last witch she talked to on the phone. She got online and checked her bank account. Her bills were paid and everything was fine.

She stopped by the Community Center and ooo'd and ahhhhh'd over everyone's projects. All the summer women were back and Laura tolerated their expressions of sympathy. She was able to stay nearly 45 minutes this time; a little bit longer than previously.

She went by the post office. Her box had overflowed and everything was waiting for her in a white corrugated box.

She went by Walker Brothers and bought groceries and that was it. She had accomplished more this day than she had for the last twenty-nine! She drove home, parked the jeep in its usual place and brought in the groceries and the mail. She put the note back on the inside wall. Every time she posted it she was torn. She knew it was big-time denial and at the same time couldn't let it go

Susan called every other night. Most of the time Laura was sober; occasionally, she was drunk or dulled by the meds but those conditions seemed to occur less and less often. At least she was getting out once a week to run errands. On Sunday she went to church and slipped out early again. Her sorrow was still sharp.

The following Monday July 22nd

Missing—36 days. She took an old project, went to Knit Group, managed a little chatter and stayed a little longer. The note was on the door anytime she left the house. Frank Bell came by later in the week. Randy Avery and Banda had stopped by the station on their way up 287. He told Frank they would be searching whenever they had time. There had been three other missing person searches; all were successful and one was found alive. He was hesitant to tell her the news but he felt like she needed to know. She didn't say much but made sure the tape was fresh on the note she posted whenever she left the house.

The Next Monday July 29th

Missing—43 days. Most days Laura was able to get through the day without the chill pills. A glass or two of wine at night was the norm, so her visits to Lone Pine Wine were regular; a bottle usually lasted three days. Yesterday as she left for church she posted the note on the back door. When she returned, it had fallen from the door and blown to a corner of the deck. She sat in a deck chair, watching the note slowly drift back and forth; finally retrieving it and chunking it in the trash. One more step.

She put house in order, packed up a knit project and drove to the Community Center, determined to stay the entire three hours. The parking lot indicated most of the knitters were inside. Laura took a slow deep breath and walked in the door.

All the locals were there. Hannah Simmons was back from New Mexico. It was a comforting, familiar setting with everyone talking at the same time. She was the center of attention for a few minutes, but then the old familiar routine kicked in; several different topics were being tossed around from group to group; lots of laughter, new patterns and gossip. The main topic was a trip to the casinos in Riverton.

"Laura! Please come with us this Saturday! Everyone who usually goes is going," Rosie Esposito shouted across the room. Adah and Emma Davis never went; they said it was money wasted. "We can meet here and cram into Ivy's jeep and Molly's mini-van, leave by 8:00 in the morning and be back by 5:00!"

All eyes were on Laura. She was unprepared to take such a big step and began to respond, "Oh y'all I don't think . . . ." She hesitated, then continued, "It sounds fun; let me think about it, okay?"

Rosie winked. *She'll go! I know she will. She just needs a little time!* Rosie Esposito was the most flamboyant of the Knit Groupies. "Been there, done that" is her motto and she usually has. She is the owner/ stylist of the Mountain Magic Hair Salon and meets with the knit group because the salon is closed on Monday.

Laura sat at a table, pulled out her project; hats for the elementary school kids, and got busy. She was content, relaxed; and no one made any demands. Everyone gave her the space she needed and soon she was comfortable, letting the conversations swirl around her.

He's been missing 43 days. I thought I would be miserable forever. I'm not happy but I don't feel like I'm going to die anymore. Maybe, I should go. What would it hurt?

Needles clacked, jokes were told, gossip swapped and then it was time to go. "Okay, Laura," Rosie started, "time's up. You're going, right?"

Make a decision, Laura! Don't just sit there! "Okay, I'd like to go, but I don't think I want to stay all day. How about I meet y'all here Saturday morning and I go in my own car and then way I can leave whenever I'm ready."

"That works! I'm glad you're going."

"We all are," Opal said quietly, "and if it's okay, can I ride back with you? I'm usually out of money long before I'm out of time."

"That'd be great Opal. We can ride up together too, if you want."

Opal smiled and nodded. She loved the knit group, but sometimes they got a little too rowdy and loud.

The Knit Group's visits to Riverton were always fun. It was a chance to laugh and drink and draw straws for the designated driver. The summer women's income had been a topic for discussion. They never threw away large amounts of money but they never hesitated to play the $1 slot machines and some of the table games.

Adah and Emma's income was another topic for discussion. After their father died they took over his hunting guide business and actively worked until about three years ago. Adah's back began bothering her and the recovery from overnight trips on horseback finally became too difficult. No one knew what they did for income once the hunting trips were cancelled. Knowing Adah Davis, they probably saved every penny they ever made.

Laura usually took $100 and stuck to the nickel poker machines and the quarter slots. She'd watched Hannah play Three-Card Poker and would've loved to have tried her hand but Hannah usually went through three or four-hundred dollars sitting at a table and that was too rich for her blood.

When she went to the bank on Friday to get her gambling funds she checked her balances and withdrew $500. She had never taken so much in her life. In fact she considered withdrawing more but James' next pension payment was going to be half the usual amount and she needed to sit down and work on her budget.

Everyone met at the Community Center on Saturday morning and the 35-mile trip had everyone parked and in the first casino, ready to play by 9:00. Laura had already decided if anyone questioned her change in play she would make some reference to an inheritance from Andy.

The group usually stuck together as far as casino to casino. There were three casinos where they liked to play and they usually started at the Red Eagle, agreed on a place and time to meet to go on to the Fire Horse and then everyone went their own way. Sometimes they ended up on machines side by side but it wasn't a hard and fast rule. Soon Laura found herself at the nickel poker machines and the money was burning a hole in her pocket so she switched to the quarter machines and was impressed with her winnings. When she went to meet everyone she was $110 dollars ahead! She had $610 crammed in her fanny pack. She went to the bathroom, sat in a stall and divided her money into two groups; what she would use for play and what she would take home.

Shuttles were available from casino to casino so they left their cars and hopped the shuttle to the Fire Horse. When they got out Laura asked Hannah how her luck had been. "Oh, you know, you win some you lose some, but I'm doing okay. How about you?" Hannah usually arrives in

June from Santa Fe, New Mexico and leaves at the end of September. Once a month her husband flies up to the airport in Lander in his private plane and stays 4 or 5 days. Hannah is part of the "summer contingent" at St. Michael's.

"I'm $110 ahead! I'm doing pretty well. Have you played 3-card poker yet? I've watched you play and I thought I might just try it!"

"Hey, good for you! Yeah, let's go. I lost at the Red Eagle and I'm ready to make it up so let's find a table." The routine was to play for a while and then meet up at the buffet, then play a while longer and then catch the shuttle to the next casino. Laura and Hannah went to the poker tables and everyone else went their own way. They had an hour and a half before it was time to meet for lunch.

Hannah sat down at a table with two other players, handed the dealer a $100 and ordered a coke. The dealer exchanged it for chips. The game was easy and the dealer friendly and willing to teach so after three hands Laura decided it was "now or never". She sat down, handed the dealer a $100 dollar bill and tried to act nonchalant but on the inside she was a nervous wreck.

She watched Hannah handle her chips. She was casually picking them up and letting them fall into a stack but Laura knew she was counting them. She knew exactly how much money she had. Laura tried to do the same thing and ended up scattering her pile. *Shit!* The dealer just smiled and waited as Laura stacked them into piles of five.

Laura hit three sixes! The odds were great and the dealer paid her $300 plus cash from the side bets! She was stunned. The other players cheered and Hannah slapped her on the back.

"Uh oh, Laura. You're hooked! Trips on your third hand! You're lucky, girl!

Fortune smiled through the rest of the hands and when it was time to meet everyone Laura was several hundred dollars ahead! This was too much fun! Hannah cashed out, tipped the dealer and stood up so Laura did the same and they headed toward the buffet.

At the buffet Laura was the star! Some were ahead, some were behind but no one had done as well as her. It was exciting! When lunch was over the group talked about whether they should stay at the Fire Horse or go on to the Gray Wolf. Everyone was talking at the same time when Laura noticed Opal and she remembered telling her she could have a ride back if she left early. Opal was smiling and laughing but Laura could tell she had not been lucky. This had been a good day. She'd had fun, made some money and learned how to play a new game but it was time to go home.

"Why don't y'all go on? I've had fun and I'm ahead but I think I've had enough," *a Big Fat Lie, but whatever*! "I'm ready to go on home." She noticed Opal's eyes light up. "You want a ride, Opal, or do you want to stay and come home with everyone else?"

"Nah, I'm ready. I've got $15 left and I better save it for another day."

They caught the shuttle back to the Red Eagle, tipped the driver and found her jeep. Laura felt exhilarated! She hadn't felt this good since way before James disappeared. Then her exhilaration turned to guilt. Good God Almighty, how could she be out having fun when James was out there somewhere?

She unlocked the doors, got in and put her head on the steering wheel. Opal reached across the seat and patted her on the back. "I have an idea you're feeling guilty right now, huh?"

Laura looked at her and said "How did you know?"

"I didn't lose my husband they way you lost James; mine divorced me 12 years ago, but it still hurt. Sometimes I felt like a widow and for a long time I didn't feel like it was right to have fun or do anything except grieve. You can only grieve for so long Laura; and only you can decide how long it will be but eventually you will start living again. That's what you were doing today. You weren't being disloyal or anything and your grief isn't over, but you were able to have a good time. That's a good thing."

Laura straightened her arms out on the steering wheel and leaned her head back against the seat. "That's exactly it! I forgot about everything for a little bit. Then the guilt hit like a ton of bricks."

The trip back to Aspen Falls didn't take long and she and Opal had the chance to talk without being interrupted. She and Laura swapped stories about crappy husbands until they arrived at the Community Center.

"Thanks, Laura. I'm glad we had the time to talk. You've got a lot of friends here in Aspen Falls. There's no reason to be lonely." She smiled and shut the door.

Missing—50 days, 57 days. She was marked it off on a calendar. She kept busy, worked on projects for the Knit Group; the secretary at Sacajawea Elementary called and asked if she could volunteer the first few days of school, she washed and ironed linens for the Altar Guild at church. She talked to Susan and Erin and Kaurie on the phone. She kept her days full. The nights were long and lonely and sometimes it seemed as if dawn would never come. She drank or took the pills but never on the same day.

On Thursday Laura got ready to go to the grocery store and noticed her fanny pack hanging on a hook on the inside of her closet door. She had never put the money back in the bank. *I could take the original $500, leave the rest and try my hand at 3-card poker again. It's 35 miles to Riverton. I could be there in less than an hour!*

No choice there! Grocery shopping could wait.

Hot damn! I'm going to Riverton all by myself! I remember how to play!

She was pulling into the parking lot at the Fire Horse less than an hour later, fanny pack cinched tight at her hips, a little zing of excitement settling around her shoulders. She found the table where she'd won the money while playing with Hannah. A different dealer was there but the table was empty so Laura pulled out a hundred and acted like she'd been doing it forever.

Twenty minutes later the $100 was gone and Laura was disappointed! *I guess I had beginner's luck. Maybe I'm not so good at this after all.* She walked around listening to the catchy tunes and watching the glittering lights. Deuces Wild! Her favorite poker game! Why not! She still had $400 so she sat down at a $1 machine, put in her money and ordered a bottle of water. The deuces were wild and soon she made up the $100 she lost at the poker table.

Why not try it one more time, and then if I don't win I'll go home and still be ahead. So she found her way back to the table and this time the dealer who was working when she won with Hannah was back on the table. Three other players were already there and a game was in progress. She pulled out a hundred and waited until the dealer could give her the chips.

She was up and down and soon the hundred was gone. *One more hundred and I'm leaving for sure.* She pulled out another hundred.

When Laura sat down the progressive was up to $4459.62. This time the hundred lasted longer. Everyone was having a good time. A new dealer walked up, ready to give the current one her break. One more hand was dealt. Laura looked at her cards and she stopped breathing for a moment. Ace, King, Queen of Spades! The dealer qualified and then the dealer began turning over the player's cards. The table erupted in screams when the dealer turned over Laura's Ace, King Queen Spade flush. Suddenly a beverage server was at her elbow, wanting to know what she wanted to drink. Several of the pit bosses came to stand beside the dealer to monitor the pay-out, and all congratulated her. She won $4500!!

You don't get your money immediately. First of all the dealer has to explain everything to the pit boss, the pit boss has to verify the win and then the tax man wants his part. Someone came with a giant check for $4500 and wanted to take her picture but she said no. She signed two different documents, one verifying her win and the other, a W2-G agreeing to pay the government 12% right then. So she walked out with $3960 plus whatever was in her fanny pack.

It was time to go! On the way to the front entrance she heard, "Hey Laura! Did you get lucky?" Gary and Marla Jenkins were walking in as she was walking out. She knew them from school.

"Oh, hey! I did okay, can't buy a "benz" but I can buy groceries. What're y'all up to?"

"We come once a month and play. After school starts we don't come as much and we come on weekends. How about you, do you come often?"

"Nah, not really, I came with my knit group last week and we had a lot of fun. I had some time to spare so I just drove over by myself. I'm volunteering the first few days of school so I should see you soon, Marla." Laura was ready to get out of there. She really didn't want anyone one to see how much she gambled or how much she won. Everyone in town knew James' pension had been cut in half so seeing her gambling, especially alone, could raise some eyebrows.

"It was good seeing y'all! Good luck!" And Laura was out the front door. She was going to have to rethink this gambling stuff. It was entertaining and the winning was great but she didn't want to be the subject of gossip. She was just going to have to stick with going to Riverton with the Knit Group and explaining she was using some of Andy's inheritance.

CHAPTER TWENTY-TWO

Every Monday she put another X on the calendar. 64 days, 71 days, 78 days. Frank let her know whenever he heard from the K9 teams. School started and she volunteered in the office; the first few days were usually hectic and Karen Parker, the school secretary, welcomed whatever help she could get. There were always crying kindergarteners, crying parents and occasionally a crying teacher or two whose class list was too long or too full of too many boys or too many girls.

At 9:30, the second day of school, Laura was behind the counter when a young woman walked in; infant in a backpack, holding the hands of a toddler with a runny nose and a crying kindergartener.

"Hi, my name is Betsy Haven and this is Maggie," she held up the hand of the sobbing little girl. "We should have enrolled yesterday but I had car trouble. My car is still down and I didn't want her to miss anymore school so today we just walked. I'm so sorry she's late." Betsy wore the harried expression common to lots of young mothers and Laura was drawn to her immediately.

"Well, hey there Maggie! We've been waiting for you!" Laura checked the kindergarten rosters. "Your teacher is Mrs. Fleming and she has a spot just for you down in her classroom."

Betsy completed all the paperwork and Maggie was enrolled, not crying and in her classroom within a short time. She kept apologizing to Laura, promising to get Maggie to school on time. Laura had seen these mothers before and her heart broke for them. Life can be hard for a single mother, scratching an existence for herself and her children. Laura gave her as much information as possible about help with breakfast and lunch on school days, bus schedules, after school care and health care at the school-based clinic. It felt good to help someone else. It took her mind off her own problems.

78 days, 85 days, 92 days, 99 days, 106 days. September started and ended; it was still hard and lonely but Laura was finding more and more to do to keep herself busy.

The Knit Group went to Riverton again; Laura went along and stayed the whole day. 3-card poker proved to be her game. Laura honed her strategies on her home computer. The computer game was a little kinder. Hannah left at the end of September and Laura lost her gambling buddy. Neither one of them shared the news of their winnings with the other Knit Groupies.

October began and the aspens started their annual fall production. The aspens in the Rockies in the autumn were stunning. They appeared as volcanic eruptions of gold cascading down the mountainsides, contrasting with the deep green of the pine and spruce. The foliage tours started and more tourists came through Aspen Falls on their way to Jackson and the Tetons. There was never a word about James. James had died 107 days ago, somewhere in the mountains above Aspen Falls, only just about the time she acknowledged he was dead something nudged her hope and she changed her mind.

Tuesday morning; no substitute job, no Knit Group, no reason to leave the house. It was time to go through her closet, clean out everything she hadn't worn in three years and take it to the Goodwill down in Lander. She had been doing this for several years but never kept the receipts. Susan said it was a good idea to find as many deductions as possible; income tax this year might be complicated. Laura acknowledged she could use the break.

She started in on her closet. Sweaters bought at Goodwill had served their purpose. It was time to take them back and find something different. Trips to the Goodwill were topics of pride around Aspen Falls. No one worried about wearing their thrifty purchases. In fact, lots of her friends tried to outdo one another in snagging couture and high dollar finds on the racks for $3.99!

Sweaters, jeans, and long sleeved tee-shirts were piled on her bed. She opened the door to James' closet and shut it immediately. He would need his clothes when he came back! *Stupid!* But she wouldn't consider giving his things to Goodwill. Not yet anyhow!

The top shelf of her closet was stacked with purses and she took them down, one by one; deciding which ones would go onto the donation pile. She chose three and started going through them, finding pens and quarters and old receipts. The second purse was a slouchy shoulder bag she had never really liked; it never would stay put and she always had to hike it back up on her shoulder. More pens, a paper clip and a folded slip of paper were in a side pocket.

When Laura unfolded the slip she saw it was a lottery ticket and she remembered when she bought it; on her last trip home from Susan's when she spent the night in Fort Collins!

I wonder if I won anything. She went to her computer and typed in the web address for the Colorado Lottery and clicked on the game. The ticket was nearly four months old, so she scrolled to the Check My Numbers section, typed in her numbers, entered search for the last four months and clicked enter.

She stared at her computer screen, opening and closing her mouth like a guppy. She erased the numbers and retyped them, coming up with the same results.

It was either breathe or pass out so she took in a huge gulp of air and stared at the screen again. She hit the jackpot on the eighth drawing of a twelve-drawing ticket. She printed out the game details, erased and retyped the numbers for the third time; the results did not change.

She didn't know what to do with the ticket. She didn't want to lay it down; she didn't want to put it back in her purse. She wasn't sure what she should do with it. So she just sat there for a few minutes and then she made four copies of the front and back. She put one copy in her purse, one in her desk and had no idea where to put the other two; maybe her lockbox at the bank. The original ticket might as well have been a snake! She was afraid to touch it, afraid she would tear it or drop it or get it wet or get it dirty! She went to the kitchen and got a zip-close baggie, put the ticket inside and zipped it shut.

Where could she put it? Several ideas, once put into action, were ridiculous, including taping the baggie to her stomach. Finally, she just put it in her purse.

Now what? She found a lined, yellow legal pad and an unopened package of pens in her desk, took them into the living room and sat in her recliner. Three diet sodas and seven hours later she had a plan. *I need to call my sister.*

"Hey you! Are you still my attorney?"

"Hey yourself, of course I am! What's up? Are you okay? Did they find James?"

"No, everything is still the same with him. So, you're still my attorney, right? Will you be at your office for the next few days?"

"Laura! Yes! What the hell's going on?"

"I need to make an appointment with you. I'm going to make some reservations and I'll call you back."

"Wait, wait! Are you okay?"

"Yes, I'm fine. I'll call you right back." Laura hung up. It was unfair to be this enigmatic, but she wasn't about to say anything about winning over the phone. She'd already made some specific plans and privacy was paramount. Money was no longer an issue, so she made reservations getting her to Wichita as soon as possible, arranged for a rental car and called Susan again.

"Okay, I'll be there late tomorrow afternoon. I'm flying in to Wichita and driving up to Sinclair. I'll meet you at your house."

"Laura, dammit! What's going on? I don't like this!"

"I'm really, really okay. Everything is fine, I just need to talk to you and I need to do it in person. Please, I know this sounds mysterious and I don't mean to be so dramatic, but I'll explain everything when I get there, okay?"

"Well! Hell! Okay, I guess I don't have any other choice. I'll be in court in the morning and tomorrow afternoon I have three appointments with clients I can't change. I can't even leave the office until five!"

"That's not a problem! I'm really okay and I'll be at your house when you get home. Leave a key under the mat and I'll see you then."

"You're gonna owe me big time! You know this is going to drive me crazy until I see you."

"Hey wait! You're the Queen of Cool! You've always prided yourself on not worrying so . . . DON'T WORRY! Everything is okay. I love you and I'll see you tomorrow."

She was finally off the phone. She called one of the Knit Groupies and told them she was going to visit her sister and she called Karen Parker to say she wouldn't be available to sub for the same reason. The post office was already closed so she wrote a note and stuck it in her box asking them to put a hold on her mail.

She packed, taking warm weather clothes and clothes to layer if it got cool. If she forgot anything she could always pick it up in Kansas.

"You won six-hundred thirty million dollars? Six-hundred thirty fucking million dollars?" Susan was standing in the middle of her living room holding the ticket, her voice high and loud.

"Stop with the f-bomb! I'm trying to quit cussing and it's my target word right now. It really sounds awful." Laura said calmly.

"Wha . . . ? Oh, good grief! You won SIX-HUNDRED THIRTY MILLION DOLLARS!"

"Yes, I did. You may pace if you like, but give me the ticket. It drives me crazy if I'm not physically holding it!"

Pinot noir and chocolate were on the coffee table. Susan refilled her glass before continuing.

"OH. I . . . . I don't have the words! I don't know what to say"

Susan gave the ticket back to Laura and resumed her pacing. Laura pulled out her legal pad. "You keep pacing. I'll read you my ideas and then we can talk about them. I have a copy for you.

"Number one, and this is the most important, no one, absolutely no one will know about this except me and you, not even Erin. Number two; I want you to figure out how to keep my identity anonymous. You know about that kind of stuff so I have confidence you can come up with some ideas. Number three, you are my attorney. I intend to pay you a salary. I want you to advise me every step of the way. I can't do this by myself and I don't trust anyone else. Number four, I want to take the payments by the annuity option; twenty-six annual payments. I've researched this; I'll get more money this way. According to the information on the website I'll get $24,255,000 a year before taxes. After taking out taxes I should get $16,978,500 a year for the next twenty-six years. Number five, I want to give away most of the money. I have a list of causes that are important to me and then I have some more ideas for individuals. It's very important no recipient knows the source of their gift. I want to decide who gets what and when and I don't want phone calls and knocks at my door with sad stories. If anyone questions my spending I've concocted a story about finding another insurance policy from Daddy! Number six, I need a new will!"

Susan stopped her pacing momentarily, topped off her glass and broke off a large chunk of the chocolate. *Number seven, what about James? I'll deal with that when and if . . .*

"Impressive! You've been busy. Give me my copy." Laura handed it over and Susan continued to pace, read, drink wine and eat chocolate. "Okay, this a decent initial plan. It all looks good and yes I can figure out what you need as far as a trust. I don't want a salary. I . . ."

"You're getting a salary. That's not a point of negotiation!"

"Okay, fine. We'll talk about it later. Have you called the lottery people? Do know how long you can wait before you claim the prize?"

"You're the only one I've called and now I hope you understand why I wouldn't discuss this on the phone. The prize must be claimed within 180 days. The numbers were drawn on June 25th so I have until December 25th to claim it."

Susan scanned the list. "I don't have court tomorrow, I have one conference I can reschedule and Lana can take care of everything else. I'll be working from here.

"We've got to get some real food. Wine and chocolate is fine for now, but I need to concentrate. I need carbs and protein. I've got meat sauce in the freezer and pasta in the pantry. That should clear my head and I need sweet tea."

"That'll be my job then," Laura started toward the kitchen grabbing the wine bottle on the way. *No use wasting it, I'll pour it in the meat sauce.*

Susan got her laptop and some legal pads, propped her feet up on the coffee table and started tapping keys, occasionally looking at Laura's notes. Her small law library was down at her office so she couldn't get to her books but she paid a fee every month to a website which allowed her to do law research online.

When Laura returned to announce dinner was ready Susan was ensconced on the sofa, surrounded by wadded balls of yellow paper, sticky notes and pencils and print-outs on the coffee table.

"Can you stop and eat?"

"Yeah, I need to; I'm getting a little fuzzy. Yum, it smells good." While they ate, she took more notes.

After dinner she went back to her laptop. Laura answered questions when asked but never asked any of her own. Her sister was the only person in the entire world she completely trusted and she knew whatever

Susan suggested would be in her own best interest. She might butt heads with her over the salary, but that's one argument Laura had no intention on losing.

At 10:30 Susan was still tapping away and Laura was exhausted. "Go to bed. I'm fine and I've still got several more searches I have to finish. Be a sweetie and bring me more tea and go to bed. Don't wait up for me. I'll go to bed when I'm satisfied I've found everything I need and I'll put it all together tomorrow.

Laura fetched the soda and went to bed. She was asleep within seconds of her head hitting the pillow and she slept the entire night, without help of pills. The effects of the wine had worn off long before she went to bed and it was the first time since before Andy died she had such a restful night.

She slept until 7:00 the next morning and was actually stretching and moving slowly under the covers when she realized the reason she was visiting her sister. She padded into the living room to find Susan asleep on the sofa, curled up under a chenille throw.

She opened her eyes as Laura walked in. "Whoa, what time is it?"

"A little after seven. I take it you didn't go to bed."

"The last time I looked at the clock it was 4:30," she sat up and rubbed her eyes. "Crap, I'm too old to pull an "all-nighter!" I'm aching all over and I don't think sleeping on this sofa is something I want to do too often. BUT! I found everything I need. It's all organized and I just need to get your opinion on my suggestions.

"Well, then, how about I make some coffee and you get the kinks out and we'll meet back here."

"Done!"

With coffee and toast, Laura was ready to hear Susan's suggestions. "I've addressed everything on your list and I think I know exactly what you want. You kept saying your privacy was important; you don't want anyone knowing where their donations were coming from. And I can't remember if you said it or not but I think you also want to remain anonymous when the prize is claimed."

"Right!"

"Then here is what you want. You want what's called a Blind Trust. All trusts must have a purpose and yours is for the health, education and welfare of the 'grantor', that's you, plus charitable endeavors. This is how it works. Susan began a detailed legalese explanation.

"Wait, wait! I need to put what you said into terms I understand. If I want to remain anonymous I set up a blind trust. The trustee has complete control but has to carry out my wishes and I can revoke the relationship at anytime. Right?"

"Basically, yeah."

"Okay that's what I want. You're my attorney and I appoint you as trustee of this blind trust. You redeem the ticket. Your control of the money is based on what I want you to do! It sounds simple to me."

"Oh, sheesh Laura! This is a big decision for you to make. Don't you think . . ."

"I've already thought about it. This is exactly what I want. I told you you're the only one in the world I completely trust. Now why in the hell would I even consider getting anyone else to handle this? No, it's you. I want you! Will you do it?"

"Yes, I would love to do this for you."

"Then I guess it's time to get busy. I have a feeling this isn't going to be a fill in the blank form."

"You're right about that. Even though you live in Wyoming and I live in Kansas this ticket was purchased in Colorado so I have to do the paperwork according to Colorado law. In this case I think all these twists and turns are a good thing. You living in one state, me in another and the trust set up in the third is going to cause a huge headache for anyone even attempting to trace this back to you."

"But I thought you said I would remain completely anonymous? How could that happen?"

"Some states have open document laws where one can request the attorney to tell the name of the beneficiary in a blind trust, however if this should happen the state would only make me reveal your name if the requester has a legitimate reason for knowing the information and in that case the state lottery official may be the only ones to see your name. We will make sure no one will need to know your name. Every letter of the law is going to be followed. I have to get busy. And by the way, you are brilliant!"

"Okay, I'll bite. Why am I brilliant?"

"You didn't sign the back of the ticket. Since a blind trust is filing a claim for the prize a winner's claimant form is required. The trust is identified on that form! You don't want your name written anywhere on that ticket. You're brilliant!"

"Thanks for the compliment but I'm not brilliant. Thank goodness I didn't think about signing it or I would have. I wasn't brilliant, I was brain-dead! And before you start I have something to say to you. I love you with my whole heart. I have no reservations about this. And the next thing I'm going to say is not an issue for discussion. As my attorney I will be paying you a retainer fee of $250,000 per year plus expenses. I've researched this, I know about retainer fees. When you need more you can bill the trust."

"Laura that is way too mu . . . ."

"No discussion! You have to write up the retainer contract, too. It looks like you're going to be using your retainer right away because you've got a lot to do! I will be at the end of the dock, I brought a swim suit and you've got plenty of books. I'm here for the duration. Take as long as you need, I've got plenty of time."

CHAPTER TWENTY-THREE

Susan stayed home one more day and went back to her office on Friday, rearranged her schedule and concocted excuses to satisfy Lana and J.T. She worked on the paperwork several hours that night and all day the following Saturday and Sunday.

By the next Monday James had been missing 113 days. Susan went to the office and returned in the afternoon ready to discuss their plans.

"I get to pace, you get to sit and listen. Let me get all the way through this and then you can ask questions.

Laura sat.

"It's ready to go! It has to be notarized but that won't be a problem. This trust has nothing to do with you winning the prize. As your trustee I can only use the money the way you tell me too. When I invest any of it I have to do so as per your directions. I've got a print-out I want you to read which explains everything. Plus I have a copy of your will for you now. She'll notarize it when she notarizes everything else.

"Here's a small but important detail. You have to name it. Don't use any kind of name which can be associated with your name or where you live. Maybe something like "The XYZ Revocable Blind Trust but we can talk about that later.

"I'm not going to manage this as part of my present law firm. Lana and J.T. don't need to know anything. I could work from home but this is one more layer in protecting your identity. I've rented a small office in Manhattan, about 20 miles from Junction City. I drove over at lunch, signed the rental contract, and got a P.O. Box and ordered some business cards. I'll go there once a week and check the mail. I rented some office furniture and a copy/fax machine. I'll work from my laptop. It's only a forty-mile round trip; about the same as driving to Junction City from here. I bought a trac phone at Wal-Mart. It's already set up. All I do is go to Wal-Mart to load the minutes and I can pay for it in cash. That phone will only be used for Trust business.

"Now, we need to . . . . Oh, Laura! What's wrong? Babe, don't cry, it's all going to work out fine!"

Laura was sitting on the sofa, a tissue pressed to her mouth and tears flowing down her cheeks. She burst out laughing. She laughed so hard she lost her breath and had to go to the kitchen for water. "Wait, wait," she choked. "I'm sorry, I'll be right back."

Susan was left standing in the middle of the room, dumb-founded; and slightly pissed.

"I'm so sorry. I couldn't help it; it's just that this sounds like some kind of a spy game!" Laura started laughing again, trying hard not to snort water out of her nose.

"Well, you said you wanted to remain anonymous and this is the best way to do it," Susan retorted, arms crossed in front of her chest.

"I'm really, really sorry for laughing. Please ignore me, I'm a dumb ass. I don't know what got into me. I can't remember the last time I really laughed and it just busted out of me. Please go on. I promise I won't laugh anymore. This is serious," she said with a goofy grin on her face.

"I could just smack you! You acted like you had completely lost your mind! So are you ready to listen or do you need to laugh some more?"

"I'm ready to listen but hey, I just won a shit-load of money. Don't you think that's a reason to laugh it up?"

Susan smiled and shook her head. "Yeah, I guess it does sound like some kind of a spy game. But this is what I need to do in order to safeguard your interests! And you probably should add "shit" to your list, that doesn't sound very nice either!" she said.

"Uh, one word at a time, okay. Keep going!"

"Okay, then don't laugh until I finish. We have to go to Denver to claim the prize. Before I claim it I want to open the trust account there. You don't need your money in a little local bank where everyone knows your business. I want it to be at the biggest bank in Denver, that way no one will know me and they'll be accustomed to handling much larger accounts; they'll think I'm just a little country mouse and pay no attention to me. I'll open another, smaller account for you to use with a debit card. You can check the balance online, the statements will come to me at the Manhattan office and I'll forward them, unopened, to you. What you do with that money is none of my business.

"Then I'll go to the lottery office. I'll have to show my identification, but my name will be on the paperwork as trustee anyway. There's no way to keep me anonymous. Spending money! You'll have spending money! Oh, my God! You are rich, you are really, really rich!" Susan stopped and hugged Laura hard. "You are going to have so much fun!"

Deep breath. "But back to the serious stuff, I'm almost done. Since this is the only trust for which I'm a trustee I don't foresee many problems handling the taxes. I know sixteen-million dollars a year sounds like a lot of money but there are people who have accounts ten times as big as that. They're the ones that need a whole office full of tax accountants. You said you wanted to give away a lot of the money so I think I can handle this one by myself and if I can't I'll ask for help."

"What about Lana and what's-his-name, your runner? Aren't they going to be curious as to why you will be out of the office one day a week?"

"I'll figure something out and I'm not going to start for a few weeks anyhow. I'll go on Saturdays. I don't want them to associate the change with your visit. So now, the serious stuff is over. Oh, wait! The name! What do you want to name it?"

"What was your example? The XYZ something or other?"

"The XYZ Revocable Blind Trust."

"Well then, I think it should be the SLM Revocable Blind Trust. SLM for 'Shit Load of Money'."

Susan laughed. "Uh, yeah. I think that works!"

They flew to Denver on Wednesday morning and took a cab to the 16th Street Mall. The mall had a kiosk with lockers for rent and they stuffed their luggage in two of them. Susan had "lawyer clothes" and "dinner at nice restaurant clothes" and Laura had "Goodwill clothes" and "substitute teacher clothes". Susan took over and within three hours Laura had "hanging around nice hotel clothes", "dinner at nice restaurant clothes", pajamas, shoes, underwear, and a three-piece set of matching luggage. Susan knew how to shop! Laura wore one of her new outfits and put her old clothes in the store bags. They went back to the lockers, retrieved their luggage, she repacked everything in her new luggage and left her old luggage stacked against a trash container. They walked out the front of the mall, hailed a taxi and checked into the finest luxury hotel in Denver and as they walked into the lobby Laura was glad she wasn't wearing her "substitute teacher clothes".

Susan checked them in and a bell man loaded their luggage onto a cart and escorted them to the elevators and up to a huge two-bedroom suite with stunning vistas of the mountains.

"Knowing you, this is not the way you will probably live from now on but this is a celebration! We're pulling out all the stops!" Susan pointed to a large gift basket wrapped in cellophane and ribbon on the bar. An envelope marked with Laura's name was pinned to the front.

"To my sister, thank you for your faith in me, thank you for your love. The world is a better place because of you!"

The basket was packed with fruit and cheese and crackers and two bottles of Pinot Noir and two big bars of gourmet chocolate.

They walked out onto the balcony and looked at the view. "I can afford this! I still can't believe I can afford this!"

"Yes, you can afford this but you're not paying for it. I am. You'll have plenty of time to spend your own money later. This is my gift to you! I have a feeling you're going to do great things, Laura and I'm lucky you chose me to help you."

Room service and a nap, in that order, were next.

"Hey you! Do you want to get up or sleep until morning?"

It was 6:45 and the sun was close to setting over the Rockies in the west. The views from the floor to ceiling windows were worth the price of admission.

"Let's do room service again. I'm too comfortable. I want to get into my new jammies and eat dinner and drink wine! I can wear my "dinner at nice restaurant clothes" tomorrow night!

"Sounds good to me. I have a few last-minute things I have to do anyway. You order and I'll work. You know what I like so knock yourself out."

It was all perfect! If only James were here to see . . . .

"Okay, so here's the deal. I'm going to be gone most of the day tomorrow. I'm having a notary come up in the morning so you and I can sign everything. Then I have to go to the bank and open the accounts. I'll come back for lunch. The lottery commission knows I'm coming. I have an appointment at 1:30 and I have no idea how long it will take and then . . . . and then it will be finished!"

"And I can get started! I have so many plans, so many things I want to do! I need my legal pad. I've got lots of ideas!"

The next morning Susan greeted the notary, looking impressive in a gray suit, burgundy pumps, black briefcase containing the ticket, still in the baggie; very lawyerly! The documents were quickly processed and the notary left, unaware of the life-changing decisions about to take place. Laura looked at her sister; very professional and in-charge. What about herself? What did a woman making over sixteen million dollars a year look like? Green and wrinkled? Laura decided she didn't care and she didn't want to look like she made sixteen million dollars a year anyway. She wanted to look like she always did, with maybe a tummy tuck and a face lift!! *Laura you silly woman!*

Susan left and Laura noticed two envelopes on the bar, marked "Morning" and "Afternoon". "Morning" contained an appointment card for the spa sanctuary. A hot stone massage, followed by reflexology and a facial! *What the hell is reflexology?* "Afternoon" contained an appointment card for the salon. Hair, nails and eyebrow waxing! Tips were included. She was happy about the hair and nails but no way on God's green earth would she ever do eyebrow waxing again! She'd done it once and for two days she looked like she was wearing red rubber arches above her eyes. *Thanks, but no thanks!*

So she showered and put on her "hanging around nice hotel clothes" and took the elevator to the spa. She'd had massages before but never a hot stone massage! *Oh, I could get used to this.* Reflexology was unique; who knew applying pressure to different parts of her feet could improve her health? *I could get used to this too! Did anyone in Aspen Falls know about reflexology? Good grief, Laura! You need to get out more!*

When she looked in the mirror after her facial there was a whole new woman looking back at her. She hadn't realized what a toll the last four months had taken on her face.

Susan called; opening the accounts at the bank was taking longer than expected and she wouldn't have time to come back for lunch and still make the appointment with the lottery commission. She wouldn't be back at the hotel until mid-afternoon.

Laura had a spa-lunch out by the pool and then went to the salon for her afternoon appointments. She wore a spa smock so she wouldn't "muss" her clothes. When the cosmetologist approached with the little pot of hot wax Laura knew it was time to go! "Oh, no thank you. I like my eyebrows just the way they are!"

She was in the suite, taking notes on her legal pad when Susan came back wearing a huge grin! "It is done!" She threw her briefcase on the coffee table, kicked off her shoes and plopped down on the couch.

"The lottery commission was wetting their pants wanting to know your identity. They don't even know if SLM Revocable Trust is a he or a she or a "they"! I guess since we were busy with all the goings-on when the winning ticket was drawn, we didn't watch much TV. The speculation on your identity was rampant. They even played footage on the news in Colorado and Kansas from the place where you bought your ticket, hoping someone would identify you. They have the video and I watched it! You were wearing a KU ball cap and sun glasses and if I hadn't already known it was you I wouldn't have recognized you myself!

"I gave them the bank information and they took care of the deposit. They deposited ONE MILLION DOLLARS into the trust account! It's to show "good faith". They want you to know you really are getting the money. The remainder of your first year's annuity payment may take up to six weeks to get into the account. This is to give them time to gather the money from all the other states participating in the lottery. From now on your yearly annuity will be deposited on the 10th of October, that's today. I went back to the bank and it was already available! Anyway, I transferred $500,000 into your personal account. Here's your debit card. Don't forget to go online and set up your security questions." She handed Laura a plastic debit card in a white sleeve.

Laura looked at the card. The activation sticker was stuck across the front. "$500,000! It's what we would usually make in who knows how many years! And I have it all at one time! This little card holds a lot of power for me. There's so much I want to do."

"That card, that account, is strictly for you own personal needs. Be careful where you use it. Don't use it at any out of the way gas station or mom and pop convenience store. It's where most fraud occurs. There is a limit as to how much you can take out per day. If you need more all you have to do is call the bank and give them some security answers. Just use your good judgment about carrying cash. Anything charitable must come from the trust. You tell me who and where and I get it done. That's my job."

"Well, what if what I want to do only costs a few dollars? Like maybe I want to buy someone a coat or something?"

"Think about it like this: Would the value of your gift cause anyone to question where you were getting your money? You live in a little town; everyone knows everyone else's business. If you suddenly start spending more money than people expect you to have you are going to draw attention to yourself. If you can help someone without drawing attention then go for it. If you see someone with a need that may cost more than what you supposedly have, let me know about it. I can make it happen so the person gets what they need and you are not associated with it. You have three accounts now; your regular account, the account with the money from Daddy and this new account. Keep using your regular account as you always have; for paying bills; ordinary stuff. Use the inheritance account for bigger things; both of those accounts are in the Aspen Falls bank. Use this account away from prying eyes and nosy locals. And think about this; the lottery payments only last for twenty-six years. You have to save enough money to support yourself after those payments are finished. You'll only be in your seventies. I'll be advising you on that too!"

"Okay, I'm still working on my list. I've got twenty-six years to do the things I want to do. I'll be careful, not spend money which would draw attention to me. Remember what I said about using a newly found insurance policy as an excuse? What do you think about that? I want to do some things for Erin, finish paying for her tuition; do the same thing for David. He's staying in the Army until he can get four years of tuition. He could retire early. They want to start a family."

"The insurance policy is a good story. Just don't over use it and don't ever tell anyone the amount of the policy. And spend some money on yourself! You could use a new jeep!"

"No!" Laura said a little too loudly. "No, I don't want to change anything about the appearance of the house in case James . . . comes . . . back. Just about the time I'm ready to admit he's dead, I get this nagging feeling he isn't. You know; amnesia, or some other silly story. So just put up with me, okay?

"Okay, you take as long as you need." *Just don't take too much longer! This is getting tedious!*

"Are we done now? Yeah, yeah, I know we've just begun but is this initial stuff done? I'm ready to put one my "dinner at a nice restaurant clothes" and celebrate!

A renowned five-star restaurant was located at the top of the hotel. They were seated next to a window where they could watch the changing views as the sun set. Susan asked for the Maitre D' and let him know they were celebrating and wanted the best of the best. The Maitre D' summoned the Sommelier and with his help the most elegant meal Laura had ever experienced was created—The Chef's Tasting Menu with Sommelier Wine Selections chosen to complement each course: appetizer, salad, a seafood course, a beef course, vegetables, dessert and a cheese course.

They sat for two hours, laughing and talking and being treated like millionaires! *Oh, my gosh! I am a millionaire! Several times over!* Laura basked in the attention and service. She wanted to remember every single detail.

"I think this should be the first of a yearly tradition. I want to come back here every year on October 10th and celebrate just like this! Thank you Susan, thank you for everything!"

"And each year will be better than the last," Susan said, her eyes sparkling with tears. "I thank God every night you are my sister and I promise to do everything in my power to help you manage this blessing."

The sommelier brought a bottle of champagne and they toasted to their promise.

"Oh, crap! I can't tell you the last time I had a hang-over!" She and Susan emerged from their bedrooms at the same time, needing coffee and Alka-Seltzer.

"There's a coffee pot on the bar but I can't even move enough to make it. I'm calling room service. Do you want anything to eat?"

"Nothing big! Good, grief, I feel like a herd of long-horns stampeded through my mouth! Ick!" Susan walked to the windows to open the drapes.

"Wait! Not yet! Let's just keep it dark in here for a little bit. I think if I looked at the morning sun right now my eyeballs would pop."

Laura called room service and ordered two pots of coffee, dry sourdough toast, a fruit plate and a box of Alka-Seltzer. When they started on the second pot Susan opened the drapes but left the sheers closed. The sunlight had to be exposed a step at a time!

The food and Alka-Seltzer did the trick. They finally felt like they could face the rest of the day.

There was no reason to stay any longer. Susan needed to get back to the office and Laura wanted to get back to Aspen Falls. By noon they were at the airport having lunch and late Friday afternoon they were back at Susan's.

Saturday morning they were on the dock having coffee.

"This is where you were when you remembered about her?"

"Yeah; the most terrifying experience of my entire life. I actually felt like I was back there. I could smell the smells and feel the textures. It was all so real."

Susan's eyes got a faraway look; she was somewhere else.

"I've only had the memory for a short time. I hated her. I was glad she was dead. I had no sympathy for her at all. The talk with Bert and Ernie just left me bewildered.

"I didn't know how to feel; but I didn't hate her as much. Finally it was replaced with sadness and, like Father John suggested; forgiveness. She wasn't trying to hurt me; in her crazy, insane way she was trying to protect me. I'll never forget those three days but I don't want to concentrate on them either. Laura, Daddy raised you and me and, like Bert said; he did a damn good job. I admired him before we knew all this and after Bert told us what he did to make our lives happy and "normal" I admire him even more. I can't let those three days change my life. When the memory pops up, I just let it hang around for awhile and leave. Maybe one day I won't think about it as much and maybe after that I won't think about it at all.

"Have you noticed when we talk about her we refer to her as "our mother"? Never "mama" or "mom". It's like she was never a real person. And that's it. That's all there is. We were, and still are, a happy family. Not everyone can say that!" Susan stared across the water. "What about you?"

"I didn't have to contend with the memory like you did. Bert and Ernie answered all the questions, explained everything. I still don't remember her. Whether Daddy was right or wrong makes no difference to me. He did it because he loved us. I'm starting to remember tiny snippets regarding asking about her and he managed to change the subject without being obvious about it. Can you imagine how difficult it was to raise two daughters; to tell them everything a mother usually would? And he never acted embarrassed or uncomfortable. I'm like you. I admired him before and my admiration for him has increased ten-fold.

"I was worried about you."

"I'm good. I know we needed to talk about it. To Daddy!"

"Thank you Daddy."

They clinked their mugs.

CHAPTER TWENTY-FOUR

Missing—120 days. Laura returned to Wyoming on Sunday morning and experienced the familiar feeling that occurred whenever she first glimpsed the mountains after a trip to the flatlands. The Rockies were calling her home.

As she walked into the house she had an unsettling feeling. *I'm different! How do I live my life now, with all this . . . . money?* She looked around the room. Nothing there was different; only her!

She studied the print-out Susan gave her explaining the details of a blind trust and was able to understand it as much as any layperson. There was a packet of information about using lottery winnings wisely including several stories describing winners who regretted ever winning the money and a few stories of winners who were able to manage their fortunes and live normal happy lives. Those piqued her interest and she spent several hours at her computer researching the sad stories of lottery winners. *That's not happening to me! I'm not going to be one of those people!*

She took up her old routine. Knit Group, substitute teaching, church and once a month trips to Riverton. She used her trust debit card to withdraw money from the ATM at the drive-through at the bank and limited herself to $500 each time. Even though it was located at the bank, the bank didn't own the ATM and so no Aspen Falls Rosie Nosies had any inkling of how much she was withdrawing. She made trips to Lone Pine Wine but finally started buying the Pinot Noir by the case online and had it delivered to the house. She saved money and gave the clerks at Lone Pine one less customer to gossip about.

127 days, 134 days. There was a red X on every Monday of her calendar starting on June 24th. Frank would call whenever he heard anything from the K9 people. Her prayers for her husband continued.

The days were easier, the nights were still hard. She had the pills refilled once and then stopped taking them. She left the full bottle in her medicine cabinet, "in case of emergency".

Missing—141 days. The aspens produced their final glorious, golden extravaganza and became tall gray-brown sticks interspersed among the dark green firs on the mountainsides.

A significant snowfall came on the first Wednesday in November and Laura was facing her next dilemma—how to use the snow blower. It was a growling, beast of a thing even when James used it. She went to the workshop and realized she didn't even know how to start it.

Overwhelmed, she let loose a crying jag of epic proportions. She sat on the floor and for the first time she cursed her husband. "Damn you, James! How could you do this to me? Where the fuck are you?" She sat there, crying and cursing until she was so cold she couldn't curse without her teeth chattering. So she stood up and slogged back into the house.

I can do this! I'm not stupid and I'm not the only woman living alone up here. I've always looked at single women with pity. Now that I'm in their shoes and I see how they manage my perspective has changed. I don't pity them! It's just the opposite, I marvel at them! I bet Adah and Emma never sat on the floor and threw a bawling fit. If they can do it. I can do it, too!

She needed to call someone. She could shovel a path from the house to the workshop but the driveway would be brutal.

"Hey there, Molly! This is Laura!" She was trying to sound as cheery as possible.

"Laura! Good morning! I hope you're all snug and warm this snowy day. What's up?"

Laura told her sob story, trying to make it sound like it was no big deal. "I'm sure I can get it done but I need someone to show me how to use the machine."

"Rick's outside doing that exact job! How about when he's finished I send him over? He can do it for you!"

"No, no, I just need someone to show me. I'm sure I can do it myself once I know how to get it started." *Dammit James! Why didn't you ever show me how to do this? Why was I so ignorant about everything you did?*

She had a pot of coffee ready when Rick Martinez turned into the driveway and tramped up to the house. She hadn't seen him since the summer when he volunteered with the search teams. He was a wild land firefighter and spent most of the fire season in the western states fighting forest fires. *I guess he figured by now they would have found James!*

"Hey, Laura! Molly tells me you need snow blowing lessons!"

"Yes, I do! James always took care of it, but I'm sure I can do it once you show me." A Big Fat Lie! *I'm not sure about anything right now, except I want my husband back!*

She offered him coffee but he said, "Nah, thanks, I'm all coffeed up right now. Let's take a look at your blower." Laura put on her heavy jacket, hat and mittens and followed him out.

"Your path looks good. If you can keep up with it, it will be easier, rather than waiting until it's deep. The longer you wait the more snow you have to shovel and the harder it is. Don't wait too long to clear the decks either. The snow looks nice and fluffy but it can get heavy and you don't want to overload them. If I were you I would get one of those snow shovels you can push. We have one and it's a lot easier than your single-handled one"

She opened the double doors to the shed and Rick gave the blower a cursory inspection.

"Not bad! It's a lot like ours and Molly can use it so I think you'll be fine."

He showed Laura where to put the gas and oil and how to adjust the choke. It had an electric start and after a few adjustments it started with no problems. Rick pushed it out onto the driveway and started blowing snow.

"I want to watch you make one swipe and then I need to do it"

"No problem, just follow me."

Laura followed him to the end of the driveway and took over. Rick watched and waited for her to finish. "Now don't try to do this all at one time. It's tiring! Take a break or two."

Laura finished the driveway with instructions on blowing around the vehicles and put the blower away under Rick's supervision, He was right, it was tiring and she realized she would have to take breaks. She started it again, while he was watching, just to make sure she knew the steps. No problems

She called Susan, "One more step for me today! I learned to use the snow blower!" She proudly told her sister about her accomplishments.

"Great! I'm proud of you. There's also another step you get to take. The bank called me today! $15,978,500 was deposited into the SLM Revocable Blind Trust! It's official; you are one hell of a rich woman!"

No response from Wyoming.

"Laura, did you hear me."

"Yeah, I did," she spoke softly. "It's just hard for me to talk right now. I'd wondered how I would feel when it finally happened and now it's hard to describe. I thought it would be all joy and ecstasy; you know; like you see on TV when someone wins the Publisher's Clearinghouse, and make no mistake, I am truly happy. But it's also damn scary!"

"It shows you're ready to take this seriously and not be frivolous about it. Everything's going to be fine!"

"I've been putting some ideas down on paper and I need to look at everything again. Can I call you tomorrow night when you get home?"

"You bet! Take care and I'll talk to you then."

Laura sat down with a glass of wine and her yellow pad of notes. After several revisions and refills she was satisfied.

"Are you ready? I have my list!"

"I'm ready. Shoot!"

"I don't want to do it all at once. I want to take my time and keep my eyes and ears open for opportunities, so for right now I have two charities and one individual on my list. I want to give three-million each to the Wounded Warrior Project and St. Jude's Children's Hospital."

"Got it. That will be simple. Now, who's the individual?"

"Her name is Betsy Haven. She's a single mom here in Aspen Falls with three kids; the oldest one is only five. She drives a crappy car that's always breaking down. Her little girl has been late to school a bunch of times and it's always because of the car. When it happens she has to walk her to school, with the two little ones in tow. I think she's on government assistance and probably unemployed. There's a school program she qualifies for that allows her to bring the two younger ones for lunch so she brings them most days.

"I want to give her a new car, four-wheel drive, with a comprehensive warranty, bumper-to-bumper insurance with no deductible and a gas card. I think a small four-wheel drive of some kind, one with built-in child safety seats. Nothing fancy, just the basics. Susan, my heart just went out to her. She's the kind of person I want to help. She just needs a chance. Can you do this?"

"I can make it happen. It will take a couple of weeks at the most. I'll google dealerships in Rock Springs and cook something up. You have a good heart, Laura; Betsy Haven is a lucky young woman."

"And I have one more, no wait, two more things I want to do. Remember when we took Erin to the airport? She said she and David were planning on coming here for Thanksgiving. I want us; you, me, and the kids to have a big Thanksgiving! I miss James but I can't put my life on hold until they find him. So I want a fun, happy Thanksgiving and that's when I want to give her whatever she needs to finish school and I want to tell David I want to pay for his school too. Whatever it takes! Both of them are so responsible. Erin is nearly finished and I know she can get a good job when she graduates. I want David to be able to go full time. They want to start a family! I want to be a grandma!"

"And I want to be Auntie Susan! This is where we use the "newly found insurance policy from Daddy" justification! Oh, Laura. This is going to be so much fun!

"Wait, wait, I said there were two more things I want to do! Erin and David were the first one. There's one more!

"I want us to go on a cruise! A fancy-schmancy one! This coming summer! At least two weeks; more if you can get the time off! I don't know where yet! Alaska, the Med, South America, Hawaii! Somewhere fun, fun, fun! Okay?"

"Yeah! Let's think about it!"

"Think about it. Hell! We're doing it! You've got enough time between now and then to work on your schedule; I've got enough time between now and then to find something just right for us. We can talk about it later!"

CHAPTER TWENTY-FIVE

Missing—148 days. Laura's days were falling into a familiar routine. She, Clara, Opal and Rosie started a Wednesday night Supper Club and took turns hosting meals at their homes and occasionally having dinner at Three Pines Café.

Thanksgiving was in seventeen days. Laura called Erin to firm up their plans. "I want to pay for your plane tickets!"

"Mom! That's a lot of money! We've been budgeting for this ever since Grandpa's funeral. You're sweet; Mom, but we can afford it."

"No, it's okay! Susan and I made out like bandits when Daddy's house sold and I want to do this for you; you can consider it a Merry Christmas in November!"

"Oh, Mom. Thank you! You've been hit so hard with Grandpa and James, all at the same time!" *If she only knew the half of it!* Laura thought. "I wish I weren't so far away, I wish I could be there for you. Lately when we've talked I've heard a different tone to your voice. You sound stronger and I'm proud of you, Mom,"

She was sitting with a mug of hot chocolate and butterscotch schnapps, enjoying the sunset, when she got a new idea. She kept a yellow pad and pencils in a drawer in the side table. She grabbed them and started writing, then researching on her computer.

"I have another idea, are you ready?"

"Go for it."

"I want to send hats, gloves, and jackets to the kids on the rez in Riverton."

"The rez?" Susan laughed

"The reservation! In Riverton! The Shoshone and Arapahoe tribes share a reservation there. I want you to find out how many kids there are; school-age and under. Then I want you to estimate how many of each size will be needed. I want you to do the same thing for the reservations in Idaho, Washington, and Kansas. I found a website online; it's a national Indian child welfare group. I'm sending you the link. You should be able to get a lot of information from that one place."

"Whoa, that's a grand idea but there could be a problem. It sounds like you're talking about a boatload of kids. Let me call you back Sunday night, okay?"

"And nothing cheap! I want them to last more than one season. Quality stuff."

Susan disconnected the call. *We're going to have to have a "sit-down". She thinks all she has to do is give someone money and everything will be okay. Life can be ugly and money doesn't always solve the problem. This isn't going to be as easy as she thinks.*

"Mom, we've been saving our vacation time so we can stay awhile." Erin called from Seattle with their schedule.

Laura got online and found seats. Normally she would not, could not, have paid so much money for plane tickets but not now! She booked non-stop flights out of Seattle to Salt Lake City on Business Class and then the necessary plane change for Rock Springs. She'd never flown Business Class in her life! They were going to be so surprised! This was too much fun! She called Erin again and gave her the itinerary.

She got back online and did something totally out of character. She found a gourmet food site in Colorado and ordered holiday foods to be delivered the Monday before Thanksgiving; a whole roasted turkey and a spiral-sliced ham and every side dish that sounded good, yeast rolls, apple, pecan and pumpkin pies, bread bowls and clam chowder. There was plenty of room in the freezer so everything could stay there until it was time to cook.

Next site: wine glasses for twelve in four different sizes, plus tumblers for iced tea and bourbon; Fiesta-style dinnerware for twelve in four different colors, with serving dishes, flatware for twelve, an eighteen-piece cookware set, and a wine rack; all with expedited delivery. Lots of people in the area shopped online so these extra deliveries shouldn't raise any eyebrows or cause tongues to wag. This was too much fun. Thanksgiving would be a clean sweep of the old, starting with the kitchen.

After ordering red and white wine, butterscotch schnapps and two styles of beer from the online website, she turned off the computer and made an extensive grocery list. Thanksgiving Day was in two weeks and one day. The holiday dinner was taken care of but she still had to feed everyone regular meals for the rest of their visit. She had never spent this much money at one time in her whole life. *I like this!*

There had been only light snows since her snow blowing lesson so it was easy to back the jeep out of the driveway and drive down to run errands. She followed her list, got empty cardboard boxes and drove back home. After putting away everything she started her kitchen transformation. She saved some favorite pieces; then the remainder was wrapped in newspaper and packed in the boxes.

Thank goodness Supper Club was meeting at Three Pines tonight because she was in no mood to cook.

The next day she cleaned out her closet, carefully checking the purses just in case, packed the clothing and the boxes in the jeep and drove to Lander. She unloaded everything, got her receipt and did some shopping. She found three great sweaters, a vest and some snow pants. *I don't have to shop at Goodwill, but I like finding bargains!*

"Hey you!" It was Susan. "Are you ready for some updates?"

"Yeah, give it to me. I'm really excited to hear what's happened with my first donations."

"Your first three transactions are done! Both charities extend their heartfelt gratitude to the Trust. They are quite aware it was a one time donation and if the Trust wishes to donate at a later time they will be contacted. You made some great choices Laura!"

"What about Betsy Haven?"

"I was able to do this entirely over the phone. An SUV meeting your exact specifications will be delivered to her tomorrow. The owner of the dealership in Rock Springs is delivering it himself! The insurance is taken care of; she'll get a new gas card worth $100 once a month. I had to think about this part before I finally came up with a solution and I think once a month is a prudent way to dole out the gas funds. My suggestion is to stay out of her way for a week or two, don't volunteer at school or anything. Despite how cool you think you are, you may not be able to keep a straight face. I don't want her seeing you seeing her with the new vehicle for a few weeks until you can hide your emotions."

"So, what's the story? What's the car guy going to tell her?"

"He's actually done this one other time so he gave me the scenario. He's going to drive up to her house, knock on the door, and give her a packet containing the car information, the insurance papers, the first gas card, the title and the keys; get her to sign for it and then leave. Everything will be explained in the packet. It will contain a short note congratulating her efforts to get her daughter to school and that the donor wishes to remain anonymous."

"Oh, gosh! This is so exciting! And you're right; I don't need to see her driving it for a little while; I couldn't keep a straight face! I'm supposed to volunteer in the office and the library every Tuesday in December so by then she'll have had the car for a couple of weeks and I can work on my poker face!"

"I'm closing the office the week of Thanksgiving. There's not usually a lot going on then so I thought I'd fly up on Saturday and spend the week with you. I'm still working on the winter stuff for the kids and we can go over some strategies. How does that sound?"

"Great, it sounds great! I'm sure I'll have some more ideas for you then."

Laura's online orders began arriving and soon her kitchen cabinets were refilled and new robes and slippers were in the closets. She cleaned out the hot tub and got it ready.

She worked on her list and it exploded with ideas. She started dreaming about it; sometimes she felt consumed by it and sometimes it wasn't fun. One concern was she didn't want to do too many projects in her own area. Too much attention would be attracted, too many questions would be asked and the risk of losing her anonymity would be higher. She got online and paid subscriptions to every major newspaper in the United States. She could read them online and use the information to target recipients.

The food was delivered on Saturday morning; thank goodness for the freezer in the shed; it was packed! She was ready for Thanksgiving! Susan called Saturday afternoon; she would be driving up Sunday morning.

Laura was returning from Morning Prayer and she and Susan drove up to the house at the same time. She helped her sister unload her usual luggage plus a large rolling briefcase.

"When are the kids getting here?" Susan left the briefcase beside the dining table and stowed everything else in the computer room.

"They're doing the same as you; flying up the night before and driving up on Wednesday morning. I can't wait to tell them about the tuition! I wish there were non-stop flights from Kansas and Washington to here but there's no such animal. If I owned my own plane I could just send it for you anytime you wanted to come up and you could land at Hunt Field in Lander! That's what Hannah Simmons' husband does when he visits her up here during the summer."

"Hold on there big sister, you've got money but not that much money! The price of the plane, even if you only leased it, plus pilot, hangar and maintenance fees would blow a big hole in your income and I know you wouldn't want to waste so much on a big toy when you could be donating to more worthy causes. Let's just keep things the way they are for the time being. I'm starving! I only had coffee and donuts this morning. Do you have anything to eat?"

"Oh, I think I can get something together!" They went into the kitchen and Laura told her about her new purchases and the food delivery. After lunch Susan was ready to talk business.

"So here's my list. There's a bunch of stuff on it, some unrelated to the Trust so I'm just going to start at the top and work down. Number One, do you still have the .38 special Daddy gave you?

"Well, yeah, why?"

"Where is it?"

Laura showed her the hidden compartment in the wall next to the back door. You couldn't tell it was there unless you knew where to look. She pushed a spot on the wall and a small section sprung open. In the opening there was the gun, extra ammo and a canned air horn.

"Ah, so this is what you were talking about when you said James had to scare away the bear. Clever! I've been worried about it ever since you told me the story. I brought my gun so we can get in some target practice before I leave. Can you kill a bear with a .38?"

Laura was baffled. "Susan, I haven't even seen a bear and besides, it's winter! They're hibernating!"

"Well can you; can you kill a bear with a .38?"

"If you shoot him in the head, yeah." *James should have carried a gun that day!* "But you've gotta be careful. Hit him anywhere else and it could just piss him off. He might run away and he might run straight at you. What's all this about?"

"Humor me, okay? I just think you need to be safe here in the house and I think you need another gun in your bedside table!"

Laura only huffed and rolled her eyes.

"Look, it was different when James was here." She hadn't wanted to bring him up but there was no way around it. "Now you're here alone and I think it's a safety issue. I keep mine loaded in my bedside table at home and that's my suggestion for you. It's no big deal, Laura. Just some extra protection. If there's not a gun store here I'll bet there's one in Lander." There were three, she had already checked.

Laura stared at her sister for a moment, without responding, then, "I have never been scared here, I think you're worried over nothing. I have Daddy's shotguns in the closet so I'll think about it. What's next on your list?"

"Okay, next is Betsy Haven. Her car was delivered and the dealer called me. Everything went according to plan. He also offered to give the trust a discount in case it wants to provide a vehicle to another family. So whenever you go back to school you'll get to see her drive up and drop off her little girl! Call me; I want to hear the details!

"I'll be there the first Tuesday in December, volunteering in the office, so I'll have a front row seat! I'll let you know. What's next?"

"This one is a biggie! It's about the clothes for the kids. Laura, you had a grand idea that is totally NOT doable all at once and it has nothing to do with money. There is one reservation in Wyoming, one in Idaho, one in Kansas and thirteen reservations in Washington! I told a Big Fat Lie to the lady at the agency when she asked me why I needed the information. I told her I was doing research for a book!

"There is no way to find that many quality jackets, hats, and gloves this late in the season for kids on sixteen reservations! I called a company I found online. The massive order couldn't be filled with current inventory. I know it's only November but most of these companies are working on their spring lines already!

"I have some suggestions. First, take care of Idaho now! They have the smallest number of kids. I'll order from the company. They have enough to cover the order if you're not picky about colors and they can expedite delivery. Then I'll plan with the supplier for next year about the other reservations.

"Second, I think we need a "runner". I'm not worried about Washington and Idaho. Those states are far enough from Kansas that my name is meaningless, but I get nervous the closer I get to Kansas. I'm just saying the closer I get the higher the risk of someone recognizing my name and getting snoopy. I could make all the arrangements and the "runner" could make the contacts. I know exactly how I could utilize a "runner" so I could continue to keep my regular office hours and still get things done in other places. The job would require an appealing salary plus expenses. Let's think about the "runner" idea, okay?" Susan saw a look on Laura's face. "What's wrong?"

Laura had barely listened. "I'm a stupid idiot! If I had just thought about it for a little while I would have realized it wasn't doable. I had it in my head the only problem was the money. I'm sorry you went to so much trouble for my hair-brained idea." Laura felt completely defeated. She'd played out this huge dramatic scenario where the kids were all toasty warm for the winter and now it wasn't going to happen.

"You stop it right now!" Susan's tone brought Laura out of her pity party and back to reality. "Don't ever stop dreaming up ways to help people. That's your job. My job is to make it happen. We have to learn you can't always solve a problem just by throwing money at it. We're really new at this and obviously very naïve. We'll learn. Don't be discouraged. It's doable; it's just going to take ten months to do it!

"And you don't have to spend all $15 million in the first month! Keep writing down ideas. We can talk about them and take our time."

"Yeah, we can. I just feel like such a dim-wit. It never occurred to me that supply would be the problem."

"Okay, you have about three more minutes to beat yourself up and then put on your big girl panties and get over it."

"How about five, I think maybe I need five minutes!"

"How about four and a glass of wine? Do you know what time it is? We've been talking quite a while."

"I have an even better idea. Why don't we try out the hot tub with the wine? A long soak with Pinot on the side sounds good!"

"No way! Too dangerous! One of my clients drowned in her hot tub doing that exact same thing. A long soak, a little dinner, then a toddy for the body and I'll be ready for sleep!"

"It's ready to go. All I have to do is turn on the jets! I'll meet you in five! Look in your closet. I ordered spa robe and slipper sets to wear over our suits so we won't freeze our asses off getting in and out!"

A soak in a hot tub on a winter's day is sublime. Your body is warm but your face isn't hot and sweaty. It's the perfect combination and Laura and Susan took full advantage, soaking and talking until it was dark. The robes and slippers made the transition from hot to cold bearable. Step out of the tub and into your robe and into the house.

They stayed in their robes and ate a light dinner with wine.

"I've hit the wall babe; I've got to lie down before I fall down." Susan's eyes were at half mast and she had a silly grin on her face. "So, are you all better? Can I go to bed and not worry about you beating yourself up anymore?"

"I'm good. You were right; we're going to make mistakes and I don't need to spend $15 million all at one time. I also like the runner idea. Go to bed and we'll talk in the morning."

"I'm on my way. I love you, good night." She weaved and wobbled down the hall and into her room.

Laura put the dishes in the dishwasher and turned out the lights. *This is going to be a great Thanksgiving!* Five seconds after her head hit the pillow she was out.

CHAPTER TWENTY-SIX

Missing—162 days.

"Let's go to the gun store, there's one in Lander with an indoor shooting range. The kids aren't coming until tomorrow and everything else is ready to go."

"I'm not going anywhere until you 'fess up! What's going on? What's your obsession with me getting a gun?"

"Look, you said the .38 wouldn't kill a bear. Put it in your beside table and get something bigger for the hidden cabinet. Something that will stop a bear, not just piss him off. And here's the deal. You're alone now. If someone breaks in you may not be able to get to the back door. Another gun next to your bed is added protection."

"Does this have anything to do with the money?"

"Yes, it does and I think deep down you already know it. We're doing everything we can to protect your identity but you need to be careful. I also think it's time you got a home security system. No one in town would give it a second thought; they'd just think you were trying to feel a little safer now that James isn't here." She chose her words carefully, she didn't say "dead".

Laura stared at her sister a few moments. "This money thing carries a lot of baggage doesn't it?"

"Yeah, but not so much you can't handle it. Now is the best time to get a security system. Please do this; I wouldn't push it if I didn't think it was important."

Laura sniffed, "Okay, then. Let's go to Lander."

"From what you've told me, I think a .357 with a 4-inch barrel will suit your needs." The gun guy in Lander asked Laura a few questions and knew she owned a .38. "You can handle the recoil and it makes a nice large wound. Why don't you try it out while I finish the background check?"

Susan brought her gun and they fired several practice rounds at different distances. The gun guy was right. The recoil was acceptable and the holes in the targets said a lot. $700 later she walked out with a new handgun and a box of cartridges.

"Feel better now?" She glanced at Susan as they were driving back.

"I will when you get the security system."

The holiday festivities were perfect. They ate, they drank, they laughed, they played word games and they soaked. They shot at paper targets on the BLM land north of the house and Erin and David agreed; a security system was a good idea now that James wasn't here. Nobody said "dead".

When Laura and Susan told them about the tuition gifts there were tears. David was planning to re-enlist and now it wouldn't be necessary. The "we found another insurance policy" explanation was accepted without question.

Laura was watching Susan pack.

"Did I tell you I have online subscriptions to all the major news papers in the U.S.?"

"Good grief! That's a bunch of newspapers! Why?"

"I don't want to concentrate just on the surrounding states. I skim the news for an hour or so every morning and take notes. I'm not ready to make any decisions yet but I'm getting some good ideas. And, I agree, we need a "runner" and I know just who we should ask. Kaurie Hidalgo! Remember her, from Kerrville? She lives in California now."

"Sure! I remember her, y'all used to work together; you talked to her before Daddy's funeral. What made you think of her?"

"We've been friends for a long time. She's very dependable, very trustworthy. She's single, she doesn't live anywhere near you or me and, unless I donate to someone in Kerrville, it's very unlikely anyone would associate her with us."

"Hmmm, you may have something there!"

"Then this is what I want to do. I'll have the security system installed and when that's done I'll call her and make plans to go to California for a visit. You work out the details for a contract, write it up and I'll take it with me. We can talk details over the phone. But, I can't go anywhere until after the first Tuesday in December! I want to see Becky with her new car!"

"Oh, that's right! Don't forget to call me."

Laura got to school early on Tuesday. She wanted to be sure she was there when Becky Haven dropped off Maggie at the front of the school. She chatted with Karen while keeping an eye on the front door. The bell rang and still no Becky. Ten minutes later she drove up; in her old car, let her daughter out at the door and drove away. Laura knew she had to curb her reaction, but she felt like she was going to explode!

"So, Maggie is still getting to school late?" Laura said; shuffling papers, doing anything she could to hide her shock.

"Yeah, poor little thing. Becky drove up in a new SUV before the Thanksgiving break but she only had it a few days. Then she was driving the old car again. She said her dad and step-mom loaned it to her while they were getting her car repaired. It doesn't look like they did a very good job because she's still late a lot."

Laura managed to stay another hour and then decided it was time for a "splitting headache". She made her apologies to Karen and drove home without crashing into anything. She walked in through the back door and slammed it so hard a picture fell off the wall!

"I don't believe this! I don't fucking believe this", she screamed. "What did she do with that car?" Laura raged, pacing back and forth in the living room. She called Susan's cell phone; no answer. She called her office and Lana answered. Susan would be in court all day. "Do you want me to have her call you on her lunch break?"

"No, it's okay. Tell her I'll call her at home tonight!"

What did she do? Did she sell it? Did she trade it for something?

Six hours later her frenzy had settled in to a smoldering rage. She called Susan again.

"Hey you!" Her cheery greeting didn't help Laura's anger. "What's going on?"

Laura told the story, her language peppered with every curse word she ever knew!

"Whoa, calm down! Just hang on a minute! This may not be what it looks like."

"Well then what the hell could it be?" Laura yelled. "How could she do that?"

"LAURA!" Susan shouted. "Laura, listen to me. You're getting way too upset. Now you're just going to have to calm down. I'll find out what happened; just give me some time to come up with a reason to call the car dealer."

By this time Laura was reduced to tears. "What happened Susan, what did she do? The car was perfect for her, perfect for her kids!"

"Babe, you've really gotta get a hold of yourself. I know this is upsetting, I'm pissed too! But you can't do this! Are you listening to me?"

"Yeah," she said dully. "You're right. I just . . . . I just can't believe it!"

"Are you going to be at school tomorrow?"

"No, the security system people are coming in the morning. I have to be at the house."

The security system guys knocked on her door at 9:00 and by 3:00 they'd installed sensors, updated the motion-detector lights on the decks and on the workshop, and mounted touchpads inside the back door and in her bedroom. A small sign with the company logo was posted beside the driveway. The system package included a panic button, which was installed beside her bed. All the safety precautions made her uneasy. She felt safer before the alarm system and the second firearm. Maybe she was just ignoring the situation; she didn't know, but she hated the fact she had to think about it at all. It made her feel a little better when one of the men said they had installed four other systems in the area. Maybe she wasn't the only one that was paranoid

Susan called as they were leaving.

"Hey, are you better today?"

"Maybe, I guess so. Did you talk to the car dealer?"

"Yeah, I told him I wanted her to have a set of heavy duty snow tires for the winter. He's going to call and ask her to bring it in to get the tires installed. Did you get the security system?

"They just left. I got every horn and whistle available including panic button beside my bed. Susan, I guess I'll get used to this but I didn't feel unsafe <u>until</u> I got the new gun and this security stuff! This is unsettling."

"You'll get used to it. I'm buying one, too."

"You? Why you?"

"The more I thought about it the more I thought it would be a good thing for both of us and I like the panic button idea. I'm getting one of those too. Is everything else okay?"

"Yeah, I'm calling Kaurie tomorrow. I'll let you know my schedule. Let's think about spending Christmas together. I'll come there; how about?" Laura hung up. No sisterly chit-chat, no Trust talk. She decided to skip Supper Club and stay home and pout. And drink her self-imposed limit of 3 glasses of wine. The bottles weren't lasting as long as she estimated. It was time to order more.

Kaurie was ecstatic. "Yes, I want you to come. I'm ready whenever you are!" Laura made plans to go to Susan's and stay until two days after Christmas, then fly out to see Kaurie and return to Wyoming on January 2nd.

She chased the dust around until she was satisfied, then sat down and stared out the windows. *I'm going to Riverton with some of the stash in my fanny pack! I'll go to the Gray Wolf; maybe I won't see anyone I know. Everyone usually starts at the Red Eagle.*

She left $1,000 in her fanny pack and hid the rest at the back of her underwear drawer. *I need to get a safe!*

Just walking in to the Gray Wolf Casino lifted her spirits. No windows and no visible clocks set the tone for a good time with no distractions.

Her favorite dealer was at the Three-Card Poker table when she sat and laid three bills on the table to be exchanged for chips. After four losing hands it was time for the dealers to rotate and she stood up while they were accounting for their money to the pit boss and shuffling new cards. *Maybe I'll play a few more hands and try video poker again.*

The video poker machines were one section over from the tables. The dealer change-out was finished and she was ready to sit down again when she saw a familiar face at one of the machines.

"Color me out okay? I'll be back later."

She walked a meandering route, keeping out of the line of sight. When she was sure she couldn't be easily observed she stopped. Betsy Haven was sitting at a $5 video poker machine next to a sleazebag-looking guy, feeding tokens into the machine. They were having a hell-of-a-time; laughing and joking and pushing at one another. Laura could see the cash balance light was on but she was too far away to see the amount.

You greedy, lying selfish little bitch! You sold that car! It was safe for your babies, safe for you; you didn't have to spend one dime on it and this is what you do with a gift like that? You pour it down the coin slot on a poker machine, $25 at a time!

Laura felt her face flush and she began to shake. She turned around and walked to a ladies restroom far enough away from the poker machines that she wouldn't accidentally run into the witch coming in to empty her greedy, lying, selfish little bladder. A small lobby was arranged inside the entrance to the restroom, furnished with sofas and chairs. Laura fell into one and covered her face with her hands.

What kind of person would do that? What kind of mother would do that to her children?

"Excuse me," a hand was placed on her shoulder. "Are you okay? Would you like some water?" One of the beverage servers was bending towards her, offering a bottle of water and a little packet of tissues.

"Oh," Laura took her hands from her face. "Thank you," she said, accepting her offer. "I'm fine."

"Hard day, huh? I have them sometimes, too." She walked out before Laura could say anything.

She's probably thinking I'm sitting here crying because I lost all my money. I lost money alright; to a greedy, lying, selfish sow! I need to get out of here before I go back out there and knock her teeth down her throat! She went to a sink and splashed water on her face.

She cashed in her chips and was looking for the nearest exit when she saw the beverage server taking a drink order from a player. "Excuse me; thank you for the water. That was very nice. Do you have to share your tips?"

"Uh, no we don't get paid much, we rely on our tips." The young woman gave Laura a puzzled look.

"Good." She reached into her fanny-pack and took out the folded $100 bills she'd planned on playing at the poker table. "You were right; I was having a hard day, until you were so kind, thank you." She tucked the money into the pocket of the server's gray and silver uniform blouse and walked out the exit. She got into the jeep and rested her head on her hands on the steering wheel. *There are more kind people than there are greedy, lying, selfish sows like Betsy Haven; there have to be. I hope she loses all that money! Every single penny! I'd rather the casino have it than her!*

She drove home and got into the house without setting off the alarms. Her code was "larsu"; easy to remember.

By the time she called Susan she was calmer. The $6 million in donations to the charities had not given her the pleasure she got when she gave that server the money. *Oh, God, don't let her be a greedy, lying selfish sow, too!*

"Hey, I know what Betsy Haven did with her new car," she said when Susan answered

"I just found out myself! How do you know?

Laura told her about seeing Betsy at the casino. "Susan, I have never been so pissed and so disappointed at the same time in my whole life. I really wanted to go beat the shit out of her. I think it's pretty obvious she sold that car!"

"That's exactly what happened! John Garza, the car dealer, called me this afternoon. He called Becky with the story about the tires and she told him she sold it. It's sitting on a car lot in Lander! I was irate but he said this is not uncommon. Many times a recipient wants the cash a lot more than the car and they end up selling it. She didn't say how much she got for it and he didn't ask.

"Laura, you and I have a lot to learn about philanthropy. This was a hard lesson and we may not be able to prevent it from happening again but we need to be a little more cautious, a little more critical the next time we do this. I'm saying "we" because I'm as much at fault as you. Neither one of us knew any better. You have to relinquish control after you give a gift it's no longer yours."

"I can't let her influence who I help. You're right I should have found out a little more about her before I jumped in with both feet; thinking I was all gold and a yard wide. I'm telling you Susan, I've never been so mad in my whole life! Never! I'm glad thoughts don't automatically turn into actions because I'd be in jail for murder!"

Kaurie Hidalgo lived in a small stone and redwood bungalow perched 300 feet high on a cliff overlooking Highway One and the Pacific Ocean in Big Sur. She fit right in with the artisan and bohemian cultures that had been gravitating to the area since the 1920s. Kaurie had been born and raised in Texas. Right after she graduated from UTSA her mother divorced her father, took half of his oil-money and moved to Big Sur. Kaurie stayed in Kerrville, teaching 2nd grade with Laura, marrying and divorcing twice; stuck in a rut so deep she could barely see daylight. Her mother's brain cancer was her ticket out of Texas. She moved to California to care for her and, like Laura and the Rockies, once she saw those wild, untamed expanses she knew she wanted to stay.

When her mother died she left the house and a modest trust fund to her daughter and Kaurie was set. She learned to make pottery and built a studio with a kiln in the back yard. She found her niche and within a few years she had customers up and down the coast and in the little tourist villages along the coast highway. She earned enough, she had enough and she was happy.

They were sitting on her deck beside a blazing fire pit, drinking local wine when Laura explained her proposal. She wasn't specific about exactly how much money she'd won; she just gave her enough information to get the point across that philanthropy was her goal and she needed help.

"I can't pass this up! This is the most exciting thing I've ever heard of! Yes, yes! I'll do it!"

"You don't even want to think about it?"

"I'm a fast thinker! Yes, I want to do it."

Laura spent the rest of the afternoon telling Kaurie about the donations she had made, including the Betsy Haven fiasco and the winter wear for the kids on the reservations. Kaurie was in complete agreement regarding anonymity.

"I feel the same as you. I don't make anywhere near the amount you apparently do but I still don't want anyone to know my income. That was the first thing the trustee told me." Her trust was managed from a bank in Los Angeles and she complemented Susan on her decision to deposit the money in a bank in Denver. "Put it where you are a little bitty fish in a great big pond."

There was a marathon conference call with Susan. Kaurie was satisfied with the contract and the confidentiality agreement. A credit card would be issued in her name to be used for all trust-related expenses and she would email an expense report once a month to Susan.

Kaurie had the same problems with visitors as Laura. Oakland, the nearest city with a large international airport, was 162 miles away, so Laura left on New Year's Day afternoon and made the drive to Oakland so she could catch an early flight to Salt Lake City the next morning. As she neared the hotel she started to see billboards promoting travel to San Francisco and Los Angeles and Las Vegas!

Las Vegas! I could go there and not run into anyone I know! Yes! I can play as much as I want with as much as I want! Her heart started beating faster just thinking about playing and not worrying who was watching! Her knees felt shaky! *If someone took my blood pressure right now it would be off the charts!*

She turned into the parking lot of a fast food restaurant and made some major changes to her itinerary. She drove to the airport, dropped off the rental car and waited three hours before boarding a plane for Las Vegas. The New Year's Eve party goers were checking out on the same day Laura wanted to check in! By 11:00 p.m. she was in a room on the 29th floor with a floor-to-ceiling view of dancing fountains, Parisian towers and Roman-inspired architecture. She called room service, ordered a double shrimp cocktail, a cheese and fruit plate, a bottle of Pinot Noir and a chocolate bar and had dinner in her pajamas.

After a room service breakfast she went downstairs. Las Vegas was no Riverton! There was beauty and opulence and 3-card poker tables everywhere! She explored the casinos using the elevated walkways to cross Las Vegas Boulevard and Flamingo Road. An hour later she was back at her own hotel with a plan; start here, spend some time and money in each of the other ones and end back here. She spotted a friendly-looking dealer at a Three-Card Poker table and started playing. She made the maximum bets every time; two hours later she cashed out, went to the next casino and, after a quick snack, across to the next one. By the time she started at the third casino she was down more than $5,000. *Well, so much for my winnings from Riverton, I just blew it!*

She found a high-limit table and bought $7,500 in chips. There were three other players and soon the banter was loud and lively. The dealer was fast and the players were generous with tips whenever they won a hand.

Laura bet the maximum and the wager for the progressive. The dealer dealt the three-card hands to the players and himself. After looking at her cards she tucked them under her final wager.

The dealer qualified and started turning over the player's cards; paying out or taking away the wagers when the player didn't beat his hand. He turned over her cards. "Straight Flush spades; Ace, King, Queen," and the table erupted in cheers. Pit bosses in suits and ear pieces came from every direction. After all the payoffs and the progressive were added up, Uncle Sam and The State of Nevada walked up and took their due. When it was over Laura was facing stacks of chips equaling more than $45,000!

"Color me out! I'm quitting while I'm ahead." She tipped the dealer and walked off to shouts of congratulations and thanks from the other players and pit bosses.

She went to the cashier's cage, cashed in the chips and was given the money in a small zippered pouch; which she stuffed into her shoulder bag. *I'm going back now and put this in the room safe! No way am I walking around Vegas with this much cash, even if it is broad daylight! I think it's time for a hot stone massage and reflexology at the spa.*

As she was crossing the pedestrian walkway she was jolted by a pain on the left side of her head more intense than anything she'd ever experienced in her entire life.

CHAPTER TWENTY-SEVEN

Pain! She moaned and tried to move. Panic! *What the hell is that beeping noise? Why can't I open my eyes? I hurt everywhere.*

"Nurse, can you come in here please? I think she's waking up."

Nurse? Where am I?

A woman's voice sounded close to her face, "Laura? Laura, honey can you hear me?" She moved her hand and someone squeezed it.

A man's voice. "Laura, my name is Carlos and you're in Las Vegas General Hospital and I'm your nurse. You were injured but you're going to be okay. Tell me if you understand me." A large hand held her smaller one.

"Ye . . ." Then a tiny squeak of pain. She tried to talk but her mouth was dry as sand and any movement caused excruciating pain in her head and shoulder. *Well, hell what doesn't hurt?* She felt something touch her lips; cool and lemony.

"I'm swabbing something in your mouth that will help with the dryness." Cool and lemony was rubbed inside her cheeks and across her tongue.

"Talk to her while I get Dr. Welch and make a phone call."

"Laura? This is Kaurie. I know you can't see me but I'm right here and so is Susan."

Someone patted her arm. That arm felt restricted somehow.

Another disembodied voice. "Laura?"

Laura recognized her sister's voice and tried to talk. "Thur-tee! Nee wa-er."

"Honey, I can't give you any water until you wake up some more. They don't want you to choke." *They? They who?*

"Laura?" Another woman's voice. "My name is Dr. Welch. You were attacked while crossing the walkway from Caesars Palace. The attacker hit you in the face and knocked you down. That's why your head is so painful and swollen. Luckily no bones were broken. Your right shoulder was wrenched when the thief snatched your purse. I have your arm in an immobilizing sling temporarily. There are multiple bruises from where you hit the pavement, but all in all I think you will recover.

"The MRI, neurologicals and other tests are within normal limits. The nurses will be applying cold compresses to your face to reduce the swelling along with medication in your IV. Just let them know what you need. I have . . .

"Wa-er, wa-er nee wa-er!"

"Water, are you asking for water?"

"Ye . . ."

The doctor replied, "I can't allow you any water until you can swallow without choking but some ice chips are okay. The nurses will monitor you closely and I'll check back with you later."

Laura nodded her head; and she never wanted to move again, the slightest attempt caused lightening flashes of pain.

"Oh," Dr. Welch added. "There is someone here who wants to talk to you. His name is Sgt. Gregg; he's a detective. Can you talk to him for a minute or two?" Dr. Welch looked at the officer sternly and held up two fingers as she turned to leave.

"Ye . . . th." Laura was trying as hard as she could to speak clearly. *I don't remember anyone hitting me!*

"Laura, my name is Sgt. Gregg. Do you understand who I am?"

"Ye . . . th, co . . . p."

"Do you remember anything about the person who hit you?"

"Nuh"

"So you don't remember if it was a man or a woman?"

"NUH!" Laura was becoming agitated. "Wa-er, nee wa-er!" *I'm thirsty dammit; can't you people understand plain English?*

Carlos shook his head at Sgt. Gregg and gestured a time-out.

"Okay Laura, I want to come back when you're feeling better. We're going to catch whoever did this to you."

Laura could hear movement and low voices. "Babe," Susan's voice, "we're going right outside and talk to Sgt. Gregg. We'll be right back, okay?"

"Nee wa-er!"

Carlos took over. "Laura, I'll stay right here with you. If you can tolerate the ice chips you'll get water soon.

They walked to the nurse's station across from the small ICU room.

"This is what we know. Security cams are all over Vegas and our techs have been working for hours on the footage. Laura left her hotel yesterday morning and . . . ."

"She wasn't even supposed to be in Las Vegas! She was supposed to fly to Wyoming from Oakland." Susan cried.

"I understand how upset you are Ms. Bennett." He touched her shoulder. "Let me finish telling you what we know. The footage from the different cams shows her leave her hotel and use the pedestrian walkways to visit two other casinos before she went to Caesars. Caesars let us view the interior footage showing her activity and apparently your sister won a lot of money. We interviewed the dealer and the pit bosses and she won over $45,000!"

"Oh, my God" Kaurie burst out! Susan stood silently, biting her lip.

"There's video of her cashing in her chips and receiving the money in a pouch. The cashier was interviewed and said the pit boss offered to call a cab but she refused. She exited the casino and was on the walkway when a man in sunglasses, a sweatshirt and a ball cap, coming from the opposite direction, smashed his fist into her face, wrenched her shoulder bag away and hauled ass towards Caesars. We have footage of him running to the end of the walkway and jumping into some landscaping but we lost him from there. We found the sweatshirt and cap in the bushes along with your sister's purse. From the time he hit her until he jumped into the bushes took less than 60 seconds. There were only two witnesses and by the time one of them decided to chase the guy, he was long gone.

"This is the third time this has happened in the last two months. It's never happened in the same place and always during the day. The two other victims were also women walking alone; both were carrying jackpot winnings, but from different casinos. Just like this case; their purses and the attacker's clothes were found nearby and nothing else in the purses was touched. It looks like the three attacks were made by different men so this is, at least, a 3-man team. Very organized, much practiced; the attacks were very well coordinated. One man appeared to be dark-skinned; the other two couldn't be identified as far as race. Average height and build. We couldn't see tattoos or other identifying marks but we believe they were all wearing gloves because there were no unexplained fingerprints on the purses. We could tell they knew where the cams were located and they were evasive as possible.

"Your sister is very lucky, Ms. Bennett. The last woman's neck was broken when the guy snatched her purse because she was wearing it across her body instead of hanging from her shoulder. Lots of women think it's a safe way to carry a purse." Susan closed her eyes, saying nothing. "The techs were unable to backtrack from this guy; he just appeared a few moments before he attacked your sister."

"Was it just his fist?" Susan asked, "Her face is so bruised."

"The video isn't that clear, however, I can ask them to review it. Please call me as soon as she is able to talk."

Two days later the swelling was down enough for her to open her eyes and eat soft foods. She hadn't lost any teeth but her jaw was very sore and bruised and it still hurt to chew. Although her shoulder hadn't been dislocated, the muscles were severely strained and she would have to wear a sling followed by physical therapy

"I'm so sorry! I can't believe I was so stupid," tears leaked from her bruised, puffy eyes. Laura had been transferred from ICU to a regular room and Kaurie and Susan were there when she was finally able to speak clearly. "I thought since it was day time and I just had to cross the street that I'd be safe. I was on one of the busiest, most visible corners in the world! I wasn't in a back alley, it wasn't late at night and I really did not think I was being foolish. I didn't want to waste time in a taxi because it would've taken me half an hour to go less than 100 yards; it looks like I wound up in the hospital trying to save 30 minutes! Please y'all. I feel like a little kid apologizing for bad behavior but I won't make this mistake again"

"Laura, babe, I know you didn't mean for this to happen and thank God you're going to be all right. Just do me one favor, okay? The next time you decide to take a side trip, wouldja let somebody know?" *Dammit, Laura! You nearly got yourself killed! How could you be such an idiot?* Susan knew she didn't sound very sympathetic; she was still dealing with the fact she could have lost her sister. When she walked into that hospital room and saw her, she was beyond frightened and once she knew

Laura was going to recover she was just flat out pissed! Everything she wanted to say sounded like a cliché, or like she was talking to a child, so she just let it go. She leaned over and put her lips to Laura's forehead. "I love you."

"Susan, I don't want anyone to know what happened. It looks like I was sneaking around trying to hide my gambling." *Which is exactly what I was doing!*

"Why don't you try this? Call one of your knit groupies and tell them you were in a car wreck; you're going to stay with me because you have to go to rehab and there's no physical therapy near Aspen Falls. You'll be good to go in six weeks!" She didn't respond to the "hide my gambling" remark.

After Laura was discharged from the hospital Sgt. Gregg asked to meet with them; hoping she could recall more details.

"Can you remember anything else? Even if it's something you think is insignificant, you need to tell me. We're at a dead end here. We haven't had one good lead and I want to catch these guys. Do you remember seeing anyone watching you? Did you talk to anyone?"

"Sgt. Gregg, I remember the table was loud and everybody was laughing and joking around and I didn't notice anyone acting suspiciously, I don't remember anyone following me. I've heard about this kind of thing happening and I figured I would remember bits and pieces but it's not like that. My memory just stops there and then starts again with waking up in the hospital. I wish I could remember what happened. Dr. Welch said I might not ever recall the actual attack. I'm sorry; I want to help but I can't!"

"Well, sometimes memories can come back long after the event."

Laura looked at Susan who appeared to have momentarily lost focus. *Yeah, we know about memories!*

"I know you're leaving in the morning so I'll contact you if I get any leads and please feel free to call me anytime. Nothing is too trivial. We're reviewing every detail and interviewing the entire group of casino staff connected with you plus re-interviewing everyone connected with the other two assaults. We're not letting this one go until we solve it!"

Susan was the perfect nurse; rehab three times a week took care of the shoulder and six weeks gave the bruises on her face time to fade. Laura used her recuperation time to scan the online newspapers and Kaurie was sent on her first mission.

In New Mexico, a house fire left a 55 year-old grandmother homeless. She was raising her four grandchildren and they were living in a shelter when Laura read the story in the newspaper.

Susan researched the local home builder's associations and found a builder. Kaurie was sent to New Mexico to start the process for a five-bedroom, three-bath fully furnished home. Everything would be paid by the trust.

It wouldn't be elaborate but would be comfortable for her and her grandchildren and during the time the house was being built the family was moved from the shelter to an apartment.

Laura prayed this wouldn't turn into another Betsy Haven fiasco. For this reason Susan had written stipulations as to how long the woman had to live in the home before it was hers.

It took nearly three weeks for Kaurie to get everything arranged. The builder's contract included a iron-clad confidentiality agreement. He called Kaurie several times with messages from the grandmother wanting to thank her and she had to give the same response each time; she was only the representative for a donor who wished to remain anonymous.

Projects like this took a lot of time and they decided three or four a year was all they could do and do it right. Making the arrangements for the winter clothing for the reservation kids was a huge endeavor and Susan was still working on those details.

"You can't save the world, babe. You've taken on a noble cause but you have to do this wisely. We have to make sure your money goes to people and places where it will do the most good. You've made some great donations."

"You forgot one thing!"

"Oh, no! I didn't forget about that witch! I'm just chalking her up as a learning experience! I'm doing everything I know to keep it from happening again. You've done something to be proud of. Take your time, keep researching and let's do two more big projects this year."

She and Susan worked on the "car wreck" story, fleshing it out with details to make it sound plausible and Erin was included with the story recipients. She didn't know about Kaurie; and Susan and Laura wanted to keep it that way. The "car wreck" happened in Kansas. No one needed to know about California or Las Vegas.

"Are you still mad at me?"

"No, not anymore! But I was really, REALLY pissed for a while. I almost lost you! You could have been killed and then I would have no family. I would be an orphan! You're not going to do anything that stupid again, right?"

"Right, no more stupid!"

The Rockies welcomed her home. Their familiar silhouette against the sky evoked the same sense of comfort and calm that called to her the first time she saw them. She looked forward to home. Earlier she called Molly Martinez with the "car wreck" story and to let her know when she would be back. As she turned on to the cul-de-sac she saw her driveway and deck had been cleared of snow. *Thank you God for Rick!*

When she first walked in it was dim and lonely in the late-afternoon winter light and after having been left to its own devices for nearly eight weeks, the dust had established dominance. Lights, television, a fire in the fireplace and a glass of wine chased away the gloom. She then called Susan to let her know she had gotten home safely.

"How's your shoulder?"

"No problems. Kansas rehab rocks! Remind me to come there whenever I need rehab after a bogus car wreck!"

Susan felt better. She'd worried Laura would have a hard time coming home to a cold empty house, but she sounded good and after a few more silly jokes they hung up.

The next few days were spent unpacking and making phone calls and seeing friends and chasing the dust. The prayer table looked sad and neglected and she didn't know what to do with it. She felt guilty when she realized she hadn't thought about James in the last few days and she had to look at a calendar to figure out how long he'd been missing. She lit the candle and said a prayer for him. *God, YOU know best. My prayer now is that he didn't suffer. My prayer now is that you guide me with this money. My prayer now is that you continue to watch over my stupid, foolish self! And help Sgt. Gregg catch the shi* . . . She modified her prayer . . . . *jerk that attacked me in Vegas!* Cursing while praying might trip up her message somewhere between her mouth and God's ear.

She called her sister.

"I haven't made my mind up on my remaining two big projects but I have a little one!" She'd been busy working on her list!

"Go for it! I finally finished with the winter clothes for the reservation kids and I'm ready for something small." The winter clothes for the kids on the reservation in Idaho had been delivered. The others were scheduled to be delivered by the following October.

"We might have to send Kaurie on another little mission. I want to donate money for training and equipment to the K-9 Search and Rescue group in Jackson. This won't take three weeks like New Mexico will it?"

"No way! She should be in and out in one day. This is an easy one. I'll call her tonight. What amount were you considering?"

"I don't know. Can you find out? I think it's been long enough they won't connect it with me."

"That's a job for Kaurie. I'll get back with you."

There were so many sad stories in the newspapers. Susan was right; she couldn't save everyone! But she could make it easier for a few. She wanted to pay off student loans, but she wanted to do it for people who would appreciate it; not those who would foolishly go out and rack up credit card bills once they no longer had loan payments. She thought about scholarships; her list was growing.

Karen called again to ask if she could volunteer in the office and she felt like enough time had passed for her to hide her feelings when Becky dropped her poor, neglected little girl off at school.

"Hey, you! It's good to see you, are you okay?" Karen said when she walked into the office.

"Oh, yeah," and she recounted the story complete with all the little details she and Susan had fabricated.

"So, catch me up on school. Any new kids enrolled? What's been going on? I didn't see Maggie Haven this morning. Is she still getting to school late?" *Butter wouldn't melt in my mouth! Well done, Laura!*

"They moved! Her mom checked her out about three weeks ago. She said she was moving in with her dad and step-mom in Montana. I hope everything goes well; being a single mom is hard."

Yeah, it's a lot easier being a greedy, lying selfish sow!

CHAPTER TWENTY-EIGHT

K9 Search and Rescue? Done! Laura donated enough money to cover a year's worth of expenditures.

Helicopter maintenance for a year? Done! At $1,600 an hour that was a big chunk of change.

College loans repaid for a new and deserving doctor in Northwestern Alaska? Done!

Under Susan's direction, Kaurie orchestrated the K9 and helicopter donations; doing it all without making the trip to Wyoming. Everything was coordinated by phone and email. The trip to Alaska only took a few days.

There were several needs in and around Aspen Falls and Laura was working on a strategy to enable her to take care of them without bringing attention to herself.

Mid-March temperatures on the eastern slope of the Wind River Range varied from highs in the forties to lows in the twenties and though it was officially spring down in the lower states it was still winter in the Rockies. Laura kept a fire in the fireplace and the house was always warm and comfortable. She moved her computer into the living room and was reading her email and watching the news when she heard a knock at the back door. She hadn't heard a car in the driveway and was a little uneasy.

Walking back through the kitchen to the mudroom she glanced toward the hidden cabinet where she kept the .357. She hadn't done any target shooting since her sojourn to Vegas and Kansas but she knew it was there, loaded and ready.

A man in a down vest and knit beanie was standing on the deck outside the door. *God in heaven, it's James!*

For an instant, the earth stopped revolving, she stopped breathing and her heart seemed to be beating right in her throat! She stood paralyzed, her hand on the doorknob, staring out the door glass.

"James?"

The earth began to spin again, her breath returned, her heart continued to pound high in her chest and her paralysis was replaced by trembling.

"James?" She opened the door to her husband who had been missing for . . . how long? She couldn't even begin to remember.

"Oh, thank God! Are you okay? Where have you been? What happened to you?" Laura babbled on the edge of hysteria. She threw her arms around him; an embrace as much as an assurance she wasn't seeing a ghost!

He stood there on the snow-covered deck, gently patting her back.

She stepped back to look at his face. *Are you real? Have I finally gone looney tunes?*

"Can we go inside? It's cold out here!" he asked.

"I . . . uh . . . yeah, sure!" She turned and walked back into the mudroom. He followed and closed the door behind him; taking off his beanie and vest and hanging them on a peg in the mudroom. She felt as if she was walking through something viscous and resistant instead of thin air. She only made it as far as the kitchen; never realizing he had asked permission to enter his own home.

"Where . . . ?" She put her hands to her mouth. She searched his face looking for an expression; an explanation!

"I've been in Texas."

"Texas? Texas!" Her voice rose two octaves. "What do you mean you've been in Texas? What are you talking about? What's going on?"

"I know I have a lot of explaining to do. Can we go in and sit down and talk?"

"Explaining? Wait a minute!" Her voice was edged with confusion and anger! "I thought you were dead, James! I thought you had fallen off a cliff or been mauled to death by a bear! There've been search teams and dogs and helicopters looking for you! Everybody thought you were

DEAD! We looked for you for weeks! I agonized over you for . . ." a quick look at the calendar. " . . . for nine months!"

"I figured something like that. I'm sorry. That's why I want to sit and explain to . . ."

This is NOT happening. I'm going to wake up any second from this nightmare!

"Like hell, we're going to sit! You're going to stand right here and tell me how and why you've been in Texas instead of rotting in some ravine up around Arapahoe!" She was screaming and crying and shaking so hard she was surprised she could put two words together to make a sentence. She felt like she'd been punched in the gut!

"Laura, please . . . !

Without conscious planning Laura doubled up her fist and, with all her strength, drove it straight into his stomach. *There you son of a bitch. Now you know how I feel!*

The look of complete surprise on his face was instantly replaced by one of pain as he doubled over and farted the loudest fart she had ever heard in her whole life! She would have laughed had she not been so royally pissed.

She knocked the breath out of him and he fell to his knees, hanging his head, drooling and supporting himself with one hand on the floor. It lasted several seconds, and then his breath returned with a giant heave and a gag and a cough.

She stood over him, fists clenched at her sides, surprised at her own fury.

"I guess I deserved that," he gasped.

That and a helluva lot more! Somebody push "Rewind" please. This . . . this . . . What the hell?

"Can we go sit down now?" He winced as he stood back on both feet.

"We're not "going" anywhere! If you need to sit you can sit right here at this kitchen table!"

Laura didn't notice the backpack he was carrying until he dropped it when she punched him. He picked it up, laid it on the table and sat down in one of the chairs.

"May I have some water, please?"

She filled a glass with water from the faucet and set it in front of him. Her hands were shaking and some of the water sloshed out onto the table.

She crossed her arms in front of her to hide the shaking and said, "Okay; you're sitting. So start explaining."

"Would you like to sit . . . ?"

"I'll stand, thank you very much; get on with it."

James took a sip of water and began. "You weren't far from wrong about the bear. Jo-Jo and I were at the other side of the lake and that's where we surprised it. We heard it crashing up behind us and I turned just about the time it took a swipe at me. It was snarling and growling and Jo-Jo was barking right back at it. It charged at me again and I started running and kept running until I realized I was lost. Where is she? Is she okay?"

Laura looked at him incredulously! "Where is she? Look out beside the driveway under a quartz rock! That's where she is. While you were running away she was fighting the bear! He gutted her, slit her belly!" She uncrossed her arms and put her face within inches of his. "She fell over the edge of a cliff and died while you were running away! The K9 team found her seven days later. She's buried across the driveway where the trail starts."

"Oh, no. I was hoping she got back home." He paused briefly and stared out the kitchen window. *Is he even listening to me? It sounds like he's speaking from a script! He doesn't even sound upset about the dog!* "I kept trying to find something that looked familiar. I'd never been so far past Arapahoe and I thought if I just kept on walking I would find a road.

"I finally heard the sounds of traffic on the highway." He stopped and hung his head. Laura did not say a word. She wasn't about to offer him words of encouragement. He could finish under his own power.

He sat like that for what seemed an eternity. "Laura, I was never unhappy with our marriage, it's just that . . . it's just that I was never really happy." Laura's knees began to shake.

"I didn't think about it much. I just accepted it as "that's the way life is"! As I got closer to the road I saw it as a way out. Up until then I didn't even know I wanted out! It was a chicken shit thing to do but by the time I got to the highway I knew I wasn't going back."

Laura said nothing. Tears were streaming down her face and she was afraid to open her mouth, afraid she would become a screaming banshee; and afraid of what James was going to say next.

He looked at her and when she said nothing he continued. "I came out on 287; started walking north, away from my life." he took a deep breath, "I hitched a ride with a trucker as far as Jackson Lake and then I got another ride going south. We went down through Kemmerer and west to Salt Lake City."

The flyers were never posted that far west.

He paused again; and again she said nothing.

"I never told you this, but before we got married I had two bank accounts. Not one, like I let you believe. When we got married we combined our checking accounts but this one was an interest-bearing savings account and I just left it alone. I was getting paperless statements in my email so there was nothing that ever came in the mail about it.

Sounds like what I did with George!

"I had the two-hundred dollars in my wallet with my driver's license so when I got to Salt Lake City I found a branch for my bank and withdrew enough money to go back to Texas. I didn't even realize I wanted to go back there until I got to the bank."

Again he stopped, giving her the opportunity to ask questions. Again, she said nothing.

He took another drink of water. "Before we got married you told me about George and I told you about the women I had been in relationships with." Laura's stomach started turning flip-flops. She didn't know what he was going to say but she knew it wasn't going to be good.

"One of those women was Sarah Jefferson. We lived together for nearly 11 years before we broke up. Then I was with Lannie for a little while; it lasted less than a year. Then you and I met. And we got married." *Not one word about "falling in love"!*

Another pause, another refusal to speak.

"By the time I got back to Texas I knew I wanted to find Sarah. She was still living in the same house we shared in Bastrop.

"Sarah broke up with me back then, it wasn't my idea. I'm going to skip all those details and get to this next point." *Details!?!* "Neither she nor I knew that when she broke it off she was pregnant!"

Yep, I knew this wasn't going to be good!

"She never told me; never tried to contact me. I found out I have a thirteen year-old son!"

Laura was leaning up against the kitchen sink and she knew it was time to either sit down or fall down. She sat at the table; as far away from him as was physically possible. Within two years of moving to Aspen

Falls, Laura had two miscarriages and finally a hysterectomy. James never expressed regret at not having children of his own.

"I didn't know it would mean so much to me! But it does. I have a son!" *And I have a daughter you were around for the ten years we've been married! Apparently, she never meant a damn thing!*

"Laura, I discovered all of this within a month after I hitched that ride. Since then I've been working in Bastrop and getting to know my son; his name is Blake. He's a lot like me!" *Poor kid!* "We get along well together. And I'm getting to know Sarah again!" *What about me? Did you ever try to get to know me?*

"Laura, I'm not coming back to Wyoming. I'm staying in Texas. With Blake. And Sarah! I know I've hurt you and I'm truly sorry. I don't expect you to forgive me. I can't come back here." *And I don't want you to, you sorry-assed son of a bitch!*

He stopped and looked at her expectantly.

"Are you finished? Do you have anything else to say?"

"Well, yes. I want a divorce!" James sounded more confident than he had ever sounded before. *Where did this attitude come from?* He didn't seem embarrassed or ashamed by his behavior!

"I know after hearing all of this you won't want to be married to me." *No shit, Sherlock! You're so perceptive!*

"I have a lawyer and he's drawn up the paperwork." He pulled a multi-page document from his backpack. *This isn't happening!*

"Since I worked for eight years after we were married and then took early retirement I think it's only fair that you get half of my social security for those eight years as well as half of eight years of my pension. *Oh, you're so generous and thoughtful. I'm already getting half of all of it! Have fun figuring that out!*

"I just want you to know I'm not going to take advantage of this situation. I know you have your teacher retirement and even though I'm giving you part of my pension and social security, I don't think it's fair for me to take any of yours." *Like you could even if you tried!*

"The house is paid off and I don't want to hurt you by taking half of it." *Oh, please SHUT UP!*

"So I'm willing to sign a Quit-Claim Deed. The house will be in your name only." *Oh, how considerate of you, you bastard!*

"I'm really sorry this is hurting you, Laura, but I think it's the best thing for both of us." *I couldn't agree with you more!*

He laid the divorce papers on the table. "Laura." *Don't even say my name!* "Once this is signed and filed I won't come back making any more demands." *Oh, if you only knew!*

"Now, are you finished?"

"Yes, I guess you want to look at the papers before you sign them. I'm staying in Lander . . ."

"GET. OUT. OF. MY. HOUSE! I don't care where you're staying! You can crawl under a rock for all I care. You can jump off a cliff! I DON'T CARE!!!"

"The paperwor . . ."

"Are you deaf as well as stupid? I said get out of my house! Don't worry about your precious paperwork! I'll look it over! You may call me in the morning. My number hasn't changed!"

She walked to the back door, glancing again at the cabinet hiding the gun! *Stay with me here, God! I need your hand to stop mine from blowing him away!* She opened the back door and stood to the side while James passed through.

"I'm really sorry, Laura. I'll call . . ." She closed the door and walked back to the living room without a word.

It was really time to scream and scream she did! She screamed, she cried, she cursed! She thought back to all the time she wasted grieving and in turmoil! As she collapsed onto the floor her eyes focused on the prayer table. *Gee thanks, God! Apparently my prayers didn't make it past the ceiling!*

She stood on shaking legs, walked to the pantry and got a jumbo-sized black trash bag. She walked back into the living room and unceremoniously dumped everything into the bag, including the rug and the table. She dragged it outside to the curb. *Maybe it will do more good in the dump!*

"Susan!"

"What's wrong?"

She told her sister the whole disturbing tale, stopping several times to blow her nose and gulp wine.

"Do you have the paperwork?" Susan was withholding her comments until she could take care of business.

"Yeah, it's still in there on the kitchen table."

"Scan it now and send it all to me in an email. Be sure you scan every page. I'll call you back when I get it and we'll go over it on the phone." She hesitated. "Laura?"

"What."

"We'll get through this."

"Yeah, right." Laura hung up and Susan waited for the email.

Susan looked over the document and then took a few minutes before she called Laura. It never occurred to her James would do anything like this. She wished the son-of-a bitch had died in the mountains. Gutted and eaten alive! Anything, but what he did! He caused such unbelievable pain and anguish!

She consciously chose to ignore the red flag warning marked "MONEY" flapping in her brain and when she was finally composed she called her sister.

"I got it. I went over everything. The dumb ass thinks he's being so considerate! I wouldn't change a thing. *I'll deal with the money later.* The arrogant idiot even signed it ahead of time! And as far as his offers for his pension and social security; take it! You don't need it but he doesn't need to know that. We can figure out something to do with it. When is he coming back?"

"I told him to call me in the morning."

"Good! Let him squirm! Make him wait until the afternoon to come back. Have the papers signed when he gets there. Give him no reason to stick around for "old time's sake"!

"Old time's sake?"

"Yeah, you know, one more "roll in the hay"! One more "motion in the ocean."!

"Over my dead body! Or his dead body! Remember where I keep the .357? I'd much rather engage in gunplay than foreplay!"

"Laura! Don't even kid around like that! I'm serious! Don't even think about it!"

"Too late! I already thought about it! Maybe I'll have it on the table when he comes back tomorrow. That'd be enough to scare another fart out of him!"

"Laura!"

"Shush! I'm only kidding; although it was fun to fantasize about it for a minute. The gun is staying in its little hidey-hole. I promise I won't use it. I'll call you tomorrow after he's gone!" She hung up!

What am I? A jerk-magnet? Do I have a sign on my back that says "Assholes Only Need Apply"? Laura drank her dinner and passed out on the couch.

He called at 9:00 the next morning. She was awake; treating her hangover, but let it ring seven times before answering. "You can come at 5:00 this afternoon. I'm busy until then." She hung up.

She took a box of black trash bags from the pantry and started in the bedroom. Every single thing he owned went into the bags. She loaded up everything from his closet and dumped in the contents of his drawers from the highboy, including two pistols in holsters and two boxes of ammo, which she held momentarily and played out a new scenario.

Whenever a bag was full she tied a knot at the top, dragged it out and threw it in the back of his pick-up; which was included in the divorce decree.

The contents of the shelves in the bathroom went into the same bags as his clothes; toothbrushes, razors and nose drops were mixed in with socks, shoes and boxer shorts. She walked around the house. DVD's, Jo-Jo's rubber frog, his favorite coffee mug; everything went into the bags and then into the pick-up.

She took another box of bags to the workshop. All of his woodworking tools, his chair; every single item that belonged to him was dumped into the bags. Everything! When back of his pick-up was heaping she shoved the rest into the cab.

Jo-Jo's grave was next to the driveway. "I'm sorry this happened to you Jo-Jo. You were a brave dog." Laura picked up the five-pound quartz rock marking the spot and threw it through the back window of the pick-up. She left the keys in the ignition.

She took off her clothes, turned on the jets in the hot tub and soaked and looked at the scenery until all the knots in her muscles had relaxed. She brought out tea bags steeped in ice water and put them on her eyes to reduce the puffiness.

At 4:00 she went inside and dressed, brushed her teeth, fixed her hair, put on make-up and took two chill pills.

He knocked on the back door at precisely 5:00. She opened the door, "Here's your paperwork! Mail me the copies when everything is filed. Where's my deed?" She did not invite him inside. He seemed to have lost the confidence he exhibited yesterday as he surveyed his pick-up and the black bags. He set his backpack down on a deck chair and pulled out the Quit Claim deed. As she took the deed and handed him the truck keys she noticed a gray SUV parked at the end of the driveway. A woman was sitting in the driver's seat.

"Laura, I . . . ."

"Go to hell!" She shut the door in his face and turned her back to the windows. She refused to watch him leave, refused to look at the woman in the gray car. After a few minutes she heard his truck start and the crunch of the tires on the driveway as he backed out. She never turned around.

"It's over. He's gone."

"I'm glad he's gone but, oh, no, it's not over; not yet, not by a long shot! There's one more thing. The search for James cost the city, county and state nearly $40,000. Those entities do not look kindly on someone taking unfair advantage of governmental resources. The Fremont County Sheriff is waiting for him down in Lander with a bill for services rendered! I'm coming to Aspen Falls. I'll be there tomorrow afternoon."

Susan stayed three days. Laura ranted and raved and got over it surprisingly fast. The day after James left she called Father Pete. She felt guilty for throwing out the prayer table.

"I should have called you. I'm sorry. My prayers never made it past the ceiling."

"God answered your prayers, Laura. Just not the way you thought he should. He kept James safe and ultimately kept you safe from James. God knows what we need. Have a little faith."

The rumor mills cranked for a while. Laura was afraid she wouldn't be able to face all those who'd put in so much time and effort searching for James; but it didn't happen. She received sympathy and support from everyone; especially Frank Bell and the Knit Groupies. James was the bad guy. She was the good guy and in just a few weeks it was old news;

no longer a topic for discussion. There were plenty of other things to talk about in Aspen Falls.

"Hey Susan!"

"What now?"

"There's a kid in Kentucky that needs a kidney!"

"We're in the organ procuring business now?"

"No, dopey, the funding is needed! She's on an organ donor list but will need cash!"

"I'll get started on it." *And I need to figure out a way to tell you that James is entitled to half of the money!*